Felicity Everett grew up in Manchester and attended Sussex University. After an early career in children's publishing and freelance writing, which produced more than twenty-five works of children's fiction and non-fiction, she began writing novels for adults in 2011. She lived for four years in Australia and now lives in Gloucestershire with her family.

THE PEOPLE AT NUMBER 9

When Gav and Lou move into the house next door, Sara spends days plucking up the courage to say hello. The new neighbours are glamorous, chaotic and a little eccentric. They make Sara and her husband Neil seem dull by comparison. Or so Sara thinks. But soon the couples become friends, sharing supper, bottles of red wine, and childcare; laughing and trading secrets late into the night. The more time Sara spends with Gav and Lou, the more she longs to make changes in her own life. But those changes will come at a price. And soon Gav and Lou will be asking things they've no right to ask of their neighbours, with shattering consequences for all of them . . .

FELICITY EVERETT

◆

THE PEOPLE
AT NUMBER 9

Complete and Unabridged

CHARNWOOD
Leicester

First published in Great Britain in 2017 by
HQ
an imprint of HarperCollins*Publishers* Ltd, London

First Charnwood Edition
published 2018
by arrangement with
HarperCollins*Publishers* Ltd, London

Extract of *Dis Poetry* Copyright © Benjamin
Zephaniah, taken from City Psalms published
by Bloodaxe Books, printed with permission
of United Agents.

A catalogue record for this book is available
from the British Library.

ISBN 978–1–4448–3569–4

Published by
F. A. Thorpe (Publishing)
Anstey, Leicestershire

Set by Words & Graphics Ltd.
Anstey, Leicestershire
Printed and bound in Great Britain by
T. J. International Ltd., Padstow, Cornwall

This book is printed on acid-free paper

But now I am no longer I,
nor is my house any longer my house.
FEDERICO GARCÍA LORCA

1

Sara's gaze drifted toward the window. It was dark outside now, and she could see her own reflection superimposed like a hologram on the house across the road. Their curtains were half-closed but the cold blue flicker of the TV could just be seen. She imagined Gavin lounging in the Eames chair with a glass of red, Lou lolling barefoot on the sofa. They might be watching an art-house movie together — or perhaps just slumming it with Saturday night telly. It was all too easy to conjure — the flea-bitten hearth-rug, the aroma of Pinot Noir mingled with woodsmoke. Even after everything that had happened, the scene still had its allure.

★   ★   ★

From their vantage point, Carol's place would be a goldfish bowl — blinds open, lights blazing, a room full of people and more arriving. Sara hoped they had noticed. She hoped their exclusion would hurt, but she doubted it. Her focus shifted, once again, to her own face, a ghostly smudge in the sheen of the windowpane.

★   ★   ★

Eighteen months earlier

The first time Sara saw their car, she thought it had been dumped, it looked so incongruous among all the people carriers and Volkswagens. Its rear wheel was perched on the kerb, while its front ones were skewed at an alarming angle. It was a red and grey vintage Humber with a missing hubcap, a slew of rubbish in the passenger footwell and a baby seat in the back. Over the next few days, however, she spotted the car a number of times; not always so erratically parked, but usually within a stone's throw of her house.

★ ★ ★

She was standing outside Carol's, debriefing after the school run, when she noticed her friend's concentration drift.

'Check out our new neighbour,' Carol murmured, nodding toward the other side of the street.

Sara glanced casually across. Got up in a boiler suit and headscarf, like Rosie the Riveter, the woman was struggling to steer a wheelbarrow of debris down the front path.

'She's seen us,' murmured Carol. 'Smile. Wave.'

Sara did so, regretting the aura she knew they must project, of complacency and cliquiness. The woman acknowledged them with an anxious smile.

Her house was the semi-detached twin of Sara's. Bay windows, stuccoed porches, steep gables mirrored one another brick for brick and tile for tile, but while Sara's house exuded bourgeois respectability, number 9 was a mess — peeling paint, rotten window-frames, sagging gutters. Still, they were doing it up now, and as noisy and dirty as the process continued to be, it was to be welcomed. As were the neighbours themselves. On an impulse, Sara left Carol to mind the boys and crossed the road.

'Looks like hard work!' she said, opening the gate. Her neighbour trundled the barrow out onto the street, up a makeshift gangplank and tipped its contents into the skip. She reversed back down and lowered the wheelbarrow to the pavement, before holding both hands out in front of her as if about to play an imaginary piano. It took Sara a moment to realise that she was demonstrating a tremor brought on by the exertion of pushing the barrow.

'Goodness,' said Sara.

'I know!' said her neighbour, then, after wiping her palm clean on her overalls, she held it out.

'I'm Lou.'

'Sara.'

Saah-ra. The syllables seemed to ooze like syrup, speaking of bedtime stories and ballet lessons. Not for the first time, she wished she were called something else.

'And can I just say, I feel terrible,' she added.

'Why?'

'Well, you've been here, what, a week . . . ?'

'Two.'

' . . . And we haven't been round to say hello. I kept meaning to, but you always seemed so busy.'

She was sounding like a curtain-twitcher now.

'Oh God, it's me who should apologise. We've had our heads up our arses. The building work was meant to be finished before we moved in but,' she shrugged apologetically, 'you know how it is.'

'Oh, totally,' Sara said.

'And then, just when we thought things couldn't get any worse, the art-handlers fucked up and we had to store a million quid's worth of Gav's artwork, with half the house hanging off!'

'Gosh,' was all Sara could think of to say.

'Anyway,' Lou made to pick up the barrow again, 'we'll sort something soon . . . '

'Pop in later if you want,' Sara blurted. 'It's just me and the kids.'

★ ★ ★

Lou arrived on a waft of expensive, grassy perfume. Her hair was damp and she had changed into an embroidered shirt and jeans. There was something equine about her, Sara thought — a wariness that invited soothing. She had only brought one of the children — an angelic-looking child with shoulder-length, white-blond hair.

'Sara, this is Dash.'

'Hi, Dash,' Sara said, and was treated to a sunny, yet slightly unnerving, smile.

4

'Patrick! Caleb!' She then called over her shoulder. The trill and clatter of the Xbox continued unabated. Sara turned apologetically to Lou, 'Perhaps she should just go through. They're pretty tame.'

'*He*,' Lou corrected her.

'Oh!' Sara recoiled in embarrassment, 'I thought . . . the hair.'

'It's Dash*iell*,' said Lou, 'as in Hammett.'

'Of course. Gosh. I don't know how I . . . *obviously* you're a boy, Dash. Sorry. It was only because of the . . . '

' . . . Hair. Yes, it does confuse some people.'

Lou's neutrality on the issue, her complete lack of embarrassment or rancour only made Sara feel worse. Her own two children had by now appeared, Patrick, the younger one, skidded to a stop in his socked feet, ahead of Caleb, who followed with the world-weary lope of the pre-adolescent.

'So this is Dashiell,' Sara said, the colour still high in her cheeks. 'He lives next door. Dashiell, these are *my* boys, Caleb and Patrick.'

★   ★   ★

Sara led Lou to the kitchen. It was the best room. The only room really, that she felt truly reflected her taste. Neil had wanted to economise on the re-fit, but egged on by Carol, Sara had gone all-out, sourcing artisanal tiles to set off the cherry-red Aga and agonising over subtly different shades of sustainable hardwood flooring. She had been vindicated, too. Eighteen

5

months on, the stainless-steel work surface had acquired the odd dent and the cupboard fronts were scuffed, but the room still had a warmth and integrity to it. Even today, with the sink full of dirty dishes and the boys' lunch boxes spewing rubbish across the table, it looked lived-in rather than squalid. So accustomed had she become to fending off compliments, in fact, that it came as something of a surprise when Lou offered none. Instead her visitor cast an appraising eye around the room before meeting Sara's, with an inscrutable smile.

'Well,' Sara said, 'what can I get you?'

She had been about to list a variety of herbal teas, when Lou shrugged and declared herself equally happy with red or white. They were soon installed at the kitchen table, a bottle of Shiraz nestling among the empty pasta bowls. While Lou knocked back wine like Ribena and enthused about the vibrancy of the neighbourhood, Sara studied her guest's appearance. She was not quite beautiful. Everything was just a fraction off; the eyes too wide-set, the nose a tad flared. Yet she had managed to make a virtue of these defects — a flick of eyeliner, a discreet silver hoop through one nostril — so that mere beauty no longer seemed the point. Her hair, now almost dry, had resolved itself into a short mop of corkscrew curls, which she thrust around her head as she talked, as if the weight of it irked her.

★　★　★

When their kids hadn't turned up at Cranmer Road, Sara had assumed they must have sent them to a private school, but Lou told her this wasn't the case.

'We thought we'd wait for the new school year, rather than pick up the fag end,' she explained. 'Where they were before was so tiny, and the curriculum was so different. I say curriculum . . . ' She laughed and shook her head.

'Where was that?' Sara asked.

'Oh, didn't you know? We were living in Spain. A little village in the mountains, not far from Loja.'

'Sounds idyllic,' said Sara.

'It was,' agreed Lou, with a wistful sigh. 'I pine for it, but Dash is starting Year Six in September, so we had a decision to make.'

Sara wondered if they had made the right one. She knew plenty of local parents who, faced with the scramble for places at the mediocre state secondaries in their borough, would have considered a mountain shack staffed by a goat-herd to be a better bet.

'I'd love to live abroad,' she said, 'but Neil's job isn't very portable . . . '

'Oh there's always a reason *not* to do things.' Lou tugged a tendril of hair in front of her eyes and examined it, before letting it spring back into place. 'What you have to do is look for the reasons *to* do it.'

'That is so true. I'm just a bit of a ditherer, I suppose. It's such a big leap, isn't it? And I'd be worried about not fitting in.'

'Mmmm . . . ' said Lou ominously.

'Was that hard, then?'

'Yes and no. They're very straightforward, the Spanish. If they don't like you, they tell you to your face and their kids throw stones at your kids.'

Sara clutched her cheeks in mute dismay.

'It's harsh, I know,' Lou went on, 'but it's kind of preferable to that awful thing the English do of keeping a poker face and making you guess what you've done wrong. Anyway, the flipside is, if you can turn it around, you've got friends for life.'

'And how *do* you turn it around?'

'Oh you work hard and you make yourself useful . . . and you tell your kids to throw stones back.'

'Seriously?'

'Seriously. Stopped overnight,' Lou replied, straight-faced. 'And, thank God, because that first winter was *hard*. You can't be self-sufficient in a community like that. It's all tit for tat. You harvest my olives, I'll fix your generator, sort of thing.'

'How fantastic,' said Sara.

'It is. There really is no better system when it's working well. Everyone rallies round; there's a sense of community. You share your surplus produce so there's no waste.'

'Like a commune.' Sara stared wistfully out of the window at the serried garden fences of their own little enclave, dividing neighbour from neighbour as far as the eye could see. When she looked back, she was astonished to see Lou pressing her middle finger to the bridge of her nose, apparently holding back tears.

8

'Lou?' she said.

'Sorry.' Lou took a deep, shuddery breath. 'I don't know where that came from.'

Sara maintained a tactful silence, embarrassed, yet also thrilled that Lou seemed about to confide in her.

* * *

'We had four-and-a-half blissful years in Riofrio. We made some very, very good friends. People I'd trust with my life.'

'I'm sensing a but . . . ?'

Lou took a gulp of wine and composed herself.

'It was a misunderstanding really. There isn't a court in Spain that would have ruled in their favour . . .'

'A *court*?'

'Oh, it's nothing terrible, honestly. As I say, a misunderstanding. If we'd had any money, we could have proved it . . .'

Sara frowned and sat forward in her seat, warming to her role as confidante.

* * *

Their neighbours, Dolores and Miguel Fernandez, had a smallholding further down the hill, Lou told her, a few sheep and an orchard. Miguel helped Gavin do the wiring for his studio and she and Gav pitched in at harvest time. So far, so neighbourly, but then the Fernandez decided to farm trout. A bit greedy really, according to Lou,

9

because they were doing just fine as they were. But there were grants available and it looked good on paper.

'Typical Spain — to hell with the integrity of the landscape, bugger the ecosystem — if it ekes out a few more euros, go for it. The irony was,' she hugged herself and looked at the ceiling, blinking back tears, 'Gavin helped them build the tanks. Worked flat out, even though he was meant to be getting his exhibition together for the Venice Biennale.'

★   ★   ★

It had only been up and running a week when they realised it was a disaster, she recalled. The constant whirring of the pumps gave Lou migraines, they didn't know what to do with all the free trout (God knows they weren't going to eat it, not the way those pellets smelled). The tanks were an eyesore. But they kept quiet because the Fernandez were their friends and they could see the bigger picture.

'And then one weekend,' she spread her hands wide, like a child, 'all the fish died and they said it was Gavin's fault.'

Sara shook her head.

'I know. Crazy,' said Lou, 'but they claimed it was the residue from his studio.'

'Residue?'

'Gypsum, from the plaster of Paris. Of course you don't know his work, do you?'

Sara shrugged apologetically.

'Well he's been using it for years. Anyway, he'd

hosed down his studio floor, and they claimed it ran down the mountain and contaminated their tanks.'

'Oh dear.'

'Never mind that the farm next door's using God knows what on their rape. Never mind that Miguel's an alcoholic and he could have just put the wrong chemicals in. We're the newcomers, so it's our fault, right?'

Her hand flexed convulsively on the oilcloth and a single tear brimmed over and tumbled down her cheek. Sara's throat tightened in sympathy. She reached out to cover Lou's hand with her own, but somehow suffered a failure of nerve and went instead for the tissue box.

'Thanks,' said Lou, honking noisily into the paper handkerchief. She met Sara's eye with a brave smile.

⋆   ⋆   ⋆

'Well,' said Sara briskly, after a brief silence, 'I for one am grateful to them.'

Lou looked puzzled.

'To the Fernandezes, or whatever they're called. If it wasn't for them and their stupid trout, you wouldn't be here now, would you? We wouldn't have you as neighbours.'

'*Oh!*' Lou gave her a tremulous smile.

⋆   ⋆   ⋆

The doorbell rang and Sara glanced at the clock.

'Shit!' she said. 'Guitar.'

11

And with that, the spell was broken. Lou was a neighbour she hardly knew, the kitchen looked like a bomb had hit it and Caleb hadn't practised *Cavatina* all week. She flew down the hall and let the guitar teacher in, noticing, even as she burbled apologetically to him about the chaos, the flicker of interest he betrayed as he passed Lou in the hall. It was the kind of glance Sara herself never elicited — not sexual exactly, though there was that in it — more a look of recognition. You are of my kind, the look said, or of the kind to which I aspire. And whilst appearing oblivious, Lou nevertheless managed both to acknowledge his need and to remain aloof from it. Sara felt a pang of envy.

★ ★ ★

Standing on the doorstep, Lou and Sara both started speaking at once.

'I can't tell you how . . . '

'I'm really glad you . . . '

They laughed and Sara deferred to Lou, who shrugged as if suddenly lost for words.

'*Thank you,*' she said, finally, and they both laughed with relief. Lou had got as far as the garden gate, when she turned back, as if a rash new idea had occurred to her.

'We're having a few people over on Saturday, a little get-together to christen the house. Why don't you come?'

2

By the time they had settled the boys and let themselves out of the front door, the street lamps were turning from nascent pink to sodium orange. The Victorian semis loomed tall and narrow in the navy dusk, like nuns having a conflab. The dead hand of gentrification had not yet touched all of them. For every topiaried bay tree, there was a satellite dish, for every tasteful leaded light, a PVC porch. Gav and Lou's place had yet to declare itself. The skip at the front provided some intriguing clues — an ugly fifties fire surround, a naked shop mannequin — but it was too soon to say for sure what kind of people these were.

★ ★ ★

'Bloody hell!' hissed Neil, as they stood on Gav and Lou's doorstep, waiting in vain for someone to hear the bell. 'What did you want to bring the Moët for?'

Sara shrugged.

'It's all we had left.'

She had made a point of opening the last bottle of Sainsbury's Soave, earlier in the evening, partly to settle her nerves, but mainly to make sure the Moët was all they had left. She knew, if she were honest, that Neil had tucked it at the back of the fridge on the off-chance he

13

might soon have something to celebrate. He was plotting a boardroom coup in the housing association where he worked and he was pretty sure, he had told her over dinner the other night, his grey eyes animated, his jaw churning salad like a cement mixer, that he now had enough people onside to oust the finance director. This would remove the final obstacle between him and the CEO's job he had long coveted. Sara had looked at him and seen little trace of the humble, idealistic undergraduate with whom she had fallen in love.

★ ★ ★

If she had told him, back then, that he would be buying Moët to toast his ascendancy to a boardroom, any boardroom, he would have called her a fantasist. Yet here he was, looking every inch the smart casual capitalist in his Paul Smith shirt and Camper shoes. He still had a plausible shtick on why his running Haven Housing would be the tenant-friendly outcome, but it seemed to her that the tenant-friendly outcome was inseparable these days from the Neil-friendly outcome. He had started at Haven wearing jeans and button-down shirts. Gradually, the jeans had gone and a tie had crept in ('tenants like a tie', he'd said). A brief spell of chinos and sleeveless pullovers had given way to the era of the suit. Suits went down better with 'stakeholders', whoever they were. Scratch the suave surface, though, and you'd find the idealist beneath, still fighting the good fight, still

14

standing up for the underdog. He wasn't a cynic, her Neil.

★   ★   ★

She pushed the door, tentatively, and it opened.

'I think we're just meant to go in,' she said.

It was still unclear whether the event was a soirée or a rave. All day she had kept her ear cocked and her eyes open, but there hadn't been much to go on. The household had seemed to slumber until well after two, which, for a young family on a summer's weekend, struck Sara as a significant feat. Then, when most people were beginning to wind down, they suddenly sprang into action. From her vantage point at the kitchen window, she could see Gavin hacking branches off the lime trees at the bottom of the garden with what must have been a blunt saw, because his torso was running with sweat. The temperature had to be in the mid-twenties, and, as it had seemed the whole of that summer, the humidity was high. Their fence was too tall and their shrubs too unkempt to afford anything but the odd glimpse of the kids, but she could hear their excited shrieks and yelps. Music blasted through the open windows — something kitschy and seventies, Supertramp maybe — but, occasionally, Lou would kill the volume and Sara would hear her call out, her tone plaintive, yet with a stridency that somehow managed to penetrate the rasp of the saw.

'Ga-a-av?'

When he had stopped and turned towards her,

15

face glowing, chest heaving, she would ask him some trivial question or other, more to prove her entitlement to do so, it seemed to Sara, than because she really needed to know the answer.

★ ★ ★

By six o'clock, he was still perched in a cleft of the third and final tree, sawing at a stubborn shred of bark tethering the last substantial branch to its trunk. If it were Neil up the tree, and the two of them were having a 'get-together' that night, however impromptu, she knew she'd have been going spare.

★ ★ ★

She had dithered about a babysitter, and in the end done nothing, because she didn't really know what the deal was. She'd decided she'd just keep an eye out and when enough guests had arrived, they'd wander round. There was the problem of what to wear, but seeing the way their hosts had gone about things, she reckoned it had to be pretty relaxed. By eight, she was showered, and semi-got-up in her For All Mankind jeans, a silk camisole and strappy sandals, which she'd changed for Birkenstocks, as soon as she saw the look on Neil's face. She could, she knew, have stared at his Coldplay T-shirt until it burst into flames and he still wouldn't have got the hint, so in the end she'd just told him as nicely as she could to change it.

The hall was deserted. Tea lights on every step of the uncarpeted stairs threw juddering shadows up the wall.

'Place could go up like a tinderbox,' muttered Neil. The throb of seriously amplified music came from deep within the house. Closer at hand, the hum of party chatter made Sara's stomach clench with anxiety. She poked her head around the door of the living room; a bearded man in a rumpled linen suit was sitting on a Scandinavian-style leather sofa rolling a joint on an album cover as if it were 1979. What she could see of the room was an odd combination of mess and emptiness. The walls were hung haphazardly with artworks. One alcove was crammed from floor to ceiling with books. In the other, a hydra-headed chrome floorlamp loomed behind a beaten-up Eames chair. Fairy lights were strung through the antlers of a stuffed stag's head above the fireplace. There was a smell of curry and pot and a faint mustiness, which suggested that the age-old damp problem that had long beset the house had not necessarily been cured. In another corner of the room, she now picked out, amid the gloom, a man in a pork-pie hat and a woman in Rockabilly get-up. They were clutching cans of Red Stripe. She smiled at them tentatively and ducked back out again. She shrugged at Neil.

'Kitchen?'

★ ★ ★

They blinked as they entered the strip-lit room. It was as busy and vibrant as the living room had been underpopulated and dull. The decibel level alone was intimidating, and for a moment, confronted by what seemed to be an impenetrable wall of bonhomie, Sara's instinct was to run. These people were not locals — they looked as though they had been flown in from an avant-garde New York gallery. Here were septuagenarians in skinny jeans and twenty-somethings in tweed. Here were Baader Meinhof intellectuals, kohl-eyed It girls, preening dandies and scrofulous punks. Sara felt instinctively for her husband's hand and steered a course through the mêlée, until she reached safe harbour beside the kitchen table. Neil went to put the Moët down, but Sara gave him a warning look.

★   ★   ★

There had been no attempt to prettify the kitchen, or create atmosphere. It was just a watering hole and looked, as far as Sara could remember, exactly as it had when the house had gone up for auction. Perhaps Lou and Gavin had spent all their money converting the basement, or perhaps, seventies retro being back in fashion, they considered its brown floral tiles and yellow melamine cupboards a stylistic coup.

★   ★   ★

'Ooh, champagne! Crack it open then.'
    'Carol, hi!' Sara was a little surprised, herself,

18

at the grudging tone of her own greeting. Carol was wearing one of her Boden wrap dresses, accessorised with earrings, tights and nail varnish in the precise jade green of every third zigzag. Her short ginger hair had been freshly coiffed. She looked like a home-economics teacher who had wandered into a seedy jazz club and — unworthy impulse — Sara did not want to be seen with her. Not that Carol wasn't a great girl, she was. She was stalwart and practical, clever and kind. She was as good for a heart-to-heart as she was for a cup of couscous. There had been confessions over the years and there had been tears. Carol ran a mean book group and threw a decent dinner party and if the guest lists for both tended to overlap, and the conversations repeat themselves, her hospitality was never less than generous. She was, however, no Bohemian.

★ ★ ★

Even now, as Sara reluctantly filled Carol's glass with champagne, Carol was assessing the fixtures and fittings.

'Do you think this kitchen's retro, or just old?'

'I don't really know,' said Sara. She was trying to eavesdrop on a nearby conversation about rap music and misogyny, but with Carol prattling in one ear and Neil and Simon talking football in the other, it was impossible.

'I thought it'd be state of the art,' Carol went on. 'Fancy having the builders in all this time and the kitchen still looking like this.'

'They've been making a studio, Carol.'

19

'Oh yes, I forgot he's an *artist*.' Carol widened her eyes satirically and then returned her gaze to the sea of much-pierced humanity surrounding her.

'Do you know any of these people?' she asked. Sara shook her head. The thing was, though, that she wanted to know them, and if Carol stuck to her like glue, that wasn't going to happen. The crowd was starting to thin a bit now, as guests topped up their drinks and wandered out to the garden. Carol leaned in to make some fresh observation.

'Hold that thought,' Sara said, laying an apologetic hand on her friend's arm, 'I'm busting for the loo.'

★   ★   ★

Walking down the steps to the garden, she could at last make sense of the intensive tree pruning that had gone on earlier. A gazebo had been erected at the far end, which had been filled with cushions and kilims. Paper lanterns winked with promise from within. You had to take your hat off to Lou and Gavin; they knew how to create a sense of occasion. She supposed it was some sort of chill-out zone and wondered what might take place there as the evening wore on. There would be more pot, certainly, but would there be other drugs? She wondered what she would do if someone offered her cocaine — turn it down, she supposed. There were the kids, for one thing and besides, she'd only do it wrong and look an idiot.

★   ★   ★

20

There was still no sign of the hosts, but clusters of people were milling about on the grass, drinking, smoking, weaving their heads, serpent-like, to trip-hop. Most of them seemed to know each other. This must be how it felt to be a ghost, Sara thought, as she floated from one huddle of people to the next, hovering on the periphery, smiling hopefully, yet never quite plucking up the courage to introduce herself. A few guests made eye contact, one or two smiled back and shuffled aside to accommodate her, but their conversations were too bright and smooth and fluent to allow her an entrée — it was like trying to wade into a fast-flowing stream. It was a relief, then, to bump into an acquaintance from a few streets away, who, it turned out, had done an art foundation course with Lou, but who now wanted to talk school catchment areas. After twenty minutes nodding and smiling, shifting her weight from foot to foot, and twirling the stem of her glass, Sara had had enough. She made her excuses and was threading her way back through the throng towards the house, when she met the host coming down the steps.

'Top up?' he said, tilting a bottle of wine towards her glass.

'Thanks,' she said. 'You're Gavin, aren't you?'

'Guilty as charged.'

He filled her glass and started to move off again.

'We're neighbours, by the way,' she added, quickly.

'Ahhh,' he said, turning back and re-engaging with genuine interest, 'you must be *Sara*.'

21

3

Gavin apologised for taking so long to be neighbourly and explained that he had been like a dog, circling round and round in his basket, except in his case, his basket was his studio and it had had to be 'not so much hewn from the living rock, as dug out of the London clay.' He nodded in the direction of the basement, which was still cordoned off with blue tarpaulins. At close quarters, Sara was relieved to discover he was only moderately handsome. One eyelid drooped fractionally, making him look faintly disreputable, and an otherwise fine profile was marred by a slight overbite. He spoke with a Lancastrian burr, which made everything he said sound vaguely sardonic, and prompted a certain archness in Sara's response. She didn't believe, she told him now, that the basement-conversion was a *studio* at all, but one of those underground gymnasia, beloved of Chelsea oligarchs. He said he'd happily prove her wrong, but not tonight, because he didn't want just anyone — jerking his head towards his increasingly unruly party guests — traipsing through. At this whisper of a compliment, Sara felt a flutter of excitement in her belly.

★   ★   ★

'So what is it *you* do, Sara?' he asked after a pause.

'I'm a copywriter,' she said.

'Great! Advertising. Must be fun.'

'Oh it's not Saatchi's or anything,' she said quickly, 'it's really boring. Just in-house stuff for companies mainly. And consumer-y bits . . . '

He nodded, and turned his head, scanning the garden for someone more interesting to talk to, she assumed.

' . . . But I write,' she added quickly, 'just for myself, you know.'

'Cool,' he said, turning back to her. 'What sort of thing?'

'Short stories, the odd poem. I've started a novel, but it's run out of steam.'

'You should talk to Lou.'

'Oh?' said Sara warily.

'Yeah,' he replied, nodding, 'she'll give you a few pointers — depending on the kind of thing it is, of course.'

'Lou's a writer?'

'A writer-director.'

'What, *films*?'

'Yeah. She's working on a short at the moment. Terrific concept.'

'She never said . . . '

'Oh, she wouldn't. She's very humble, my wife. One of those quiet types that just beavers away in the background and then comes up with this gob-smackingly amazing thing. Know what I mean?'

'Mmm,' said Sara miserably. She had only just got comfortable with the idea of Lou the style maven, earth mother and muse; now, it seemed, she had to contend with Lou the creative genius.

'Well . . . ' Gavin looked around for more glasses to fill. It suddenly seemed imperative that she detain him.

'What do you make of *Spanish* cinema?' she blurted.

He looked taken aback.

'I'm no connoisseur,' he said, 'Almodóvar can be fun, but he's so inconsistent.'

'I know what you mean,' Sara agreed, hoping she wouldn't have to elaborate. 'And doesn't it get on your nerves how sloppy they are with the subtitles?' she rolled her eyes despairingly. 'Some of the French films I've seen . . . '

'You speak French?' He looked impressed.

'I get by,' she replied, then shrugged.

'*Ce qui expliquerait le mystère subtil de votre allure,*' said Gavin, with a very passable accent and a twinkle in his eye.

'Er . . . yeah, okay, I did it for A level.' She pulled a rueful face. 'I'm a bit rusty.'

There was a pause, then they both burst out laughing.

'Great!' he said, shaking his head. 'I love it.'

'Good joke?' Neil appeared at Sara's elbow.

'Oh hello,' she said, trying not to feel annoyed with him. 'Gavin, this is my husband, Neil.'

They shook hands.

'It's ten thirty,' Neil said to her, meaningfully.

''Scuse me,' Gavin said, touching Neil's shoulder, 'if it's that time, I should probably be helping my missus with the food. Great talking to you, Sara.'

24

He walked away, still shaking his head and smiling.

★ ★ ★

'Don't you think it's time we left?' Neil said.

'Why?'

'Well, the boys are on their own, for one thing.'

'Go and check on them, if you're worried.'

'Are you having that good a time?' He seemed surprised.

'Yes, because I'm not stuck in the kitchen with Carol and Simon.'

'They've gone now,' he told her. 'They said no one talked to them.'

She felt a twinge of guilt.

'*I'll* go and check on the boys,' she said. 'You, you know . . . put yourself about a bit. These are our new neighbours.'

He glanced doubtfully at the clusters of people — the beautiful, waif-like women, the men with statement sideburns and recherché spectacles.

'All right,' he said with an unconvincing air of bravado. He raised his glass to her and she felt a pang of love for him. It reminded her of the day she had left Patrick in Reception for the first time — the brave smile he had given her, that she knew would become a major lip-wobble as soon as she walked away. Neil might be CEO-in-waiting of Haven Housing Association, but they both knew that wasn't going to cut any ice here.

★ ★ ★

25

The boys were fine. Patrick was snoring lightly, sweat glistening on his top lip. Sleep had stripped back the years, restoring the cherubic quality to features, which, by day, he worked hard to make pugnacious. She turned down his duvet and smoothed his hair to one side with her palm.

Caleb was in bed reading Harry Potter, his eyelids drooping.

'Good party?' he said.

'Not bad.'

'It's very loud.'

It was. They were having a Hispanic interlude. Sara could feel the salsa rhythm pulsing through the brickwork. They had a bit of a nerve really, subjecting people to this when they had only just moved in; a lot of families nearby had young kids. She suddenly wondered whether that was why she and Neil had been invited — so they wouldn't complain about the noise.

'I'll ask them to keep it down,' she said. She went to kiss him, but he pulled the duvet up over his face to prevent her. She smiled sadly and stood up.

''Night, Mum,' he called, as she went downstairs.

''Night,' she called back, in a stage whisper.

★　★　★

Their front door was shut now. She leaned on the doorbell, but she knew she didn't stand a chance of being heard above the racket. Then she noticed that the gate to the side passage stood open. She hurried through it and into the garden, just in time for the music to come to an abrupt stop. For a moment she thought she had timed her return to coincide with the end of the party, but something in the atmosphere told her that was wrong. The guests had formed a circle around the edge of the grass. As she squeezed her way through to the front, she saw Lou and Gavin standing close together in the middle, Lou's face inclined submissively against Gavin's shoulder. At first she thought they must have had a row, but then she noticed a guitarist sitting on a stool in front of the gazebo. There was a hush of anticipation. Rat tat tat; three times the musician slapped his soundboard and the loudness of the cracks belied the absence of an amplifier. Then he summoned a high-pitched, tuneful wail from his upper chest and started to thrum and sing the opening bars of a tango. Sara felt a shudder of embarrassment as Lou and Gavin flung their arms out at shoulder level, intertwined their wrists and began to dance. As the virtuosity of the guitarist and the commitment of the dancers became apparent, however, she found herself spellbound. Lou and Gavin circled the improvised dance floor, their ankles weaving intricately in and out of one another's path, Lou's slinky red dress flowing around Gav's thighs, as they embraced and parted, attracted and repelled one another. The crowd clapped along, not in a spirit of solidarity but of daring; an egging on of something dangerous and illicit. Despite lacking the polish and timing of professional dancers, Gavin and Lou had something even more compelling — a quality

27

that utterly faced down any ambivalence or awkwardness in the watching crowd — they really meant it. As they glanced off each other, brought their cheeks together and their thighs together, closed their eyes and jutted their chins, the sexual chemistry between them was flagrant. It was like watching a cataclysm; a slow-motion car crash with pulverised metal and shattered bone and rending flesh, and knowing that one shouldn't be watching, but being unable to tear one's gaze away. Sara could feel it undermining her, as she stood there, cutting away the ground beneath her feet.

★　★　★

The dance finished, one of Lou's legs high on Gavin's hip, the other trailing, her posture limp in surrender, and the audience erupted, clapping and whistling their appreciation. Laughing now, Lou hitched her other leg around Gavin's waist and he spun her round, a gleeful child where moments ago had been a femme fatale. Sara clapped too and smiled, but she felt upset.

She went in search of a drink and found Neil, reclining on a beanbag inside the gazebo; he hauled himself guiltily to his feet when he saw her coming.

'That was awesome, wasn't it?' He was grinning, in a slack-jawed foolish way. She realised he was stoned.

'Yes. Very impressive,' she said.

'Did you see that guy? Fucking amazing. His fingers were just a blur.'

'You must have been the only one watching the guitarist.'

'I might ask him if he could give Caleb a couple of lessons.'

'He won't want to teach Caleb. He probably doesn't even speak English.'

'Well I'm gonna see if he's got a CD we can buy anyway. He's gotta have a CD. Talent like that.'

'Don't,' she said.

'Why not?'

'It's embarrassing.'

He looked a bit hurt, so she slipped her hand into his. His palm felt clammy.

The music had started up again.

'Dance with me,' said Neil. He pulled her in towards him and nuzzled her neck.

'I thought you wanted to get back,' she said.

'Just one dance.'

It wasn't a good track; neither fast enough to pick up a beat and move, nor quite slow enough for a neck-encircling smooch. They revolved self-consciously on the spot, his hands holding her hips limply, hers clasping first his shoulders, then his elbows, in an effort to encourage him into some kind of rhythm. Fortunately, most people had gone back to refill their glasses, so their only companions on the lawn were a pixie-ish woman who danced with a strange wrist-flicking action, and a little girl wearing fairy wings over her pyjamas.

The track came to an end and Sara kissed Neil lightly on the lips and lifted his hands off her hips.

'Right then,' he said, looking around in a daze, 'shall we say our goodbyes?'

'I'll catch you up,' she said.

★   ★   ★

Sara stayed at the party for another hour or so, but she felt like a spectator. Lots of people smiled at her goofily, but no one offered her any drugs. She danced on the periphery of some other guests, who politely broadened out their circle to include her; one man even wiggled his shoulders at her in an 'I will if you will' invitation to freak out to Steely Dan, but despite having consumed a whole bottle of wine over the course of the evening, she found she couldn't commit to it, and drifted off to the kitchen. Here she stood by the table, absent-mindedly feeding herself parcels of home-made roti, dipped in lime pickle, until it dawned on her that Lou and Gavin had retired for the night, and she might as well go home.

4

Sara stood at the bedroom window watching the neighbourhood wake. She saw the man from the pebble-dashed semi walk his scary dog as far as the house with the plantation blinds and allow it to cock its leg on their potted bay tree before heading back home. She saw Marlene from number twelve, ease her ample behind into her Ford Ka and head, suitably coiffed and hatted, for Kingdom Hall. She saw a bleary-eyed man bump a double buggy down the steps of the new conversion and set off towards the park. She saw Carol's front door open . . .

'Where's *she* off to,' she murmured. A faint groan came from under the duvet.

Sara watched her friend cross the road carrying an envelope.

'Oh, my God, she's not . . . She is! She's sending them a thank-you note.'

Neil hauled himself up to a semi-recumbent position.

'Can you believe that?' She turned towards him with an incredulous grin.

'Christ yeah, good manners.' He shuddered.

'Oh come on,' Sara protested, 'they didn't even enjoy themselves, you said.'

With the pillows piled up behind him, wearing an expression of lofty tolerance, Neil's profile might have been carved into Mount Rushmore.

'Maybe it's something else.'

31

'What else *could* it be?' Sara eyed him sharply.

'A birthday card?' Neil shrugged and picked up his phone.

'Don't be daft, they've only just met.'

All the same, she didn't like the idea of Carol stealing a march on her. *She* was the one on the fast-track. Everything Carol knew about Lou and Gavin, she knew because Sara had told her. Their children's ages and genders; the family's recent migration from Spain; the medium in which Gavin worked; these nuggets she had doled out, with more than a frisson of satisfaction, keeping the confidences — the trout and the tears — to herself. The idea that the two women might have established their own rapport was ridiculous. They had nothing in common.

'What happened, anyway, after I left?' Neil didn't lift his eyes from the phone, nor did his lightness of tone betray much curiosity, and yet he was eager to know, she could tell.

'Not much,' she said, returning to bed and yanking the duvet towards her. 'Gavin and Lou disappeared. I talked to a couple of people, had a dance. Came home.'

'Disappeared where?' Neil said.

'To bed, one imagines,' said Sara, sounding a little prudish, even to her own ears.

'What,' Neil said, '*bed* bed?'

'You saw them,' she said, 'that dance looked like foreplay to me.'

'Really?' Neil looked appalled and delighted, like a randy schoolboy.

'Bit much, don't you think, at their own party?' she muttered.

Neil shrugged.

'Maybe they couldn't help themselves.'

★ ★ ★

They lay there for a while in silence. The cacophony of kids' TV from downstairs competed with the buzz of a hedge trimmer outside. Neil returned to his phone, but the theme of sex hung in the air between them. Sunday morning was their regular slot and she guessed from the intense way Neil was scrolling through the football results, that he had an erection. She felt aroused herself, but it was all mixed up now with Gavin and Lou and their stupid tango. She felt hungover and annoyed and horny. She sighed huffily and flopped a hand down on top of the duvet. With every appearance of absent-mindedness, Neil clasped her wrist and started to stroke it gently, whilst still apparently absorbed in the match report. It was the lightest and most casual of caresses, but he couldn't fool her — he wasn't taking in a word he was reading. She closed her eyes and tried to enjoy it, but she kept thinking of the party: the strange atmosphere; the music; the extraordinary behaviour of the hosts. Neil was nuzzling her neck now, burrowing his hand beneath the bedclothes, working his way dutifully, from base to base. A tweak of the nipple, a quick knead of the breast, then onwards and downwards. She threw her head back and tried to surrender herself to pleasure, but she couldn't get in the zone. She moaned and wriggled, took his hand and, after demonstrating how and where she would like to be touched, closed her eyes, only to find her thoughts invaded once again by Gavin and Lou, this time, naked, Gav's head at Lou's crotch, her face contorted with ecstasy. Appalled, she banished the image, stilling instantly the butterfly quiver of her nascent orgasm. By now, Neil's cock was pulsing against her thigh. To self-censor, she reasoned, would be to disappoint them both. No sooner had she given herself permission to go there than she *was* there, on the other side of the party wall, in their bedroom watching them fuck, like dogs, on the floor, Gav thrusting harder and harder, Lou's hands beating the floorboards, head jerking back, sweat flying everywhere, groaning, screaming, coming, coming, coming.

'Oh God! Oh God!'

★   ★   ★

She opened her eyes and the room and the day fell back into their right order, but still there was a muscular twitch against her leg and a misty look in the eye of her husband. She touched his shoulder and, with the air of a family dog given a one-off dispensation to flop on the sofa, he clambered on board, and could only have been a few thrusts shy of his own orgasm, when the bedroom door burst open. Sara turned her head in annoyance, ready to remonstrate with whichever son had forgotten to knock before entering, but found herself, instead, eyeball to eyeball with a strange nappy-clad toddler, whose shock of blond curls and penetrating blue-eyed stare made her gasp in recognition.

★ ★ ★

'Well, that was interesting . . . ' Sara called, breezing back into the house some fifteen minutes later and poking the front door closed with her foot. There was no response, so she followed the appetising scent of cooked breakfast into the kitchen and stood in the doorway, arms folded.

'They hadn't missed her!' she said.

Neil continued frying eggs.

'No idea she was even here. Pretty shocking really. Poor little thing's not even three. Hey, you'll never guess what her name is.'

Neil didn't try.

'Zuley, short for Zuleika,' she told his impervious back. 'I can't decide whether I like it or not.'

'You can get back to me,' he said.

'I wonder where they got it from . . . '

'*The Bumper Book of Pretentious Names?*'

'She must have tagged along with Dash and Arlo. Voted with her feet. It's not exactly child-friendly round there. You should see the place — weirdos crashed out on every sofa, overflowing ashtrays, empty bottles . . . God knows what she could have put in her mouth!' Try as she might, she couldn't quite banish a grudging admiration from her tone.

'*Anyway,*' she said, her mouth pursed against a smug grin, 'upshot is . . . we're invited round for dinner later.'

'Can you set the table, please?'

Coitus interruptus seemed to have rendered Neil selectively deaf.

★   ★   ★

Sara shuffled aside the Sunday paper, clattered plates and cutlery onto the table and called the boys. They hurtled into the room — a tangle of limbs and testosterone, jostling each other for the best chair, the fullest plate, the tallest glass. Dash won on all counts, even snatching the tomato sauce out the hands of his younger brother and splurging a wasteful lake of it onto his own plate, before Arlo had a chance to object.

'Er, we take turns in this house . . . ' Sara said firmly, and was met with Dash's signature smile — sunny and impervious — more chilling, by far, than defiance. He was a handsome specimen, no doubt about it, and possessed of an easy, insincere charm, but she wondered that she could ever have mistaken him for a girl. Neither his physique nor his behaviour struck her, now, as anything other than self-evidently Alpha-male. Arlo, on the other hand, had the unhappy aura of the whelp about him. Slight of build and weak of chin, he had his mother's rabbity eyes, without her intelligence, his father's thin-lipped mouth, without his redeeming humour. He was the kind of kid, who, even as you intervened to stop sand being kicked in his face, somehow inspired the unworthy impulse to kick a little more. She was touched therefore, and not a little humbled that,

36

long after the older boys had left the room, Patrick sat loyally beside this 'friend', whose friendship he had not particularly sought, prattling cheerfully, while Arlo chased the last elusive baked bean around his plate.

★ ★ ★

'So that'll be quite nice, don't you think?' Sara said to Neil when they were alone again and she was stacking the dirty plates in the dishwasher, 'dinner tonight. Just the four of us?'

'We were only round there last night,' said Neil.

'Yeah, us and fifty other people.'

'I just don't get what the hurry is.'

'There isn't any *hurry*, but nor is there any reason to say no. Unless we *want* to say no.'

'And in fact you've already said yes.'

'Well, not *yes* as such. I said I'd ask you.'

'Thanks very much. So now if we don't go, they'll think I'm a miserable bastard.'

Sara raised a meaningful eyebrow.

With a sigh, Neil returned to his task of scraping the leathery remnants of fried egg from the base of the pan.

'Neil, they're nice, interesting people and they want to be our friends. I'm trying, I really am, but I'm struggling to see anything negative in that.'

Neil shrugged resignedly. He was a simple soul really — affable, straightforward, curious. He had constructed a credible carapace of manliness, which, on the whole, he wore pretty lightly.

37

When he picked up a work call at home (which he seldom did), it was impossible to tell whether he was talking to his PA or to the Chairman. This, really, rather than the recent improvement in tenant satisfaction ratings, or the number of newbuilds completed under his jurisdiction, was the reason he was a shoo-in for the big job. The downside of his instinctive and wholly laudable egalitarianism, however, was, in Sara's view, his reluctance to recognise that some people just *were* exceptional.

★ ★ ★

'Eleven o'clock, absolute latest, okay?' he muttered to Sara, as they stood on Lou and Gavin's doorstep for the second time in twenty-four hours.

'Hell-o-o-o!' Neil said, as Lou opened the door and you would have thought there was nowhere he would rather be. He handed his hostess a bottle of wine and kissed her on both cheeks — a little camply, Sara thought.

'I brought dessert,' Sara told Lou, when it was her turn, 'I thought, you know, with all the clearing up you'd had to do . . . it's nothing fancy, just some baked figs and mascarpone.'

'Oh thanks.' Her hostess looked surprised and faintly amused. In truth, she didn't appear to have *done* much clearing up. The house looked only marginally less derelict than it had when Sara had delivered Zuley back that morning. Empty bottles were stacked in crates beside the front door and a row of black bin-bags bulged beside them. A wet towel and a jumble of Lego lay at the foot of the stairs. The kitchen was chilly and smelled of stale cigarette smoke. No cooking smells, no piles of herbs or open recipe book hinted at treats to come. If it weren't for the fact that Lou had obviously taken a certain amount of care with her appearance, Sara might almost have thought they had come on the wrong night, but Lou looked gorgeous — like a sexy sea lion, hair slicked back with product, eyes kohl-rimmed, in a tie-necked chiffon blouse and jeans, which could not have contrasted more sharply with the eye-popping maxi dress she had worn the night before. She had the enviable knack, Sara had noticed, of making every outfit she wore utterly her own.

★ ★ ★

Lou ushered them in and Sara and Neil sat down a little gingerly, on grubby chairs at a kitchen table still littered with half-eaten pizza crusts and spattered with juice.

'Shall I open this?' Lou asked, waving their wine bottle at them. 'Or are you in the mood for more fizz?'

She flung open the door of the fridge and pulled out a half-full bottle of Krug.

'A party with booze left over,' Neil said. 'Must be getting old.'

'Or more catholic in our tastes,' said Lou with an enigmatic smile. She filled three glasses and handed them round.

Watching her hostess pad around the kitchen, to the strains of John Coltrane, the grimy lino sucking at her bare feet, Sara found herself at once repelled by the squalor and intrigued by Lou's indifference to it. She wondered what it might be like to live like this — to dress how you pleased and eat when you felt like it, and invite people round on a whim. There was, after all, a certain charm in the larky informality of it all, in stark contrast to Carol's well-choreographed 'pot luck' suppers. Lou cheerfully admitted to being 'rubbish' at entertaining. She had once, she said over her shoulder, arms elbow-deep in washing-up water, served undercooked pork to Javier Bardem and given him worms. Once again, Sara found herself at a loss for words.

* * *

By the time Gavin bounded into the room, at 8.05, wearing jeans and a creased linen shirt the colour of bluebells, dusk had darkened the windows and Lou had brought about a transformation. She had cleared the table and put a jug of anemones and a squat amber candle on it. Around this centrepiece, she had placed terracotta dishes of olives, anchovies and artichokes, as well as a breadboard with a crusty loaf. All it took was for Gavin to draw the blinds and pour more wine and suddenly the atmosphere was one of gaiety and promise — the room felt like a barge or a gypsy caravan — some ad hoc combination, at any rate, of home and vehicle, in which the four of them were setting out on a journey. Now the informality of their reception felt less like negligence and more like a huge compliment. Gavin caught his wife around the waist and kissed her neck, glugged back most of a glass of wine, changed the music on the stereo and began to cook.

★   ★   ★

As the candles burned down and the alcohol undid the kinks in the conversation, Sara stopped worrying about her choice of outfit and Neil's unappealing habit of sucking the olive juice off his fingers, and started to enjoy herself. The tone of the evening became relaxed and confessional. She heard herself admit, with a careless giggle that she'd been intimidated when Gav and Lou had first moved in.

'By *us*?' Lou looked askance. 'Why on earth . . . ?'

'Oh, you know — the car you drive, the way you dress . . . ' Sara said, ' . . . the *stag's head above your fireplace!*'

'That's Beryl,' replied Lou, dismissively, 'no one could be intimidated by Beryl. She's cross-eyed and she's got mange on one antler. As for the Humber, I can't even remember how we ended up with that . . . '

'Damien was getting rid of it,' Gav reminded her, 'and we were feeling flush . . . '

'*That's* right!' said Lou, 'because you'd just won the Tennent's Sculpture Prize. So you see, pretty random really. *Anyway*, Madam,' she said, leaning forward in her seat and fixed Sara with a gimlet eye, 'it cuts both ways, let me tell you. That day you first spoke to me, remember?' Sara did. 'I was a nervous wreck!' Lou glanced at Neil and Gavin, as if for affirmation. 'There she was, all colour-co-ordinated and spiffy from the school run, and me looking like shit in my filthy work clothes and, what's her name? *Carol*, watching me like a hawk from across the road. I felt like I was auditioning for something. And then you invited me round for a drink and I was, like, *yesss!*'

Sara didn't know what to do with this information. She blushed with pleasure and pushed a crumb around the table with her forefinger.

'Well,' said Gav huffily, 'if no one's going to tell me how fucking marvellous *I* am, I suppose I'd better serve the dinner.'

They laughed. He had a knack for putting people at their ease, Sara had noticed. She'd imagined an artist to be the tortured, introverted type but Gav was neither. You couldn't call him charming, quite, because there was no magic about it, no artifice. He was just easy in his skin and made you easier in yours. He pottered about the kitchen, humming under his breath, pausing occasionally to toss some remark over his shoulder, and then served up a fragrant lamb tagine as casually as if it were beans on toast. When at last he sat down, he didn't hold forth about himself or his opinions, but quizzed Neil about his work, with every appearance of genuine curiosity.

42

'I just think it's great how you guys give back,' Gav said, shaking his head with admiration.

'Oh, I'm no Mother Teresa . . . ' Neil protested, through a mouthful of food. 'It's important work, don't get me wrong, and I believe in it one hundred per cent, but they pay me pretty well. And if you heard the grief I get from some of the anarchists on the tenants' associations, you'd think I was bloody Rachman . . .'

'Rachman?' Lou skewered a piece of lamb on her fork and looked up, inquiringly.

'He was a notorious private landlord in the fifties,' Neil explained, 'became a byword for slum housing and corruption. I did my PhD on how he influenced the law on multiple occupancy. It was fascinating actually.'

'Neil, you can't say your own PhD was fascinating,' Sara murmured.

'I meant *doing* it was fascinating.'

'So you're *Doctor* Neil,' Gav said. 'Very impressive. I can't imagine having the staying power for something like that.'

'It was a bit of a slog,' Neil conceded. 'Then again, I don't suppose you leaped fully-formed from your mother's womb wielding a paint-brush . . . ?'

'Too true mate, and if my mother had had anything to do with it, I'd have leaped out with a brickie's hod instead.'

He put on a broad Lancashire accent, ' 'Learn a trade, our Gavin, if you want to put food on't table.' '

'But you *do* put food on the table, as an *artist*,'

said Sara. 'Surely your parents must be proud of that?'

'What do you reckon, Lou?' He turned to his wife with a rueful smile. 'Are they proud?'

'We wouldn't know, would we?' said Lou coldly.

'Lou gets very indignant on my behalf. The truth is they don't really get it. If I was a doctor or a lawyer, I'm sure they'd be pleased, but my mum's idea of art's a herd of horses galloping through surf, so . . .'

'She knows you've done well,' Lou muttered, 'wouldn't kill her to say so.'

'Doesn't bother me,' Gav said, shrugging. 'I always played second fiddle to our Paula, anyway.'

'Is that your sister?' asked Sara. 'What does she do?'

'She's just a primary-school teacher,' Lou interjected, 'but to hear Gav's mum, you'd think she walked on water.' She mimicked her mother-in-law with unsparing sarcasm: ''Our Paula's doing an assembly on multiculturalism, Gavin. Our Paula's taking the kids to the Yorkshire Sculpture Park.' No mention of the fact that Gav's got a *piece* in the Yorkshire Sculpture Park. Never occurs to her that she might actually stop playing online bingo for two minutes and go and have a look herself.'

'*Lulu*,' Gavin put a hand on her arm, 'it's no big deal.'

Lou's eyes were glittering.

'That does seem a bit unfair,' said Sara, doubtfully.

'Not really.' Gavin shrugged. 'I mean, artists aren't very useful, are we? People don't actually need art.'

'God Gavin,' Lou fumed, 'I hate it when you put yourself down. You're an important contemporary artist, represented by a top gallery.'

'I know,' Gavin laughed, 'and I never stop wondering when they're going to rumble me.'

'What do you mean?' Neil asked.

'Well honestly, what is it I do? Just muck about really, like those kids our Paula teaches. I just haul my guts up in three dimensions; I play around with bits of old rubbish until they start to look like the things I fear or loathe or love and then I put them out there and amazingly, people seem to get it.'

'*Some* people,' said Lou.

★   ★   ★

'Well,' said Neil, draining his wineglass and placing it decisively back down on the table. 'Sara's too shy to ask, so I will. When are we going to get a look at your studio?'

'Neil!' Sara turned to him indignantly.

'Haven't you seen it yet?' Gavin seemed surprised. 'Oh no, you haven't, have you? That was Stephan and Yuki. Come on then!'

He slapped his thighs and stood up. So much for their banter last evening, Sara thought — the Chelsea oligarchs long forgotten. Nevertheless, she couldn't quell a fluttering in her stomach as she rose, unsteadily, to follow him. She only wished she were feeling her bright, articulate best, instead of fuzzy with drink. As she wove her way towards the spiral staircase which led to the studio, she tried to recall some of the *aperçus* she had read when she'd googled his latest show, but the only phrase that sprang to mind was 'spastic formalism', and she couldn't see that tripping off her tongue. Lou dried her hands on a tea towel and moved to join them, but Gav turned to her with a look of pained regret.

'Do you think maybe one of us should stay up here in case Zuley wakes up?'

'Oh . . . okay,' Lou gave him a tight little smile and turned away. Sara struggled to shake off the feeling that she had somehow usurped her friend, but that was silly — Lou must be up and down these stairs all the time, she would hardly wait on an invitation from her own husband.

★   ★   ★

Her qualms were quickly overtaken by astonishment and fascination when they emerged, not into the picturesque, messy studio of her imagination but into a stark, brightly lit space more reminiscent of a morgue. She could see at a glance that a lot of money had been spent here. There were the specialist tungsten light fittings, the open drains running down each side of the concrete floor, the coiled, wall-mounted hose and gleaming stainless-steel sinks. There were rolls of mesh, and rows of white-stained buckets, and in the centre of the room a large zinc workbench, on which lay the only evidence of what you might call, if you were feeling

46

generous, creative endeavour. Sara edged forward to get a closer look. She could see what appeared to be a rudimentary human form made out of wire mesh, which protruded here and there through a slapdash layer of fibrous plaster. It reminded her, both in its diminutive size — about two-thirds that of an actual human, and its tortured attitude — of the writhing, petrified bodies she had seen in the ruins of Pompeii.

'Gosh!' she said.

'I suppose this is a work in progress?' said Neil hopefully.

Gavin smirked.

'And if I told you it's the finished article?'

'I'd say I don't know much about art, but I know when someone's taking the piss,' said Neil affably. Sara darted him an anxious glance, but Gavin was laughing.

'You'd be right,' he said. 'Come and have a look at this.'

He led them through a swing door, into a space three times the size of the first room. Neil emitted a low whistle.

⋆　⋆　⋆

'What I can't get over,' he said afterwards, as they sat up in bed, discussing their new friends with the enthusiasm of two anthropologists who have stumbled on a lost tribe, 'is the scale of it. I mean, I knew it had to be big — all the earthworks; the noise — but I didn't realise it would be *that* big. The plumbing alone must have cost . . . ' He closed one eye, but bricks and mortar was his specialist subject and it didn't take him long, ' . . . four or five K and they must need a mother of a transformer for those lights. I'm glad I'm not paying the bills.'

'I know,' said Sara, 'but what gets me is the contrast. That really practical work-space and then you see the end-product and it's so *moving*, so human.'

'Right,' said Neil doubtfully.

'Didn't you like it?'

'No, I *did*. It's just . . . I didn't get why . . . he's obviously a consummate craftsman . . . and yet on some of them the finishing looked quite rough and ready.'

'Oh I think that's deliberate,' said Sara, 'because others were really meticulous, really anal. And I think the ones covered with the mirror mosaic-y things were *meant* to be sort of fractured and damaged in a way. Don't you think?'

Neil shrugged.

'Beats me,' he said, 'but you've got to take your hat off to him. The nerve. The confidence. To take on a mortgage like they must have, knowing you've got four dependants . . . '

'Lou works,' Sara objected.

'Yeah, in *film*,' he said. 'And then to blow a ton of money kitting out the studio like it's a private hospital, and all for . . . ' he shrugged ' . . . something so particular, so rarefied. I mean, how does he know people are going to get it?'

'Oh people get it,' said Sara, 'I've looked him up online. He's in the top fifty most collectable living artists.'

'Don't get me wrong,' Neil said, 'I *admired* it. I'm just not sure I understood it.'

'Oh *I* did . . . ' Sara said. She took a deep breath ' . . . I definitely think he's obsessed with mortality. And then I think there's quite a lot about the sacred and the profane. I mean the writhing, emaciated ones — I think must be referencing Auschwitz or something, and then you've got the ones with the wings — they're angels, obviously — but maybe *fallen* angels because there's a sordidness about them, a sense of shame. *My* favourite — the one that really spoke to *me* — was that one with all the tiny toys stuck to it and whitewashed over, did you see that? It looked kind of *diseased* until you got up close and saw what they really were. That, to me, was about childhood, about how we're all formed and scarred by our early experiences. I think he's actually very courageous.'

'Ok-a-ay,' said Neil.

5

It was the start of the autumn term and Sara had promised to show Gavin the ropes. The school run was his thing, apparently. Over the course of the summer, they had forged a firm rapport, yet finding him on her doorstep bright and early this crisp September morning, she found herself unaccountably tongue-tied.

'Hi,' she said. 'It's not raining, is it?' Gavin frowned, held out his hand and scanned the cloudless sky.

'I think we're okay.'

Sara ushered Patrick and Caleb out of the door, fussing unnecessarily over their lunchboxes and book bags to cover her awkwardness, then fell into step with Zuley's buggy.

⋆   ⋆   ⋆

The day might have been warm, but the street was done with summer. The privet hedges were laced with dust and the trees held onto their leaves with an air of reluctance. The long grass in front of the council flats had snagged various items of litter. Here and there a car roof box, as yet un-dismantled, recalled the heady days of August in Carcassonne or Cornwall, but for the commuters hurrying by, earphones in, heads down, the holidays were ancient history.

Only Gavin, in his canvas shorts and flip-flops

still seemed to inhabit the earlier season. Sara stole occasional glances at him as he strode along. She liked the way he gave the buggy an extra hard shove every few steps to make Zuley laugh, the way he gave his sons the latitude to surge fearlessly ahead, but pulled them up short with a word when they got out of hand. He might not spend that much time around his children, she thought, but he was a good parent when he did; a better one, probably, than Lou. To the casual observer he could be any old self-employed Dad — a web designer or a journalist. She hugged to herself the knowledge of his exceptionalness.

★ ★ ★

'So you didn't get away in the end?' he said. 'That's a pity.'

'No,' Sara sighed, 'Neil wanted me and the kids to go without him, but I wasn't up for a busman's holiday. We just stayed here and I took them swimming and did the museums and stuff. Lost our deposit on the cottage, but . . . ' she said, shrugging, ' . . . not the end of the world.'

She had been less phlegmatic when Neil had told her, with days to go, that he couldn't make it to Dorset after all. A mix-up over the holiday rota at work — not his fault, but if he wanted to send the right message, improve his chances of getting the big job, he'd have to lead from the front.

'Sounds like *you* had a lovely time,' she said, wistfully.

51

'Yeah. Great to catch up with old mates,' Gav agreed.

They turned the corner, passing the bus shelter where shiny Year Sevens waited for the 108 in over-sized uniforms, like lambs to the slaughter.

'Where was it you went again?'

She knew perfectly well. Tom and Rhiannon's place in the Lake District. She'd had the full account — the walk up Helvellyn, the skinny-dipping, the toasted marshmallows. She had managed to disguise her envy; had smiled, nodded, agreed with Lou that they should *definitely* all get up there some time, the six of them and that Tom and Rhiannon sounded lovely.

'The Lakes,' Gav said with a shrug. 'Weather was terrible.'

She could have kissed him.

* * *

'Neil still odds-on for promotion?' he asked, as they waited at the pedestrian crossing for the man to turn green.

'Looks like it,' she admitted, embarrassed. What, after all, could promotion mean to a man like Gavin? A man for whom success was measured in the raising of hairs on the back of a neck, the falling of scales from the eyes?

They shepherded the children across the road and quickly past the newsagent's, ignoring their clamour for sweets.

'Smart guy, your husband,' Gav said.

Sara gave him a curious sideways glance.

'No, really, I admire him,' Gavin insisted, 'he's

52

got integrity. Doggedness. Do I mean dogged?'

Sara shrugged.

'He *commits* to things — his work, his family, the community. I admire that . . . '

'So, are you a *quitter*?' Sara blurted.

'Because we left Spain, you mean?' Gavin frowned, after a pause.

Sara looked away, her cheeks hot. She always did this; overstepped the mark, said the wrong thing. A harassed-looking woman came out of her thirties semi, still tucking her shirt into her smart skirt. She waited, with barely disguised irritation, for their procession to pass so that she could reach her car and Sara gave her a meek smile of thanks.

'I didn't mean that,' Sara said now, turning back to Gav. 'Of course you're not a quitter. Your commitment's obvious. To Lou; to your work — my God, nobody could doubt your commitment to your *work*.'

'So you think I'm *obsessed*?'

'No! Good grief, but even if you were, it goes with the territory, doesn't it? Artists are supposed to be driven. I mean, can you imagine,' she added, with a manic little laugh, 'Picasso getting up in the morning and going, 'Right, Françoise, shall I reinvent modern art today, or do you need a hand with the kids?''

'I suppose . . . ' he said, doubtfully, swivelling the buggy up the ramp and through the school gate.

'No, *you're* fine. It's us mere mortals who have to worry about work-life balance.'

'But you're a writer,' Gavin shouted, above the

din of the playground, and Sara winced, hoping no one heard.

'A *copy*-writer,' she corrected him, 'day job comes first. Don't know when I last got to do any of my own stuff. For all you think Neil's such a family man, with this promotion in the offing, he's around less and less. And when he is around, his head's not around, if you know what I mean.'

'Oh, I get accused of that a lot.'

'Do you?' said Sara curiously. 'I'd have thought with you both being creatives — hey, boys, don't forget your book-bags . . . ' but it was too late, her sons had disappeared into the mêlée.

'Not by *Lou*,' Gavin replied. 'She's got a sixth sense about that stuff. She gives me plenty of headspace. And I do her. No, it's other people.'

'Oh,' said Sara, a little deflated. She couldn't imagine who else would have dibs on Gavin's headspace. Then again, there was still a lot about Gavin that mystified her. She could have gone on talking to him all day, but this was where they parted, he to deliver Zuley to her childminder, she to catch the 9.47 to Cannon Street.

'Well,' she said, briskly, 'for what it's worth, Neil really likes you too.'

Gavin gave her a grateful glance, and she saw that for all his biennales and his groupies and his five-star reviews, he was just as needy of reassurance and friendship as anyone else. The temptation to put out a hand and touch his skin was almost overwhelming.

★   ★   ★

54

'I see you've got her kids again,' Carol said, one teatime. She'd come over to see if Neil and Sara were interested in tickets for the new play at the Royal Court.

'I have, yes,' said Sara tartly, and then, in response to Carol's meaningfully arched eyebrow, 'it works really well. I have hers when she's working. She hangs on to mine if I'm late back.'

'Which you almost never are . . . '

'I'm actually under the cosh quite a bit since I upped my hours,' said Sara, irritated by Carol's sly dig. 'She's saved my bacon a few times.'

Carol twisted her mouth into an approximation of a smile and for a second Sara felt like Judas. Hadn't Carol also saved her bacon over the years? The time Caleb was rushed to A&E with suspected meningitis? The day the guinea pig disappeared?

'Anyway, if you *do* want to come,' her friend was saying now, as she handed the leaflet to Sara, 'can you let me know ASAP?'

Sara took this as a veiled reference to the last time they had gone to the theatre, when Sara's prevarication had meant the only available tickets had been for the surtitled performance for the hard of hearing. Sara smiled, closed the front door after Carol, and put the leaflet straight in the recycling.

★   ★   ★

She was sorry they were drifting apart, but sometimes you just outgrew people. Friends like Lou and Gavin didn't come along every day, and

55

she felt such warmth towards them, such gratitude that they had come into her life and made it three-dimensional and vivid. She felt she had been sleepwalking until now, lulled by the conformity, the complacency of everyone around her. How could she go to Carol's book group and discuss the latest Costa prize fodder now that Lou had introduced her to the magic realists of Latin America whose profound ideas wrapped up in hilarious flights of fantasy were like fairy tales for grown-ups? There was no doubt about it, Sara was learning a *lot*. It wasn't a one-way street, though. Sometimes she surprised herself with her own perceptiveness. She had recently aired her pet theory that Georgia O'Keefe's famously Freudian flower paintings were perhaps *just flowers* and not, as the art fraternity would have it, symbolic vaginas, only for Lou to confirm that this was, in fact, what the artist herself had always claimed.

* * *

The most rewarding aspect of their friendship, though, wasn't the head stuff, but the heart stuff. After a surprisingly short time, Sara had found herself confessing things to Lou that she had never said to anyone else, not even Neil. Lou had set the tone that first afternoon, when she had cried about the trout farm, but since then, whether surrounded by childish clamour at teatime or listening to Dory Previn beside the dying embers of a late-night fire, they had shared some of the most intimate aspects of their lives.

56

Sara didn't even mean to say half of it — it just came tumbling out, her unhappy teenage promiscuity; her botched episiotomy and its impact on her and Neil's sex life; her disappointing career and suspicion that Neil was secretly happy about it because he wanted a traditional wife. Lou was such a good listener. She had a way of asking just the right question, or upping the ante with a heartfelt confession of her own. She managed to make Sara feel both entirely normal in her anxieties and utterly exceptional in her talents. 'But you're so gorgeous, I can't *believe* you had to shag a bunch of spotty oiks to prove it,' she would say, or 'Creativity just *oozes* from you, Sara; the way you live, the way you raise your kids — I don't think you realise how inspiring that is to someone like me.'

★ ★ ★

It was true that Lou had her shortcomings, but this only made her more interesting. Sara had heard her lose it with the children on a number of occasions. She blatantly favoured Dash over Arlo in a way that made Sara wince for the younger boy. Then there was the rather complex matter of Lou's relationship with Gavin. There was a neediness in the way Lou related to her husband that didn't seem quite healthy to Sara. Surely one shouldn't be competing with one's own children for the attention of their father? Yet Sara saw this happen often. Once, she had been in the kitchen chatting amiably with Gavin while

57

she waited for Lou to get ready. The two women were going to see a film together, though if Lou didn't get a move on they'd miss the beginning. Gav had been dandling little Zuley on his lap and marching toy farm animals across the table, interspersing adult conversation with a variety of silly moos and grunts that were making the three of them giggle. They were so absorbed that it was a moment or two before they noticed Lou had joined them. Wreathed in perfume and got up like an art-school vamp, she began clattering cupboard doors noisily in what looked, to Sara, like a flagrant bid for attention. And did Zuley, at nearly three years old, really need a bottle of milk thrust into her mouth, mid 'Baaaa,' just so that Lou could pirouette girlishly in front of Gavin and solicit his opinion on her outfit?

Yet Sara wasn't quite sure she was being objective. The air around Gav and Lou fairly crackled with sexual static and it made Sara envious. If the roles were reversed, would she care what Neil thought of the way she looked? If he were absorbed in a game with the boys — well, first of all she'd pinch herself to make sure she wasn't seeing things, and then she'd leave while the going was good. No pirouetting, no eyelid-batting. All that was in the past. They'd been married fifteen years, for goodness' sake. Surely, a certain amount of complacency was natural, desirable even?

Then again . . . ever since she'd witnessed it, she'd been unable to get that tango out of her mind. It had made her wonder whether all her life she had been doing sex wrong or, worse, with the wrong person. She watched, now, as Lou leaned in to kiss Gavin languidly on the lips. Zuley, eyes rolling with pleasure as she slugged back the milk, reached up a plump fist to grasp her mother's forearm, but Lou prised the child's fingers away and gave them a cheerful shake of admonishment.

'Mummy's got to run,' she said, glancing at the sunburst clock on the kitchen wall. 'You're making Mummy late.'

★　★　★

They arrived five minutes into the film, just as the opening credits were starting. It was a gritty, low-budget number, which had got four stars in the *Guardian*. Sara took a little while to acclimatise, but half an hour in, she was starting to enjoy it; Lou, on the other hand, seemed to be growing restless. She kept shaking her head and laughing under her breath at things Sara didn't think were meant to be funny. Finally, after what seemed to Sara a rather moving scene, Lou groaned loudly and rested her head on Sara's shoulder.

'Do you want to leave?' Sara whispered anxiously. She couldn't have been more mortified by Lou's reaction if she had made the film herself. Lou nodded and, muttering apologies, they climbed over the laps of their fellow audience members before escaping to the bar.

'I had a feeling it'd be like that,' said Lou (Like what? wondered Sara). 'I nearly said something when you suggested it, but I thought, give the guy a break.'

'Do you know the director?'

'He was in the year above me at St Martins. Very talented. Always wanted his name up in lights and now he's got it. Just a shame he had to compromise the integrity of the film.'

'Compromise how?'

'Oh everything. The aesthetic, the soundtrack, the casting,' said Lou. 'That grainy, cine-film thing? I mean, sorry, but yawn.'

'Mmmm,' said Sara.

'And the lead actor? Totally unbelievable in the role. Straight out of RADA, but, you know, he's up and coming. Getting him's a coup, so . . . '

'Right,' Sara nodded, thoughtfully. 'Who would you have cast?'

'Oh an unknown,' said Lou. 'I'd never compromise the integrity of the film for a 'name' actor. It's just not worth it.'

Sara took a sip of her drink and tried to appear nonchalant. 'So, I've been dying to ask: what's your new thing about?'

'What's it *about*?' Lou frowned humorously, and Sara blushed. 'Well, it hasn't got a plot as such. It's not that kind of film. But I suppose, if I had to sum it up . . . it's a sort of urban fairy tale.'

Sara nodded. 'And it's a short?'

'Yes. But a short film has to work that much harder to earn its keep. No indulgences. No flights of fancy. Every frame counts. And because shorts aren't really made for a mainstream audience, there's a . . . I won't say higher . . . a *different* expectation on them to deliver.'

Sara nodded again.

'So, forgive my ignorance, but who actually watches them?'

'Well, there are all these amazing festivals now . . .'

'Sundance?'

'Sundance is a bit old hat, but there are lots of other really interesting ones all over the world: San Sebastian, Austin, Prague. You just hope to premiere your film at one of them and get good notices . . .'

'So that's who they're for, the critics?'

'Well, no,' Lou said, 'they're for everyone.'

'But they don't go on general release?'

'Well, you're not really looking for bums on seats . . .'

'What are you looking for?'

'Well an audience . . .'

'But not a *big* audience.'

'A discerning audience.'

'Ah . . .'

'And enough money to make your next film. Making the things is a doddle compared to financing them. I sometimes wish I'd studied accountancy . . .'

'Lou . . .'

'Yes?'

'I was wondering . . .'

'What?'

'Oh, no, you're busy . . .'

'Come on, out with it. Gav said you'd got some writing on the go. You want me to have a look?'

Sara smiled hopefully. 'I would *love* to know what you think.'

'It'd be an absolute privilege.'

'You might hate it. If you hate it, you've got to promise you'll say so . . . '

'How could I hate it? I would *tell* you, though, of course I would. Not to would be a betrayal of our friendship, but I can't imagine someone as clever and sensitive, and *off-beat* as you, could possibly write anything bad.'

Sara glowed with pleasure. Was she off-beat? She certainly hoped so.

★   ★   ★

It turned into another late night. They were pretty well-oiled when they tumbled out of the taxi and Lou eagerly accepted Sara's invitation of a nightcap. Neil must have only just gone to bed, because the wood burner required only a little stoking to send flames licking up the chimney again. Sara put Nick Drake on the stereo, broke out the Calvados and the conversation turned, once again, to matters of the heart. Sara found herself reminiscing, dewy-eyed, about Philip Baines-Cass, the boy who'd played opposite her in a fourth form production of *Hobson's Choice*.

'He wasn't really good-looking,' she remembered fondly, 'but he had this incredible charisma. He was the kind of person you couldn't *not* look at. He was clever but cool and you didn't really get that combination at my school. I'm kind of surprised he didn't go into acting actually — he seemed like he was made for it.'

'Probably a computer programmer in Slough,' Lou chuckled. 'Go on . . . '

'Well, so he was this . . . amazingly gifted actor and I was this stilted little am-dram wannabe, and there was this one scene where we had to kiss, and I would be literally shaking as it got nearer. On the one hand, I was dreading it, because every time we did it in rehearsal, everyone whistled and slow-handclapped and stuff; but on the other hand . . . '

' . . . You couldn't wait.'

'Exactly. So, anyway, it comes to the big night and the play's going really, really well. You can sense the audience is on our side. Even the rubbish people aren't fluffing their lines and our big scene's coming up and I'm just crapping myself. But then it's like someone flicks a switch and I think, 'Fuck it'. I just go for it. You could have heard a pin drop. It was amazing.'

Lou grinned. 'How long did you go out with him for?'

'Oh, we didn't go out,' Sara replied, 'he had a girlfriend.'

'But you got a shag at least?'

Sara shook her head.

'He wanted to. At the after-show party, but I was a virgin.'

'I thought you said . . . '

'That was afterwards. I overcompensated,' Sarah laughed, but she found herself welling up. 'He was really mean. Called me a frigid little prick-tease and got off with Beverly Wearing right in front of me.'

'What a cock!'

'I know. But the funny thing is, even though he was a total cock, I've always wondered what it would have been like. It's kind of haunted me, because I never really enjoyed it with any of the others. I think I was just trying to show him that I wasn't . . . what he said.'

'Well, at least you did — show him, that is.'

'I don't think he even noticed, to be honest. I was never girlfriend material for someone like him. I only came on his radar because of the play, and the one chance I had with him, I blew. I still think about that kiss . . .'

It was true, she did still think about it; more and more lately. The trouble was that the harder she tried to recall the facial features of Philip Baines-Cass, the more they tended to meld into Gavin's.

★ ★ ★

There was a pause while Lou tipped herself out of the armchair, drained the last of the Calvados into their glasses, and shuffled backwards on the hearthrug until her back met the sofa.

'Funny, isn't it?' she said, taking a thoughtful sip. 'How different it all could have been, I mean same for me. God, I shudder to think of it! *I* was almost with that computer programmer from Slough.'

'You!'

'I know! Imagine. He wasn't *actually* a computer programmer, obviously; nothing quite that bad.' They chuckled. 'His name was Andy. He was a very sweet guy, and he's loaded now. My Mum never misses a chance to slip that into the conversation: 'I saw Andy Hiddleston at the weekend, Louise. Did I mention he's a property developer?'' She rolled her eyes. 'She's never quite forgiven me for breaking off the engagement.'

'*You* got *engaged*?'

Lou nodded, delighted with the incongruity of it all.

'Until I went for my interview at St Martins and realised the world had other plans for me.'

'Poor Andy!' Sara sniggered.

'I know,' agreed Lou, 'he didn't take it very well,' she shook her head and grinned fondly, 'then again; I'd only have made him miserable. Can you imagine? Me in a double-fronted, Bath-stone villa with a monkey-puzzle tree and a waxed jacket . . . '

' . . . Two-point-four children . . . '

' . . . A Range Rover . . . '

' . . . And a lobotomy!'

Sara started giggling and found she couldn't stop. She forced the back of her hand to her mouth in an effort to control it.

'Come along, Camilla, we'll be late for pony club!' said Lou in a plummy accent.

'Now then, Nicholas, don't cry,' joined in Sara. 'All big boys hef to go to boarding school.' Lou beat the hearthrug in merriment. Tears ran down Sara's face.

'Introducing . . . the new . . . Chairwoman of the . . . Townswomen's Guild,' Sara tried to say, but it came out as a series of gulps and squeaks. 'Mrs Andy Hiddle . . . ' she gasped, then keeled over on the rug, insensible with mirth.

6

It was hard to concentrate the next day, partly because of the hangover, but mainly because, somewhere along the line, Sara had lost even the small shred of enthusiasm she'd once had for her job. She found herself reading and re-reading the same phrase — *'I don't really have a preferred supermarket and tend to use whichever is most convenient'* — until the words merged into one another and ceased to hold any objective meaning. For a stopgap job, NPR Marketing had taken up an awful lot of her time. Other creative types who had joined when she did had long since moved on. Anders the miserable Swede now wrote voice-overs for *Masterchef*; Tracy Jackson was a lobbyist for the Green Party. But NPR had granted Sara two generous periods of maternity leave and, although her game plan had been to return after Patrick's birth for no longer than her contract dictated, five years had somehow elapsed and she was still sitting at the same desk, in what was essentially a cupboard, opposite the talented but cynical Adrian Sutcliffe.

★   ★   ★

A part of Sara had known for a long time that her and Adrian's relationship was unhealthy. They were co-dependants, facilitating each other's inertia through corrosive humour. As long as they channelled their creative energies into satirising the futile nature of their work, the slavish ambition of their less talented colleagues and the passive-aggressive behaviour of their workaholic boss, Fran Ryan, they could kid themselves that they were, respectively, a novelist and a journalist *manqué*.

'Eyes front,' said Adrian now, 'Rosa Klebb at three o'clock.'

Sara snapped out of her reverie and battered her computer keyboard with a flurry of random keystrokes.

'On my way to Gino's,' said Fran, 'can I get you anything?'

'Ooh lovely,' said Sara, 'tuna melt for me, hold the mayo.'

'Why do you let her do that?' said Adrian, after Fran had gone.

'Er . . . because it's lunchtime and I need something to eat,' said Sara, with the interrogative upward lilt she had picked up from her children.

'You know what she's up to, don't you?'

'She's getting my lunch?'

'Yeah, so you don't leave the building.'

Before Sara could make a suitably acerbic retort, Fran had popped her head back into the office.

'By the way, can I tell Hardeep that you'll ping the survey across by close of play today?'

'Yep. On it,' Sara said, picking up her biro as she spoke, ready to throw it at Adrian as soon as the door had closed.

Lately, Sara's boredom was making her rebellious. Neil's promotion was practically in the bag, and he had hinted on numerous occasions recently that she might at last like to 'free herself up' from the rigours of work, which she took to mean free *him* up from the necessity to dash round Waitrose after a hard day at the office. She had resented the suggestion at first, but since Lou had been so encouraging of her writing, she was beginning to harbour serious ambitions in that direction. When Fran returned with her sandwich at one thirty, she didn't bother to minimise her computer screen; instead, she doubled the font size.

As the front door banged shut behind Nora's father, the draught wafted an empty plastic bag up in the air. Nora watched it as it rose and seemed to inflate itself with his very absence, before floating back down and lodging between the banister rails. She started to sing quietly,

'Bye baby bunting, daddy's gone a-hunting, she sang, over and over, until the words became, not words, but sobs.

'One tuna melt,' said Fran, barely able to tear her eyes from the screen. Sara scrabbled in her purse and handed Fran a fiver, which she took, without shifting her gaze.

'It's okay, I don't need any change,' said Sara, pointedly.

'No, right,' said Fran, remembering herself.

'Er . . . well, bon appétit,' she added, giving Sara a terse little smile before she left the room.

'The worm turns!' said Adrian, with grudging respect. Sara nodded in haughty acknowledgement and took a greedy bite of her sandwich. A large gobbet of mayonnaise dripped onto her jumper.

★ ★ ★

On the train home, she spotted Carol's Simon getting on further down the carriage. Normally she'd have lowered her eyes to her Kindle, certain in the knowledge that everything they had to say to one another could be covered on the short walk between the station and their road, but she had hatched a plan and was bursting to tell someone, so she called out his name.

'Oh, hello, Sara.' He started to thread his way through the carriage towards her. She could tell from the look of portentousness on his face that he had some news of his own to impart. 'I expect you've heard . . . ' Sara prepared herself for the death of a pet, or a recurrence of Carol's sister's ME.

'What?'

'Cranmer Road got a stinking OFSTED report. One step away from special measures.'

'Shit!' Sara remembered her words to Gavin, as he'd urged a reluctant Arlo over the threshold on the first day of term: 'Don't worry, it's a really lovely school. You won't regret it.'

'Carol must be doing her nut.'

'Oh, I think she's secretly quite pleased,' said

Simon, 'she's been looking for an excuse to go private for ages.'

Sara stretched her lips into a smile.

'It was the numeracy that did it, apparently,' Simon added, 'that and inadequate special needs provision.'

'Inadequate special needs? That's a travesty,' spluttered Sara. 'They bend over backwards at that school . . .'

Simon raised a didactic finger. 'Ah but special needs includes GAT, you see.'

'GAT,' repeated Sara dumbly.

'Gifted and Talented,' said Simon, patiently.

Of course. The middle classes were in revolt because they thought the Head was squandering resources on the thickies instead of hot-housing their little geniuses.

'Ridiculous,' she said.

'Well, I'm not so sure . . . ' Simon demurred. Then, sensing an ideological rift opening up, asked quickly, 'How's work?'

'Oh, you know, alright.'

Suddenly, Simon was the last person with whom she wanted to share her burgeoning literary ambitions. She could just imagine the smirk on his face as he relayed the news to Carol that she'd given up work to write a novel.

⋆ ⋆ ⋆

She expected better of Neil though.

'I'm not saying, don't do it,' he said defensively over dinner, 'I'm just querying the timing, is all.'

70

Sara tried not to wince at the Americanism. They seemed to be creeping into his vocabulary lately. She wasn't sure if he had picked them up from watching back-to-back episodes of *Breaking Bad*, or from reading American business manuals, but, either way, they didn't enhance his credibility as a literary adviser. He seemed to think she should do a course. As if creative writing was something that could be taught, like car maintenance or Spanish. And yet, the most irritating part of this suburban inclination of his to kowtow to 'teachers', was the fact that it piqued her own insecurity. She didn't want some second-rate novelist picking over her work. She much preferred Lou's bold exhortations to 'just go with it', to 'trust the muse' and 'tap into whatever's down there.'

Now she found herself becoming tearful with frustration. She planted her fork in what remained of her quiche and tried not to let her voice quaver.

'I don't think you realise what it's like for me,' she said. 'I'd like to see you spend eight hours a day writing consumer questionnaires.'

Neil looked up in dismay and Sara realised, with a mixture of satisfaction and shame, that the tears had clinched it for her, as they always did with Neil.

'No,' he said, apparently overcome with contrition, 'you're better than that. I totally agree. Go for it then. You'll have six whole hours a day while they're at school.'

Sara was about to point out that creativity wasn't necessarily something you could turn on and off like a tap, but thought better of it.

'It certainly won't hurt to be around more,' she said, 'especially with the school on the slide.'

'What do you mean?' said Neil.

'They've had the thumbs-down from the inspectors,' said Sara, rolling her eyes, 'so expect a mass exodus. Carol's already looked at St Aidan's, apparently.'

'We don't have to copy Carol.'

'It's not Carol I'm worried about,' said Sara, 'it's her influence on the others.'

'Carol is a bad influence on the other parents,' Neil affected a pedagogic tone.

'I wish you'd take this seriously. Carol wraps Celia round her little finger.'

'And I should care because . . . ?'

'Celia's Rhys's mum, and Rhys is Caleb's best friend.'

'I think you're making a meal of it. Boys aren't like girls. It's easy come, easy go.'

★   ★   ★

But the damage was done. Sara could only look at Cranmer Road with a jaundiced eye now. As she and Lou sat in the school hall, the following week, waiting for the Harvest Festival to begin, her eyes roved critically around the display boards. BE KIND TO OTHER'S read one poster, its misplaced apostrophe less worrying than the conspicuous indifference of the Year Ones to its message. When the piano struck up the opening song, and the children joined in with their warbling falsettos, Lou dabbed a sentimental tear from her eye, but

Sara felt like crying for a different reason. The 'orchestra' consisted of three recorders and a tambourine; the harvest gifts, displayed on a tatty piece of blue sugar paper, were mostly dented cans of Heinz soups and dubious-looking biscuits from Lidl. This spoke eloquently to Sara of the disengagement of the middle-class parents. The only item of fresh produce was the pineapple she had donated herself. Most distressing of all was the palpable unease among the staff. Gone, were the wide smiles and big encouraging eyes. Gone was the sense of camaraderie and fun. To a man and woman, they wore the weary, defeated expressions of an army in retreat.

★   ★   ★

As they stood together afterwards, drinking instant coffee from polystyrene cups, Sara was astonished by Lou's effusiveness.

'I can't tell you how relieved I am,' she said.

'Oh?' Sara dragged her gaze from the clusters of muttering, Boden-clad parents dotted around the room and forced herself to focus on Lou's beaming face.

'I can see the kids just blossoming here,' she said, 'there's such a buzz. It makes me absolutely certain we've done the right thing moving back.'

'I'm glad,' said Sara. She felt vindicated, now, in her decision not to worry Lou and Gavin with the news of the bad OFSTED. She couldn't imagine what kind of regime the kids had been subjected to in Spain — some draconian hangover from Franco's time, perhaps — but if

73

they thought Cranmer Road was a happy seedbed for their young, then who was Sara to disagree? Unfortunately, a dissenter was already heaving into view.

★ ★ ★

Celia Harris was a sweet woman without political nous or cynicism. She and Sara had bonded at the nursery gate and Caleb and Rhys had been close friends ever since. Celia was a Cranmer Road stalwart. She had overseen fundraisers and socials and accompanied every school trip that either of her bright, speccy children had ever been on. The news of the OFSTED report would, Sara knew, have hit Celia like a hammer blow. She loved the school, but she loved her children more. Like a football player who would lay down his life for his club until moved to a rival team, Celia's allegiance, though fierce, was also fickle. And seeing her now, brow knitted, flat, conker-coloured boots squeaking over the parquet, Sara could tell that she was already on the transfer list.

'Sara, hi,' she said, grasping Sara by the elbow and leading her out of Lou's earshot. All the time they were talking, Sara could see Lou over Celia's shoulder, sipping her coffee and trying to conceal her curiosity.

★ ★ ★

'I was thinking,' Lou said, later, her hands at ten and two on the vast steering wheel of the

Humber as she drove them all home, 'Gavin should go in and do some art with the kids sometime. He'd get a real kick out of it.'

'Yeah,' said Sara, 'definitely.'

★ ★ ★

It had been three weeks since Sara left work and four since she had entrusted her novella to Lou for some critical feedback. Her first day of freedom was spent billowing duvets and scouring mildew off the shower curtain. When Neil had asked her, on his return from work, how the book was going, she reminded him sharply that she was writing a novel, not a board paper. The next day, after rearranging her desk a number of times, experimenting with the height of her chair and opening and closing the window, she sat down purposefully in front of the computer to re-read *Safekeeping*.

★ ★ ★

She had finished the closing paragraph with a sigh of satisfaction. It wasn't half bad, for a first draft. In fact, its competence was, in a way, its main problem. She knew that what she had written was only the skeleton of a larger, more ambitious work that she must flesh out and bring to life, but it was hard to see, from her very partial standpoint, where she should insert new material, and what, if anything, could go. She had heard the phrase 'kill your darlings', but there was barely a line in it that she wasn't a little in love with, so that would mean dumping the lot. She really did need Lou's feedback now, and, despite her reluctance to hassle her friend, whom she knew to be struggling with creative decisions of her own, she decided to take the bull by the horns.

She knocked and rang next door to no avail. However, the Humber was parked outside, and when she peered through the letterbox, she caught a distinct whiff of toast, so, finding the door unlocked, she decided to take her chance.

'Hi? Only me . . . ' She pushed open the kitchen door. The room was empty. Four crumby plates stood on the table, one of which had a mashed cigarette stub on its rim. There was a heady perfume hanging in the air and an unfamiliar suede jacket slung over the back of one of the chairs. They had company. She was about to leave with even greater stealth than she had come, when she heard footsteps tripping lightly up the basement stairs.

'White, one sugar; black without . . . ' Lou was muttering, like a mantra, under her breath. 'Oh my God, Sara! You frightened the life out of me.'

'Sorry, you did say if there was no answer I should . . . Listen, you're busy. I'll leave you to it.'

'That's okay, we were just having a coffee break. Why don't you join us?'

There was a difference in Lou that Sara couldn't put her finger on. Her appearance was as carelessly stylish as ever — hi-tops, threadbare jeans, a hip-length kimono over a skimpy vest — but it was less her appearance than her demeanour that had changed. She had a slightly self-conscious air, as though acting a part in one of her own films. Watching her, Sara could almost read the stage directions: *Lou loads the coffee percolator and stands on tiptoe to reach the cups from the shelf. She is a sexy young woman in the prime of life.*

'Actually Sara,' Lou handed her two cups of coffee to carry, 'it's good you popped round because I was going to ask you . . . I can't see us finishing much before teatime here . . .'

'Would you like me to pick up the boys?'

'You read my mind!'

'No problem. You can tell the childminder to drop Zuley round too, if that helps.'

Lou flashed her a grateful smile. It didn't seem to occur to her to explain what on earth was going on.

★   ★   ★

They descended into Gavin's studio. The concertina doors had been pushed back and the white studio walls glowed copper pink in the autumn sunshine. Sitting on the wooden deck outside, smoking cigarettes and talking in low, business-like voices were Gavin and two people whom Sara identified, even before she had heard their accents, as foreign. The man's glasses were thin and rectangular and his scarf was knotted in an arcane and distinctively European manner. The woman's hair was cut in a razor-sharp bob, with a short, Plantagenet-style fringe. Her black-clad, raw-boned body was oriented towards Gavin like an Anglepoise lamp. On the floor around their feet was a heap of expensive-looking photographic equipment. Lou approached the threesome with a surprising air of diffidence.

'Dieter, white with sugar, and, Korinna . . . ooh, sorry, it's hot and er . . . ' (an afterthought, obviously) ' . . . meet Sara, our gorgeous next-door neighbour.'

Sara felt deflated, hearing herself so described. She would revisit the phrase many times that day, trying to decide why. The 'gorgeous' part was fine, if a little condescending, but why next-door neighbour? Why not friend? Best friend, even, given how much time they had spent in each other's company lately; given that Sara had pretty much burned her bridges with Carol and Celia; given that, as far as she was concerned, 'neighbour' didn't even begin to cover it.

'Hi,' Dieter shook her hand. Korinna flicked her a cursory smile and then switched her attention back to Gavin, who, gratifyingly, made full eye contact with Sara, grinned and said, 'Hello, you.'

'Dieter's a journalist for *Das Kunstmagazin*,' whispered Lou, when the business talk had resumed and Korinna had finished her coffee and begun setting up a tripod. 'He's doing a spread on Gav to coincide with the Berlin show.' *What Berlin show?* Sara thought — she always felt as though she was running to keep up.

'Mmm,' she murmured. 'Lou, now might not be the best time, but I was wondering if you'd had a chance . . . ?'

Lou was collecting her visitors' cigarette stubs

in her hand and hooking the empty coffee cups onto her forefinger.

'Sorry?' she said distractedly.

'Doesn't matter,' Sara replied. 'I'll talk to you later when you pick the kids up.'

'Yes, do.' Lou smiled and crinkled her eyes affectionately.

'See you later then,' Sara said, to the company in general, but her exit went unnoticed amid the aggressive pop and flare of Korinna's lightmeter.

★ ★ ★

That afternoon, with a lot of soul-searching and frequent recourse to the online thesaurus, Sara rewrote her opening paragraph four times. At 2.55, when the time came to leave for school, she made a couple of last-minute changes, and realised that she had inadvertently returned it to almost the exact form of words she had started with.

★ ★ ★

Teatime was stressful. Amid howls of protest, Sara had eventually chucked the boys off the Xbox and sent them into the garden with a football, so that Zuley could watch CBeebies in peace. They hadn't been there long before she heard a groan and a burst of satirical applause that told her the ball had been kicked over the fence. To her surprise, despite the fact that it had gone over on Lou and Gavin's side, the children traipsed back indoors in disconsolate mood and

Caleb admitted, when pressed, that Lou had confiscated the ball because it had 'damaged a camera or something.'

'Oh dear,' said Sara, wondering whether she should have taken a more active part in supervising the game — though how that would have been possible, when she was cooking spag bol for five, was another question. At any rate, her feelings of negligence were soon compounded, when she discovered Zuleika, winded and tearful in the hall, and learned that she had come a cropper playing 'horsey down the stairs with the big boys.'

'Caleb?' she called reproachfully. 'Patrick?'

★ ★ ★

By the time Neil got home, she had barricaded herself and Zuley in the kitchen and was reading *The Very Hungry Caterpillar* for the fifth time, whilst easing the monotony with a third glass of Pinot Grigio.

'What the hell's going on?'

'Oh, hi,' said Sara. 'What do you mean?'

'You do realise they're roller blading on the landing?'

She would wait in vain for Lou to retrieve the children, Sara now realised. The expectation must have been that she would return them after tea, but somehow, what with the highly exclusive nature of the photography session and the ambiguity around the damaged camera, she hadn't quite liked to.

Now, though, leaving Neil to restore order in

the wrecked living room, she called up the stairs to Dash and Arlo that it was time to go, and hurried ahead with Zuley slung on her hip. She stepped between the lavender bushes that formed the boundary between the two front gardens and, seeing that the curtains were open and the living room inhabited, she knocked on the window and waved. It seemed they neither heard nor saw her, however, and she stood there, smiling hopefully out of the darkness, a little perplexed and embarrassed to be witnessing, with Zuley, the strange scene within. Korinna was sitting barefoot at one end of the sofa, knees drawn up to her chin, gazing at Gavin, who was perched at the other end, making a sketch of her. Dieter and Lou were slow dancing on the rug in front of the fire, as if it were gone midnight. Dieter looked the worse for wear and was nuzzling Lou's neck, but Lou's face was blank and emotionless. She might have been waiting for a bus.

'Looks like we'd better ring the bell,' Sara said briskly to Zuley.

By this time, Dash and Arlo had arrived and were already battering the front door with their lunch boxes.

'Lou!'

'Mu-um!'

'Hurry up. I need a piss!'

The door opened and they fell inside.

'Hello gorgeous!' said Gavin, and Sara coloured with pleasure, before realising that he was talking to Zuley. His daughter clambered into his arms, without a backward glance.

81

'Thanks a million,' he said to Sara, 'you've been a life-saver. Come and have a drink?' He was smiling, but his eyes had a glazed look.

'Oh . . . no, better not. Neil just got home. Thanks though.'

She hovered by the open door.

'Okay then,' said Gavin.

'Okay then.'

★ ★ ★

That night, Sara dreamed she was at one of Neil's board meetings, which was being chaired by Korinna, in a Minotaur headdress. The last item on the agenda was Sara's novel. She was supposed to read an extract from it, naked, from the top of the filing cabinet, but when she tried to speak the words, no sound came. She woke stressed and exhausted and, later, had only just shaken off the feeling of discombobulation, when she was wrong-footed again, by Lou's substituting herself for Gavin on the school run.

'Oh!' she said.

'Sorry, you've got me today,' smiled Lou. 'Gav's gone to Berlin.'

'Don't be daft,' said Sara awkwardly, 'it's always a treat to see you.' She bundled the boys out of the door and, when she had shut it behind her, was surprised to be given a spontaneous kiss on the cheek from Lou.

'What's that for?'

'I read your manuscript last night.'

'Oh God.'

'Clever girl.'

'You liked it?'

'I loved it.'

Sara felt she might melt with happiness.

'It's great, Sara. Original, heartfelt, quirky.'

'Hey, steady-on.'

'No, honestly. I was so excited I had to wake Gavin up and read bits to him.'

'Oh my God!' Sara crushed her cheeks with mortification and pleasure.

'I want to go over it with you in detail. I've got some suggestions. Can we get together at the weekend?'

★ ★ ★

At the school gate, the Deputy Head was greeting the children as they arrived. Sonia Dudek was a favourite of Sara's. She had cut her teeth in Caleb's Reception class, and had progressed from Tiggerish ingénue to senior manager in four short years. Now she was smiling, greeting the children by name, attempting to bolster the morale of doubting parents.

'Hi there,' Sara said, flashing her a sympathetic smile. Sonia smiled back, then, seeing Lou, caught her by the elbow.

'Oh, Ms Cunningham. Can I have a word about Dash?'

The bell was ringing, so Sara hurried on with the other children, struggling to master her curiosity. Doubtless, Dash was being selected for the new 'Gifted and Talented' programme and good luck to him, she told herself firmly.

Once she had seen the boys into class, Sara waited outside the school gate for Lou, but after ten minutes there was no sign of her, so she walked home alone. As she turned into her street, she saw Carol getting out of her car. Mindful that a rift was growing between herself and Carol that could all too easily become an unbreachable chasm, Sara had issued a vague invitation for the weekend. She could tell from the way Carol now stood, four-square, in the middle of the pavement, with a slightly forced smile on her face, that she was going to be pressed for a day and time.

'Hi Sara, how's the novel?'

Sara sighed. You couldn't keep anything to yourself on this street.

'Early days,' she said.

'What's it about?'

'About?' Sara wrinkled her nose disdainfully.

'You know, what genre? Thriller? Chick-lit? What?'

'Oh God, well . . . I suppose, inasmuch as it's *about* anything, it's a sort of . . . coming-of-age novel.'

Carol made a 'get you' face and Sara felt a pang of irritation.

'So, were you thinking Friday or Saturday?' Carol asked. 'Because Saturday would work better for us. Less chance of Simon nodding off.'

'Could I get back to you? Only Saturday's ringing bells . . .'

'Friday then. I'll just have to prod him awake.

Only I need to know, for the babysitter . . . '

God, she was like a fucking terrier.

'No, let's go with Saturday,' Sara said, thinking to herself that if the worst came to the worst she could always come down with a mystery virus.

★ ★ ★

By the end of the week, Gavin had returned to the school run.

'Oh hi,' Sara said, more pleased than she cared to admit to find him on the front step. 'How was Berlin?' She pulled the door shut behind her and had got as far as the garden gate before Gavin laughed and said:

'Aren't you forgetting something?'

'Oh God, what an idiot!' She turned away briskly so he couldn't see her flaming face, put her key in the latch and called, 'Boys, come on, it's ten to . . . '

★ ★ ★

It was fascinating hearing Gavin talk about his trip. The gallery was a former warehouse in the east of the city, he said, 'very cool'.

Sara admitted that she had never been to Berlin.

'Oh you've got to go,' he said. 'We should go next year, the four of us. Stay in this boutique hotel that Lou loves in Friedrichshain. The clubs are fantastic.'

Sara glazed over for a moment, imagining herself gyrating to techno in a Berlin night club,

85

under the influence of who-knew-what stimulants, with an important contemporary artist and his film-maker wife.

' . . . So, what do you reckon?' Gavin was saying.

'Oh gosh, well, I suppose we could try for February half-term . . . ' said Sara, flattered by his tenacity.

'No . . . ' Gavin frowned in affectionate bemusement, 'I meant about Greenwich Park, tomorrow, if the weather holds?'

She must stop zoning out like this, it was embarrassing.

'Oh, right.'

'Us boys can kick a ball about and you and Lou can talk about your book, which sounds fantastic, by the way.'

'Oh God, it's only a first draft. There's, like, a million things I need to change . . . ' Her voice trailed off as she noticed his reproachfully raised eyebrow. She smiled and blushed, 'but yeah, the park sounds great.'

7

It was a perfect autumn day and Greenwich Park had never looked lovelier. As she strolled hand in hand with Neil down Blackheath Avenue, Caleb and Patrick chicaning in and out of the bollards on their skateboards, Sara felt imbued with a sense of wellbeing. She couldn't actually be happy, she knew, for happiness was unselfconscious, and this wasn't, but she was as near as dammit. She enjoyed thinking of her life as a novel in progress and, since Lou had told her she mustn't shilly-shally when people asked her what she did, but must say loud and proud, 'I'm a writer,' it seemed legitimate. As she half-listened to Neil explaining what he had found unsatisfactory about the latest Sebastian Faulks novel, she scrolled through a mental playlist of appropriate soundtracks for the day. The Kinks? Too obvious. The Smiths? Too ironic. As they reached the end of the avenue they paused to take in the cityscape, unfurled along the river like a theatrical backdrop, St Paul's to the West, Canary Wharf ahead, the Dome to the east, the greensward of the park falling away gently beneath them, and it came to her: Saint Etienne's 'London Belongs to Me'. Neil stood behind her, encircling her waist, his stubbly chin pressing against her cold cheek, and she turned to him and buried her face in his warmth, filling her nostrils with his peppery Neil-ish scent. She was weighing up whether to turn the embrace into a snog, when a familiar voice said:

'Hey, you two, get a room!'

She sprang guiltily away.

'Hello, mate,' said Neil, turning warmly to greet Gavin.

'Hi Gav,' Sara said, giving him a feeble wave.

'What have you done with the ball and chain?' asked Neil.

'She took the kids to the swings,' Gav replied. 'I'm supposed to liaise with you.'

'Liaise?' Sara said, grinning.

'That's what she said, 'Liaise with them and bring them down here, Gav.''

'I don't believe you,' laughed Sara. 'Lou doesn't 'liaise'. She wouldn't know how.'

'What does she do, then?' Gavin tilted his chin at her, smiling.

'She 'hooks up',' Sara said, 'she 'scouts out'.'

'Nope,' Gavin said, shaking his head, 'you've got her all wrong. She's a big liaiser, is Lou. She's forever fucking liaising. I say to the kids, 'Where's Mum?' And they go, 'She's liaising, Dad.''

Sara shook her head, laughing.

'You kill me,' she said.

Neil grinned politely.

'Anyway,' said Gavin, 'Patrick and Caleb have got the right idea.' He nodded towards two dots careering down the hill towards the playground.

'Hey, wait for us!' bellowed Neil, galumphing after them, leaving Gavin and Sara to bring up the rear.

* * *

The fine autumn weather had brought out the whole of Greenwich, and the playground was packed. Young mums in angora beanies and Ugg boots were psyching teenage hoodies into giving up their swings for little Olivia or Ethan. Grannies in quilted jackets fretted alongside hijabed Somali women at the bottom of the slide. Six-figure dads guarded all-terrain buggies while their wives debated Montessori versus Steiner over the sandpit.

* * *

'Jesus!' said Gavin. 'Needle in a haystack.'

But Caleb and Patrick homed in on their friends like a couple of heat-seeking missiles and Sara found Lou nearby, chatting to Neil as she rocked Zuleika back and forth on a springy horse.

'Hi,' she said, her heart lifting as Lou enfolded her in a perfumed embrace.

'I have to get out of here,' Lou said, laughing cheerfully, 'it's too much.'

'Oh sorry,' said Sara, 'have you been here ages?'

'No, just feels like it,' she said, plucking Zuley off the horse and delivering her into Gavin's arms, before either of them had time to protest. The next thing Sara knew, Lou was steering her out of the mayhem towards the tearooms.

* * *

They carried their cappuccinos over to a quiet table in the corner, next to a bad painting of the Cutty Sark. The windows were steamed up and a trellis intertwined with plastic ivy screened them from the bustle of the room. Lou burrowed in her bag and brought out a moleskin notebook.

'So . . . ' she said, 'your book.'

Sara snorted with laughter.

'What?' said Lou.

'Just, you know, 'my book'!'

'Sara! You have to stop putting yourself down. You're not doing yourself any favours. It's really competitive out there. Nobody wants to hear from an author who's not got the courage of her convictions. Do you respect my opinion?'

Sara wiped the smile off her face and met Lou's eye. 'Yes.'

'Well, I'm telling you that this is a really remarkable piece of writing.'

'Thanks.'

★   ★   ★

Lou went on to give Sara a detailed critique of her work: her characters were compelling; her style lyrical; her flashbacks well-timed. Lou thought the childhood Nora might have a different voice to the adult one — her vocabulary would be limited, she pointed out. A child of seven would probably not use the word 'egotistical'.

'Good point,' said Sara.

'But the only significant flaw, as I see it . . . ' said Lou and Sara braced herself, ' . . . is that you bottle out of the rape scene.'

'Well, I wanted it to be ambiguous . . . '

'*I* think you didn't want to write it.'

'Um . . . maybe.'

'The thing is, Sara, writing's scary. You have to be prepared to go deep.'

Sara nodded.

'And when your brain's shouting, 'No, no, I'm not going to think that thought; it's too dirty, it's too scary, it's too painful, that's when you must make yourself think it and make yourself *write* it.'

'Well, I was sort of going on the basis that the best horror movies leave something to the imagination.'

She might as well have said 'The dog ate my homework.'

'Have you seen *Antichrist?*'

Sara shook her head.

'You should.'

★ ★ ★

By the time they had finished, the chill cabinet was down to its last sad egg sandwich and was being refilled with clingfilmed cream teas.

'So,' said Lou, shovelling clutter back into her leather duffel bag, 'do you know where you're going with it now?'

'Yes,' said Sara, 'absolutely.'

Lou picked up her phone, dialled and held it to her ear. Sara laid a hand on her forearm.

'Thank you,' she murmured, her eyes pricking a bit.

Lou patted her hand magnanimously as she started to speak into the phone:

'Hi, we're done,' she said. 'Where are you?'

She rolled her eyes and hung up.

'I might have known.'

★ ★ ★

They were sitting at a trestle table overlooking the river. Gavin and Neil were each nursing a pint, and if the empty crisp packets and cola bottles all around them were anything to go by, the children had been well-catered for. The boys had long since got bored with throwing stones in the water and waving at the passengers on passing tourist boats and had contrived a homemade skate park on the pavement from a couple of stray traffic cones and a beer crate. Zuley had fallen asleep on Gavin's lap, her sweetly pouting mouth connected by a gossamer strand of drool to the lapel of her father's coat. Seeing the women approaching, Neil scrambled eagerly to his feet.

'What'll it be, guys? Name your poison.'

★ ★ ★

The low sun was hot, and against a mother-of-pearl sky, even the Isle of Dogs looked picturesque. There seemed little to take issue with, and the women installed themselves happily at the table and awaited their drinks. They had another round and then another, their tolerance of the shriek and rattle of the boys' hijinks increasing in inverse proportion to that of their fellow drinkers, most of whom were driven away within the hour. The conversation moved from small talk, via highfalutin' debate to ribald anecdote. Gavin, it turned out, was privy to some hair-raising art-world gossip. Of course, it had all quietened down now, he said, but the things that used to go on in the old days at the Colony Room Club, you would not believe. Sara wasn't sure she *did* believe them. She thought herself reasonably broad-minded but, for the life of her, she couldn't see how some of the sexual practices Gavin described would be physically possible, let alone pleasurable. Still, she laughed along, not wanting to seem like a prude and hoping he wasn't sending her up. She was relieved when the conversation evolved into a more serious debate on whether fetishism could also be art, although after three glasses of Sauvignon Blanc, her opinions, which she was surprised to find quite decisive on the matter, proved harder to articulate than she would have liked.

★ ★ ★

At last, the sun dipped behind the tower blocks and cranes, casting fingers of gold across the roiling black water and turning the sky briefly fluorescent. Sara hunched her shoulders against the cold. Her teeth had started to chatter, but she wasn't going to be the first to call time on what had been a magical day. She stole a glance at Gavin, wondering, as she found herself doing

93

often, what he was thinking. The expression on his face was contemplative, but changed, as she watched, to one of disbelief, and then dismay.

'Bloody hell, she's pissing on me,' he said.

As Zuley woke up and realised what she had done, she cried and struggled. Gavin tried to stand up, a cola bottle got knocked over and deposited its dregs on Lou's Orla Keily scarf. The boys became rebellious when instructed to quit what had become a fiercely competitive game that had been nearing its climax. For a moment, things looked like they would turn ugly. And then a strange thing happened, Gavin whipped out his iPhone and called a taxi; he distracted Zuley with a stale potato crisp out of the ashtray and made a joke about having been pissed on by women all his life; Lou corralled the boys and persuaded them that the big and clever thing would be for them to travel home on the top deck of the bus with her and Sara. There would be a short intermission, and then the party would reconvene at Gavin and Lou's place, complete with roaring fires and takeaway food. What was not to like? In its wit and resourcefulness, the plan felt like a rabbit out of a hat, a triumph of the creative over the banal, and proof, if proof were needed, that Gavin and Lou were a class act.

★　★　★

It was in this spirit of hard-won camaraderie that Sara and Lou, Caleb, Patrick, Arlo and Dash all trudged the last half-mile from the bus stop to their road, the older boys keeping their spirits up by composing a rap whose sexual precocity and casual misogyny would have made their mothers' blood run cold had they not been deep in discussion about the challenges of raising sons. But as she neared her own front gate, Sara's blood ran cold anyway for standing on the path, dressed smart casual, and carrying, respectively, a box of Belgian chocolates and a bottle of Montepulciano, were Carol and Simon.

'Shit!' she said under her breath. 'Shit! Shit! Shit!'

'What?' Lou asked.

But by now they had drawn level.

'You did say seven . . . ?' Carol said.

'I did. But you know what? No point me pretending — I'd completely forgotten. I'm really sorry.'

Carol's face fell.

'Well I'd better go and tell the babysitter we won't be needing her . . . '

'Come to ours!' said Lou.

'What?' Carol looked at her wildly.

'Why not? This is our fault, really. We hijacked them, didn't we, Sara?'

Sara tried for a smile.

'Only, it was such a gorgeous day and we ended up staying out much longer than we meant to. We were going to get a takeaway from that new place. You really would be very welcome to join us.'

★   ★   ★

95

Sara watched Carol wrestle with the choice. Would she opt for the moral high ground or go for the riskier pleasures of an evening off-piste? The latter, it turned out — they'd have to pay the babysitter, anyway, and it was ages since she and Simon had had an Indian, so, why not? Sara glanced at Simon, whose rictus of barely disguised horror must have mirrored her own.

8

'Oh,' said Gav, opening the door, 'hello.'

'Have you ordered the food yet?'

Lou hurried past him to the kitchen, leaving Sara to signal with a comic widening of her eyes that this turn of events was not of her choosing. The boys stampeded upstairs. Carol, following Sara's lead, hung her coat on the newel post and they trooped through to the kitchen, where they found Neil on the phone to the Moti Mahal. Everyone crowded in the doorway and watched him change the order with patient good humour, once, twice, three times, under Lou's overexcited supervision.

'Forty-five minutes,' he said, hanging up. 'Hope you're hungry.'

* * *

'That's very kind,' Simon said to the room at large. 'We'd have been happy just to stay for a drink.'

He sat down unhappily at the kitchen table and shrugged his waxed jacket onto the back of his chair.

'No problem,' said Gavin, 'the more the merrier. We've been meaning to get you round for ages, haven't we, Lou?'

Lou nodded eagerly and Sara could only wonder at her disingenuousness in making such a claim. It had, after all, been months since the housewarming and Carol was no fool. She sat, now, fingers laced on the laminated tabletop, glancing around the kitchen with the conspicuous curiosity of a robin after a snowfall. What must she make of the kitsch coloured cocktail glasses, the Mexican death mask, the bobbly, hand-knitted tea cosy? Sara smiled to herself. That had been her, in the beginning — she recognised the air of bewilderment, of dismay, actually, that the rules of good taste should be so wantonly flouted. She got it now, though. She stood up, abruptly, and walked over to Lou and Gavin's fridge, flung it open with a proprietorial air.

'Anyone else for a beer?'

She handed them round, pausing for a moment to watch Carol wrestle with the cap. The wine and chocolates sat unopened on the table, like props from the wrong play.

★ ★ ★

Gavin cued up a track on the iPod.

'This is nice,' said Carol. 'What is it?'

'They're called Midlake,' Gavin said, pleasantly, 'Texan band.'

Simon took a slug of beer. 'Glorious day, wasn't it?' he said.

'It was,' agreed Gavin. 'We sat out and had a pint, by the river. Can't say fairer than that, can you, in October?'

'Yes, I'm afraid we got a bit carried away, after the first couple of drinks,' Sara said.

Nobody asked what she meant.

'What did *you* do today?' Gavin asked Simon.

'Oh, you know, thrilling stuff,' Simon replied. 'Took Holly to clarinet. Went to Waitrose. Raked up the leaves.'

'Oh,' Lou looked crestfallen, 'I *love* the leaves.'

'Is anybody cold?' asked Gavin. 'Do we need more heat?'

People glanced at one another doubtfully, but Gavin got up and adjusted the thermostat.

Carol turned to Gavin.

'So, do you work at the weekends?' she asked him. 'Or are you nine-to-five, like a — '

' . . . Stiff?' Gavin said. 'Kidding. Just kidding. No, it varies a lot actually. But the materials I use can be quite time-critical, so once I start, I have to see it through.'

'He works all night, sometimes,' said Lou.

'So you sleep in the day, I suppose?' Simon concluded, with unerring logic.

'Well, in theory,' said Gav, 'but with three ankle-biters in the house, it's not always easy.'

'I make sure they keep it down before midday,' put in Lou, quickly.

'Must be rather nice to be your own master,' said Simon. 'I'm not sure I'd have the self-discipline. How are you finding it, Sara?'

'Me?' Sara was surprised to find herself bracketed with Gavin.

'Haven't you transitioned from wage slave to creative recently?'

'I suppose I have . . . transitioned,' she said doubtfully, 'but I'm not sure I'm quite a creative. More of a tinkerer, really, an *aspirer*.'

'Er, *Sara* . . . ' Lou fixed her with a reproachful look.

'Oh, yes, sorry, I forgot.' Sara banged her hand loudly on the table. 'I'm a *writer*, so you can all fuck off!'

Carol and Simon looked slightly taken aback.

'Can we read it then, your novel?' Carol asked, after a moment.

'Oh, God,' Sara shuddered, 'I don't know about that. I'm not sure I'd really want . . . It's very raw, still, isn't it Lou?'

'Oh, so *Lou's* read it?' Carol's tone was jokily aggrieved.

'I wanted a professional opinion.'

'What's it like?' Carol asked Lou. 'What did you think of it, *honestly?*'

'I'm not sure it's *like* anything,' said Lou. 'It's simply a remarkable piece of writing. An original voice.'

'So it's publishable then? In your opinion?' Carol wanted to know.

'I don't know whether 'publishable' is really the point,' said Lou.

Sara bristled. It was certainly the *point* as far as she was concerned.

'I think what Sara's doing with this piece of writing is finding her river,' Lou explained.

Carol looked nonplussed.

'*The Artist's Way?*' said Lou. 'Julia Cameron. Fantastic book. What she says is that you must push through the negativity and self-criticism that dam up your creativity and just let it flow. Be your authentic self. Write or sing or dance or paint with your whole being, without guardedness or cynicism and without trying to second-guess an audience.'

'Sounds a bit hokey to me,' said Carol. 'I should have thought having an inner critic was rather important, otherwise what's to stop any Tom, Dick or Harriet inflicting their so-called 'art' on the world? No offence, Sara.'

'Why would you *want* to stop them?' Lou asked. She held Carol's gaze and her eyes glittered.

Carol opened her mouth to reply and Sara felt her own go dry in sympathy. She felt sorry for her old friend, yet she could not suppress an unworthy glee. It was good to see Carol on the back foot for a change. It was good to see her cosy metropolitan assumptions bump up against the beautiful, twisted logic of Lou and Gavin's world.

'Well, I'm afraid I think this idea that everyone's an artist, if you just, you know, put them in touch with their *muse*, or whatever, doesn't wash.'

'I don't think that's really what I meant,' said Lou. Her tone was emollient, but a vivid pink dot had appeared on each of her cheeks. 'I was talking about creativity. Are you telling me the capacity to create isn't something we're born with?'

'Not if I'm anything to go by,' said Carol, with a staccato laugh, '*I* haven't got a creative bone in my body.'

'Of *course* you have,' said Lou, irritably.

'She really hasn't,' Simon confirmed, as though it were a source of pride.

'You see, that, to me, is shocking,' said Lou. 'That you could have internalised that message about yourself. What an indictment of our so-called education system.'

'I haven't internalised anything,' Carol said. 'I had a perfectly good education.'

'Wall to wall A stars.' Sara nodded towards Carol, in corroboration.

Lou sighed and shook her head, as if contemplating a life of utmost deprivation.

'You jumped through all their hoops,' she said, 'succeeded on their terms; and yet you came away with the mistaken belief that you lacked, that you could *do without*, one of the key attributes of a meaningful life.'

'Well I don't happen to think it's done me any harm,' said Carol briskly.

'You're missing the point.'

'I don't think my life's any less meaningful than yours.'

'That's exactly what I'm — '

'I mean, who says creativity's the be all and — '

'*YOU* ARE *CREATIVE*!' shouted Lou.

There was a shocked silence.

'*Whoa*, Lou,' said Neil, 'tell us what you really think.'

Sara winced. For a moment, it seemed as though Neil might have crossed the line, but then Lou tittered, and looked a little shocked at herself. The titter became a laugh, which became a guffaw, and then the others joined in, tentatively at first, then heartily, so that a casual observer, witnessing the scene, might have mistaken them for a group of people having a good time.

102

* ★ ★

The curry arrived and was served up in its foil trays. A mismatched handful of cutlery was clattered onto the table. It must all have been a far cry from the evening Carol and Simon had been expecting, but they helped themselves with enthusiasm from the foil trays, attesting frequently to the deliciousness of the meal. A whole new line of conversation was eagerly pursued, on the fluctuating standards and delivery radii of the local Indian takeaways.

★ ★ ★

The irresistible aroma of tikka and bhaji brought the children crowding round the kitchen door, like Dickensian waifs to a chophouse. Egged on by the others, Dash launched a commando raid on the table, sneaking in on his hands and knees while the grown-ups chatted, before rearing up to snatch a piece of naan bread and run away. The second time this happened, Sara was aware of Carol trying to catch her eye. She could sense the battle lines being drawn, tell that her allegiance was being sought on behalf of the forces of civilisation against the forces of barbarism, but she was not playing ball. Lou and Gav had gone the extra mile, and Carol was a guest in their house. It was not her place to criticise. Sara averted her gaze and found herself, instead, watching Dash cram bread into his mouth for comic effect, not thinking for a moment to share it with his co-conspirators. The

103

sight revolted her. Lou was forever trumpeting Dash's exceptionalness and Sara couldn't deny that he had a vivid imagination. She had overheard him devising blood-curdling games of dystopian make-believe with Caleb and Patrick, which she found as disturbing as they found them exciting. Nor could she deny that she had felt a pang of envy the other day when Lou had been buttonholed by the Deputy Head. But if giftedness came at the expense of humanity — if its flipside was self-centredness, as it seemed to be in Dash's case — well, Sara told herself, she would rather her boys were kind than clever.

* * *

Neil had ordered far too much. The half-full foil trays sat coagulating in front of them long after their appetites had been satisfied and the conversation had dried up. No one made a move to clear the table.

'Well, thanks so much,' said Simon, patting the sides of his coat vaguely, as if to reassure himself it was still there, 'we should probably get back now; let the babysitter get off . . . '

No one pointed out that it was still only 9.45.

'Sure you won't stay for a . . . er . . . ?'

'No, no thanks. Lovely dinner. Top notch. We'll have to have you back, won't we, Caz? No don't get up, we'll see ourselves out . . . Cheers then, thanks. Bye . . . bye.'

The sound of the front door closing prompted sighs and relieved laughter.

'God!' Lou mugged at Sara.

'I'm sorry,' Sara said, biting her lip. 'Completely forgot I'd invited them. Thanks for getting me off the hook.'

'*Sort* of,' said Lou.

'It was *fine*,' said Gav, magnanimously. 'Top notch!'

They all collapsed again, except for Neil, who stretched his lips in an unhappy smile.

9

They moved through to the living room. Lou put a record on and Neil squatted in front of the hearth and coaxed the fire back to life. Sara nestled herself into a corner of the sofa and watched Gav roll a joint. Apart from the occasional thud and muffled shriek from the kids upstairs, the room now felt cut off from the world — a haven dedicated to adult pursuits. Gav struck a match and lit up, before handing the joint, in a gesture of ostentatious generosity, to Sara. She lifted it gingerly to her lips.

'He's not a bad bloke, Simon,' Gav said. 'What is it he does again?'

Sara, who was focusing hard on inhaling, shook her head.

'Banking, isn't it?' Lou hunkered down on the hearthrug, her back against the sofa, and intercepted the joint on its way back to Gav. After a token puff she passed it back to Sara.

'Venture capital.' Neil flopped back into the Eames chair, satisfied that the fire was now roaring again. 'Sara, I'd go easy if I were you.'

She glared at him and took an extra toke.

'Ven-ture . . . cap-i-tal,' said Gav slowly, as if weighing the meaning of each word. 'What *is* that?'

'Sounds a bit *Boy's Own*, doesn't it?' Sara giggled.

There was certainly no need for Neil's priggish interventions. The weed was quite innocuous and seemed to be having no discernible effect.

'It does!' Gav turned to her and beamed. 'I can see it now. The pith helmets, the infernal chirrup of the cicadas, the heat . . . the damned heat.'

Sara sat up straight on the sofa and shielded her eyes, scanning an imaginary horizon.

'Pass the spy-glass, Carruthers,' she said, 'I think I see an investment opportunity.'

'You two,' said Lou, shaking her head indulgently. She reached across the hearth-rug to pass the tail end of the spliff to Neil.

★ ★ ★

The fire crackled and hissed. The music surged melodically. Sara sighed and stretched and Lou reached up and caught her hand. She held it, gently, experimentally, and when she was ready, she released it again. They had reached that milestone, Sara realised, when they were comfortable in one another's company not saying anything, just being. It felt much later in the evening than it could possibly have been and Sara was reminded of the tableau she and Zuley had witnessed when the Germans had been visiting: the waxen faces, the strange power play, palpable even from behind glass. She was, she realised, being inducted into a cult, but it was one that held no fear for her; she welcomed it. She was only now beginning to discover how tender and resonant and sweetly complex life was meant to be.

★ ★ ★

107

Neil leaned forward and made to pass a fresh joint across her, to Lou.

'*Whoa!*' Sara said, rearing up from her semi-comatose state to intercept it. 'Not so fast.'

'I wouldn't, if I were you, Sar,' Neil warned her.

'You're *not* me, though, are you, Neil?' she replied. 'And the funny thing is . . . ' she stopped for a moment to enjoy the irrefutable logic of her retort, ' . . . if you *were* me, then you *would*, because I'm going to.'

She put the joint to her lips, drawing on it a little more deeply than she might otherwise have done. Neil held out his hand with an air of exaggerated patience and, in defiance of him, she took a second drag. She had only just exhaled, when the genius of what she had said fully struck her.

'Jam today!' she announced.

Gav glanced at her with affectionate puzzlement.

'Come on, people! *Alice in Wonderland*. Or is it *Through the Looking Glass*? Anyway, you can't have it.'

Lou turned round and patted Sara's knee affectionately.

'You can have it yesterday, or tomorrow, but not today, because today never comes. Or is it tomorrow? Anyway, it doesn't matter. It's exactly what Neil just said. He couldn't *be* me and still do what he thinks I *should* do, because by the time he *was* me, he'd be doing what I *do* do . . . '

'I knew you'd overdo it,' Neil said with a sigh.

Sara frowned crossly.

'I don't know what you mean. What does he mean?' She appealed to the other two, but they had both dissolved into fits of helpless giggles.

'Oh come on guys,' she said huffily, 'you're just . . . you're just . . . ' but she could no longer remember what they were 'just'. Her lips were buzzing and her head felt like a boulder balanced on a blade of grass. The small adjustment required to rest it on the back of the sofa reverberated through her body like an earth tremor.

'Here we go,' said Neil.

'Would you like a glass of water?' asked Lou.

'I think I'll just . . . ' Sara closed her eyes and flapped her hand in front of her face. That felt worse, much worse. No amount of wishing it so was going to make this go away. Like a geriatric with brittle-bone disease, Sara began a three-stage manoeuvre to get off the sofa. The fire was unbearably hot. The stag's head regarded her disapprovingly.

'Do you need a hand?' Gavin sat forward.

'I'm okay,' Sara muttered, picking her way through the wine glasses and drug paraphernalia on the rug.

★ ★ ★

The toilet seat was pleasantly cold beneath her bottom. Somewhere in the distance, a children's game seemed to be getting out of hand, but she was in no state to intervene. Her head dangled not far above the dingy lino and she was only just the right side of needing to vomit. With a

109

mammoth effort, she turned on the cold tap and swivelled her body so that she could scoop water into her mouth from the adjacent sink. She swivelled back and the room righted itself slowly like the wheel of an abandoned bicycle, coming to rest. The inside of the door was covered in a collage of clippings — a black-and-white photo of a sumo wrestler texting on an iPhone; a newspaper headline: 'GOD IS CONCEPT SAYS DEAN OF ST PAUL'S'; a postcard of some kittens dressed in dungarees and neckerchiefs, with fishing rods slung over their shoulders. Sara belched loudly and stared at the floor again. She might have been there three minutes or ten, she didn't know. At last, she hauled herself to her feet and squinted at her reflection in the tarnished antique mirror above the basin. She looked startled.

★   ★   ★

'Feeling better?' Lou asked, as Sara walked back into the room.

The album had finished, but the crackle and clunk as it circled the turntable seemed of a piece with the indolent melancholy in the room. The fire was wheezing and collapsing in on itself.

'Kind of,' she said, sinking down onto the sofa again. She closed her eyes. She could hear Neil talking to Gavin in a low voice. He was saying how much he would love to walk the Camino de Santiago in Spain. Gavin asked him if he was religious and Neil said he wasn't but that he could really see the attraction of Catholicism

110

— the devotion; the self-flagellation. This was news to Sara. If she had been feeling more robust, she'd have reminded him that he had baulked at paying twelve euros to look round the Duomo in Florence, but, instead, she kept quiet and learned.

★   ★   ★

She learned that her husband had more on his mind than asset bases and sustainable-development plans; she learned that he now understood, in a way he never had before, that his ambition to succeed in a conventional career had stemmed from a desire to please his mother. She learned that he wished he had studied music instead of politics, and that a couple of years ago he had joined Facebook, with a view to reconnecting with the members of Busted Flush, the band for which he had played bass in the late eighties. All of this, he had, unaccountably, neglected to tell her. But Gavin and Lou would do that to a person — tease out their hidden desires, the ones they had forgotten about or never given voice to. They had done it to her. She knew now that her creativity was a force to be reckoned with, that she had a talent for female friendship, that she was highly responsive to sensual pleasures: food had never tasted so good; music had never moved her so deeply; sex — well, it was back on the agenda at least.

★   ★   ★

Yet, even as Lou and Gavin cracked Sara and Neil open and exposed in them fresh layers of curiosity and desire, they guarded their own enigma. Time and again, just as Sara thought she was starting to figure them out, to get a handle on their elusive shtick, they would slip away from her, like satyrs luring her deeper and deeper into a forest. Sara could never tell what was heartfelt and what was ironic in Lou and Gavin's lives. The antique pokerwork sign hanging in their kitchen, 'GOD BLESS OUR HOME', she had taken to be tongue in cheek and had conveyed as much in her tone when she commented on it, only to feel like a hard-boiled cynic when Lou told her the sign was a talisman with protective powers against the evil eye. Dolores Fernandez had put a curse on Gavin for killing the fish, she'd said, and the sign gave her comfort.

★ ★ ★

She must have fallen asleep. When she woke, a song was playing on the stereo that was so dirge-like that Sara thought it must be on at the wrong speed. Lou was swaying to it in a trance-like state. Gavin was still slumped on the sofa, studying the album cover, but Neil was sitting on the edge of the Eames chair, hands clasped around one raised knee, studying Lou beadily, as if she were of intense sociological interest. Sara had the distinct impression that she had missed something.

'Hello,' he said at last, sliding his eyes over to her. 'Okay?'

112

'I'm fine,' she replied, touchily.

'Maybe we should think about going.'

'What time is it?' she asked.

Neil shrugged. 'Late.'

'Well . . . ' Sara struggled to her feet. Her face felt hot; her extremities cold. The fire was almost out. 'Thanks for a really great day, guys.'

Despite all the intimacy, the silences, the sharing, she felt suddenly shy.

Lou, eyes still glazed, secret smile, swayed over to her and draped her arms around Sara's neck. Sara succumbed awkwardly to the rocking motion of Lou's dance and then, when the moment felt right, extricated herself.

'See you, Gav,' she said, and he moved his head in a small gesture that seemed, to Sara, fraught with meaning.

'Great!' Neil said, 'Great times.'

They paused briefly, in the doorway, then, remembering that Lou and Gavin didn't observe the normal protocols, they let themselves out into the chilly night.

10

The last things Sara saw as she closed the blinds that night were the calico linings of Carol's John Lewis curtains drawn against her like a reprimand. She was pretty much resigned, after that night's fiasco, to being struck off Carol's Christmas-card list. She could try to make amends, she supposed, go round with some peace offering and apologise, but she'd only end up getting herself in more trouble. At some point Carol would try to draw her into a bitch-fest about the state of Lou and Gavin's front garden or their children's manners, and Sara would have to tell her to get a life, which wouldn't serve community relations any better than the gradual drifting apart that now seemed inevitable. Nevertheless, as the first pink streaks of dawn rent the sky behind Carol's chimney pots, Sara felt a vague pang of loss.

★   ★   ★

Lou had become Sara's more-or-less constant companion now and, really, the sort of things they did together were much more her. Carol had been great at getting that hot ticket for the Donmar Warehouse, but she always made such a business of how much you owed her and what time the last train left Charing Cross, that it felt like an outing with the Girl Guides. Lou managed to conjure fun out of the very air. One night they'd go to a local gig in a grungy pub, another to a poetry reading on the South Bank. At weekends, while Neil and Gavin took the boys for a kick about, Lou bundled Zuley in her buggy and the three of them went rummaging through vintage shops in Brick Lane, where Sara marvelled at Lou's knack of turning up the one Biba dress among the racks of tat. She couldn't have been doing so badly herself, though, because Neil had commented approvingly that Lou had had a positive influence on her sense of style, a back-handed compliment that she was inclined to accept.

Even the weekly Thursday evening trip to the leisure centre for the boys' Taekwondo class had been converted by Lou into an opportunity for female bonding and beautification. In the old days, Sara used to sit in the café with a cappuccino and the *Guardian* crossword, but now that Dash and Arlo had joined the class Lou had other ideas. First the two women powered up and down the fast lane of the swimming pool, Lou striking out with a stylish crawl, Sara flailing along in her wake. Then, after thirty lung-busting lengths, they would repair to the sauna, where the dim lighting and lingering scent of eucalyptus created an air of intimacy.

'I love this part,' Sara had said on their last visit, sinking with relief onto the slatted bench. Lou climbed nimbly onto the hotter, higher tier, crossed her legs and closed her eyes. Sara cast an envious glance at Lou's physique. Her thighs were taut and firm and even the unforgiving

Lycra of her Speedo swimsuit couldn't quite disguise the fullness of her breasts. Somehow Sara's own hibiscus-print two-piece felt fussy and middle-aged by comparison. She measured a handful of flesh on either side of her waist and sighed.

'You look great!' said Lou, without opening her eyes. 'I wish I could get away with a bikini.'

'Oh behave!' said Sara. 'You're skinny as anything.'

'I know, but I've got stretch-marks.'

'They're nothing to be ashamed of,' said Sara. 'I've got a couple myself.'

'I bet you don't look like the bloody *A to Z*.'

'I'm sure Gav doesn't mind.'

'Gav's weird,' Lou smirked, 'he actually *likes* them. Once, when we were making love, he said they reminded him of those channels you get on the beach; you know, where the water runs down to the sea.'

'That's so beautiful,' said Sara.

'He's always had a bit of an Earth Mother thing. Couldn't get enough of me when I was pregnant.'

Sara tried for a smile.

'Which was fine by me, because I was a total shag-bag from day one. You'd think nature would *lower* your libido once you're knocked up.'

Sara shrugged, unwilling to confess that in her case, nature had done just that. She had felt too sick for the first three months, too breathless for the next five and for the last one, the taut dome of her belly had repelled all advances like an over-inflated spacehopper. The sauna door creaked open and a stout West Indian woman

116

plonked herself down next to Sara.

'You know at the end of the pregnancy, when the colostrum starts to come in, ready for breastfeeding?' Lou gave Sara a significant look.

Sara widened her eyes to indicate that she had caught Lou's meaning and no further elucidation was necessary.

'I know I shouldn't have let him,' Lou grinned, apparently impervious to the fact they now had company, 'but oh my God!'

Sara smiled nervously and threw a propitiatory glance at the woman.

'He developed quite a taste for it,' Lou said. She leaned down and added, in a resounding whisper, 'Comes to something when it takes you longer to wean your husband than your kid!'

Sara groaned.

'I'm joking,' Lou wiped away a trickle of sweat from her cleavage. '*Sort* of joking!'

Their companion wrung out a wet flannel and slapped it on her head in disgust.

'I wonder what the time is,' Sara said, half standing to get a look at the poolside clock. 'It's quarter-past. We should probably make a move. The boys'll be wondering where we are.'

'Oh, just five more minutes,' begged Lou. 'This'll be our last chance to hang out for a couple of weeks.'

'Why?' said Sara.

'I start filming Monday.'

'Oh.'

'I know,' said Lou, 'I can't believe it either.'

* * *

Lou's nocturnal working habits and the fact that Gavin's job occupied so much physical and psychological space in the house, had allowed Sara to forget, for practical purposes, that Lou was a filmmaker. The topic seldom came up for discussion. Lou liked to grow her ideas, like mushrooms, in the dark, and ever since Sara had been politely rebuffed when she'd offered to read Lou's script, she had been too daunted even to enquire how things were going. Only the bluish circles beneath her friend's eyes and her occasional disappearance to take a mysterious phone call had betokened a woman with more on her mind than packed lunches and overdue library books.

'So you've got everything lined up? The cast and crew and . . . whatever?'

Lou gave her a funny look.

'Of course you have,' Sara shook her head at her own foolishness. 'Where actually is it? The shoot?'

'Well, it's set in London, but my DP's Belgian and the only way he can fit it in is if we shoot it there. He's found a great location though, so no one will know the difference.'

Sara opened her mouth to ask what a DP was, but thought better of it. Filmmaking seemed to be a milieu in which it was very easy to put one's foot in it. Better to wait until the film was in the can and then offer a thoughtful response.

'Well, I'm here,' she said, screwing the lid onto her miniature bottle of spring water, and standing up, 'if Gavin needs any help, I mean. Not *here*, obviously. There. Next door. Or I will

118

be. You know, in case he . . . well, he'll have his
hands full, won't he?'

★   ★   ★

And then Lou was gone and Sara pined for her;
physically pined, in a way she hadn't done for
anyone since Amanda Durham, her best friend
in Top Juniors had gone to stay with her father
in Calgary for three weeks. But at least in
Amanda's case there had been a farewell
sleepover to soften the blow, when they had
gorged on Minstrels and listened to Duran
Duran and Amanda had rehearsed ways in which
to torment her new Canadian half-sister. In
Lou's case, there was no such send-off and Sara
couldn't help feeling a little sidelined in the rush
to creativity. She was sure there was no slight
intended; she knew Lou and Gavin well enough
now to see that they flew by the seat of their
pants and that sometimes the basic courtesies of
suburban life got forgotten. Why else would Lou
have allowed her film crew to park their transit
van outside Sara and Neil's house, so that they
had to ferry their big Friday night shop a full
twenty yards to their own front door? Why else,
when Sara and Neil stopped on the pavement,
straining under the weight of multiple carrier
bags, and waited for Lou to introduce them to
her variously pierced and tattooed co-workers,
would she merely offer a distracted, 'Hi,' before
returning to check her inventory with said
workers? Why else would she fail to acknowledge, even by text message, the good luck card

that Sara had handmade for her by Photo-shopping Lou's face onto a picture of Alfred Hitchcock, brandishing his trademark cigar? 'HOPE IT GOES WITHOUT A 'HITCH'!' she had written inside, and then posted it through the letterbox, rather than risk disturbing Lou in some late-night conflab. Later, she worried that the card had been crass. Maybe Lou hated Hitchcock and had perceived some unintended comparison with his work.

★   ★   ★

Hurrying alongside Gavin on the first school day of Lou's absence, Sara's nervous prattle failed to elicit much response. After a prolonged silence, during which he steered the buggy grimly up and down kerbs, the children surging around him like a pack of Huskies, she had a stab at what she thought the problem might be.

'Missing Lou?'

He gave her an odd look.

'Sorry. Silly question. Of course you are. Never mind. Two weeks will go in a flash.'

'No, *I'm* sorry,' he said, smiling at her, 'I'm being an arsehole. And to be honest, it's not so much that I'm missing her, it's more that I'm stuffed without her.'

Sara shot him an inquisitive glance.

'Don't get me wrong,' he said quickly, 'I'm all for it; the film, obviously. I'm just really up against it myself at the moment. And I could *definitely* have done without her volunteering me for this Year Six art project.'

'Oh dear — is that this week?'

Gavin mimed holding a pistol to his head and pulling the trigger.

'Great for Year Six though,' said Sara, 'getting to meet a real artist.'

'A real artist!' Gavin emitted a scornful puff of vapour into the cold air.

'What do they want you to do?'

'All I know is that it's got to tie in with the Picasso exhibition they're going to on Friday.'

'Oh, are you going to that? Me too,' said Sara happily. 'Seriously though, this week, if there's anything I can do.'

'How's your fibreglass sheathing?'

'Not what it once was,' Sara laughed. 'No, I meant domestically. If you need me to have the kids over, or anything.'

'You're sweet, but Lou'd kill me if I took you away from your novel. Bad enough that I've squashed *her* creativity; I don't want to turn into some sexist parasite that exploits all the women for miles around . . . '

'Is that what she thinks?' Sara pricked up her ears. 'That you squash her creativity?'

'Nah, not really,' said Gavin, 'it's just difficult, two artists living together. They don't recommend it in the guidebooks.'

'Don't they?' Sara said, before she noticed the look on Gavin's face, and swiped his arm playfully.

'She never gives the impression that she's anything other than a 100 percent supportive of you,' she said.

'No, she is. She is. I'm incredibly lucky, don't

get me wrong. She's completely in tune with me. Understands what I'm trying to say before I know myself. *And* she guards me from the vampires.'

'The *vampires?*'

'Oh, you know, all the people who want a piece of you. The ones who think that your work speaks to them and them alone.'

Sara wondered whether she fell into that category.

'I would have thought it was nice to make that connection with people,' she said.

'It is,' he said, 'it is nice. But sometimes those people don't know where the boundaries are.'

Sara instinctively took her hand off the handle of the buggy and put a bit of space between herself and Gavin.

'But you know,' he went on, 'Lou's got to do her thing as well, obviously, and then we've got three incredibly gifted, idiosyncratic kids who also need room to flourish, and sometimes you just think, *Jesus!* I can't breathe, you know? That's why I look at you and Neil and think it must be lovely to have the balance that you guys have.'

'The *balance?*' said Sara.

'Yeah, you know. He's doing his breadwinner thing, and you've got the domestic front covered, but you're also doing a bit of writing; *plus*, you had the good sense to stop at two kids and, yes, I'll come clean and admit that sometimes I envy you.'

'Hmmm,' said Sara, doubtfully, 'I'm not sure we're quite as yin and yang as you think.

Sometimes it feels more chalk and cheese, to be honest.'

'Well, you seem like a pretty good fit from where I'm standing,' he said.

Sara gave him a strained smile.

* * *

The boys had already assimilated themselves into the free-form, fifteen-a-side, multi-racial football game that will dominate the playground of any inner-city primary school from which it hasn't been banned in the interests of health and safety.

'Okay then,' said Gavin, brushing Sara's cheek with his 'catch you later,' and he pushed the buggy towards the gaggle of younger, more raucous mothers, of whom Mandy, Zuley's childminder, was one. Sara stood watching from a distance, as the women flocked round Gavin, the childminder signalling her superiority in the pecking order by pawing his arm and baying with red-lipsticked laughter at everything he said. She didn't know how the woman had the brass neck, really. It should have been obvious that Gav was way out of her league. You couldn't fault his manners, though — it was to his credit that he played along with such good grace.

* * *

After a minute, she remembered that there was no point waiting for Gavin, because he was staying on to do his Picasso thing, so she made her way towards the school gate again. It was a short walk, but a lonely one. A couple of months ago, it would have taken her a good ten minutes to cover the same ground. Any one of five or six women wearing a Uniqlo puffa jacket or pastel duffel coat might have stopped her for a chat, or to invite Caleb or Patrick for tea. But most of her friends had bailed out along with Carol and Celia, and the ones who hadn't were career women, who would be halfway to the station by now, too busy checking their emails to notice that the once-desirable school to which they had chosen to send their luckless offspring, was in terminal decline.

11

'Do you think our relationship has balance?'

Sara stood in front of the mirror, massaging moisturiser into her neck.

Neil looked up, the light from the laptop glinting off his reading glasses.

'I don't know what you mean,' he said.

'I mean, are we two halves of a whole?'

'We bring different things to the table,' he said hopefully.

She frowned at him.

'Are you going to put that thing away?'

'Are you going to stop asking cryptic questions?'

He flipped the computer shut and took off his glasses.

She got into bed, feeling surprisingly shy. It was as if her non sequitur had somehow brought sex onto the agenda. Perhaps sensing her unease, Neil put a comradely arm around her and she relaxed a little. She tried again.

'Do you think marriage should be, you know, something that *works*, somewhere in the background, so everyone can get on with what they're doing?'

He was stroking her shoulder and it was getting on her nerves.

'Or should it be this big difficult, passionate thing with . . . Can you not do that please?'

'Sorry.'

'There's some quote I read once that said it should be full of mud and stars and love and hate or something like that.'

'I don't think there should be hate, ideally.'

Sara sighed and slid down the bed, out of his embrace.

He slid down next to her and patted her upper arm in a conciliatory way.

'I'm sorry, Sar, I'm just not really getting you. Try me again.'

'It doesn't matter.'

'I *love* you,' he offered tentatively, 'if that helps.'

★   ★   ★

Sara was, by now, aware that she had developed a crush on Gavin. It was a banal and tawdry impulse on her part, but it wasn't shame that prevented her, when having sex with Neil that night, from closing her eyes and pretending she was with her best friend's husband — it was the impossibility of suspending her disbelief. Neil was not an ungenerous lover and there was nothing wrong with his technique. Whole minutes would be allocated to Sara's gratification, the focus of attention shifting by subtle degrees, towards her clitoris, which Neil had learned to massage not from above, with his fingertips, which tended to set her teeth on edge, but from below, with the heel of his hand, whilst kneeling dutifully between her splayed legs. In this way, nine times out of ten, she could be guaranteed an orgasm of satisfactory depth and intensity, before Neil moved on to the main business of the evening.

When Sara thought about sex with Gavin, however, it was as a different order of endeavour altogether. Here, the mud and stars came into play, and when she conjured the act itself, it was as a collage of fleeting and thrillingly transgressive images to do with pain and pleasure and shame; Gavin leaving bite marks on her nipple, plunging his fingers into her anus, coming, disgracefully, in her face. That was the storyboard, but the soundtrack was sublime — an operatic aria, a Leonard Cohen song, the divine liturgy of the Greek Orthodox church.

★   ★   ★

'Gav's been in school this week, helping out with the art,' Sara said, when Neil returned from the bathroom — he had excellent post-coital hygiene, she'd say that for him.

'Oh?' said Neil.

'He's a bit disappointed in it.'

'I wouldn't worry too much about that. It's only art. I'm more concerned that Caleb's in Year Six and he's never heard of long division.'

'Well, he wasn't only talking about the art. He was talking about the ethos of the school.'

'What's up with it?'

'There's no passion, he said; the teachers are on autopilot. It's a glorified babysitting service.'

'I shouldn't think Gav really knows what he's talking about.'

'I should think he's got more of a clue than

127

you. When was the last time you set foot in a classroom?'

Neil glared at her.

'Okay, sorry, that's unfair, but I have to say, I think he might be right. I went through Patrick's book bag the other day and all I could find were pages and pages of colouring-in.'

'I hope he stayed inside the lines.'

Sara gave him a sarcastic smile.

'I just don't understand how a school can go downhill so fast,' she said. 'I mean eighteen months ago, it was 'good with some outstanding features'.'

'Well, if you're worried, do something about it,' Neil said.

'I will,' said Sara. 'I am.'

★ ★ ★

It was pouring down on the morning of the trip but Sara had opted to take a telescopic umbrella, rather than conceal her carefully chosen outfit under an unflattering raincoat. As she struggled along New Cross Road at the rear of an unruly line of Year Sixes, she was already regretting her decision. The umbrella kept blowing inside out, obstructing her view of Gavin, who in any case was right at the front, chatting away to Kate Harrison the Year Six teacher.

'You don't mind, do you, Sara?' Kate had said. 'Only I could do with a safe pair of hands to round up the stragglers.' With that, Sara had been banished to the back of the crocodile along with Caleb, who, being ten years old and

128

separated from his best friend, minded very much. He had been paired instead with Engin, an ebullient Turkish boy who combined the curiosity of a toddler with the build of an all-in wrestler. Thrilled to be out in the world, Engin was at a loss to understand Caleb's surly indifference and kept trying to engage him, first with chatter, then by clowning around and finally with outright naughtiness.

★ ★ ★

It was standing room only on the train and every inch of available handrail was taken. Sara had no choice but to clamp her wet brolly between her knees and hold onto her two charges by their hoods, all too aware that if Engin went down, so would the whole carriage. The train smelled of damp upholstery and morning breath. Its windows were blank with condensation, and there was nowhere to look but at other passengers' backs, or shoulders or jutting elbows. If she craned her neck, she could just about see Gavin, in his classic raincoat, slung between the luggage racks like an elegant bat. She wondered whether he was growing a beard, or just hadn't shaved. Either way, it suited him.

★ ★ ★

As she ushered Caleb and Engin through the mechanical barriers at Charing Cross station, the rest of the party was already lining up for a headcount. She waved frantically and Kate

Harrison widened her eyes and tapped her watch. Sara chivvied the boys across the concourse in time to join the back of the line as it snaked off towards the Strand. The gallery appeared now, on the far side of Trafalgar Square, like a citadel glimpsed across a hostile plane. Routemasters loomed, commuters jay-walked, horns sounded, pigeons scattered. If they could just get across before the lights changed, but no, the green man was flashing and they were marooned on a traffic island, watching the rest of their party meander into the distance like a colony of ants.

★ ★ ★

At last, flustered and red-faced, Sara ushered her charges up the gallery steps and into the Learning Zone, where the other children were already sitting cross-legged on the floor in front of Picasso's *Still Life with Lemons*. A young woman wearing a lanyard over her denim shirt waister waited with exaggerated patience for Caleb and Engin to be seated and Sara slunk shamefaced into the background.

She scanned the perimeter of the room for Gavin, but he was nowhere to be seen and she had all but given up on him, when a voice whispered in her ear.

'What kept you?'

'God!' she squealed. 'You scared me.'

He squeezed her elbow, and snickered, the mild disruption earning them both a reproachful glance from Kate Harrison, which Sara met with a triumphant smirk.

'I can't believe you made me do this!' Sara plonked herself down beside Gavin on the top deck of the river bus. She felt giddy with the spontaneity of it all; the fearlessness.

'You should *thank* me,' Gav said, 'I saved us from Art History Woman. She was killing those kids, *killing* them, I tell you. And look at 'em now — happy as Larry.'

He nodded towards their four charges, who were leaning over the railings, pointing out landmarks to one another, their animated faces wet with spray from the boat's churning wake.

'We're going to be in trouble when Kate Harrison realises it wasn't just a toilet break.'

'I just feel bad for the ones we had to leave behind,' replied Gav, as if they were refugees from a war zone.

'Oh come on, she wasn't *that* bad.'

'Did you know, childwen,' Gav's impersonation was spot-on, 'that as well as being a pwint-maker and cewamicist, Picasso was also a playwite?'

If Neil had been there, Sara knew, he'd have objected on several counts: political incorrectness, sexism, inverted snobbery. But he wasn't, so she threw her head back and laughed, and she was still laughing when the wind blew a strand of hair across her mouth and Gav leaned across to remove it.

★ ★ ★

Sara remembered the champagne in the nick of time. As she took it out of the freezer compartment and transferred it to the bottom shelf of the fridge, it creaked ominously and a large bubble, the kind that had no business being in a bottle of champagne, rose slowly along its length. She straightened up and caught sight of her reflection in the dusk-darkened window. She was pleased with what she saw. The new top was flattering, if a little risqué. As she moved across to pull the kitchen blinds, she noticed Gavin trying to light a bonfire on the other side of the fence. He was grubbing around in the dark, but what little kindling he could find seemed to be dampening, rather than fuelling the flames. She smiled to herself and, hurrying through to the living room, snatched the box of firelighters from the log basket and called up the stairs,

'Neil, Gav needs a hand with something. I'll see you there, okay?'

*   *   *

'Having fun?' she said, emerging into their garden via the side gate.

Gavin looked up sharply. His hair was standing on end and he had a smudge of soot on his cheek. It was obvious that, until now, fun had not been on the agenda. Seeing her, he smiled and took the firelighters, almost as though he had been expecting her to bring them. Sara watched, hugging her elbows for warmth as he re-laid and lit the fire. Then they stood side-by-side and watched it spread its pool of brightness over the

132

grass, throwing sparks up into the navy foliage.

'Er — would it be bad manners to ask what the hell's going on?'

'Lou wants to christen our paella pan. This is how they do it in Spain — outside, on an open fire.'

'Nice,' said Sara, but at the prospect of alfresco dining in November she was unable to quell an involuntary shiver.

'Here,' Gav undid the sweater from around his waist and held it open, as if she were the child and he the parent. She dived into it, relishing the ripe, mushroom-y scent of him. As her head emerged, she felt his hand touch the nape of her neck. She turned towards him, like a flower towards the sun.

'Hello stranger!' The sound of Lou's voice made her spring guiltily away again.

'Hi!' she said. 'I *missed* you.'

'I missed you *too*,' Lou replied, and they hugged awkwardly.

'Good trip?' Sara asked, stepping back and rubbing Lou's upper arms briskly.

'A-mazing!' said Lou. 'I'll tell you about it over dinner.'

'Which looks fabulous, by the way. I don't think I've ever eaten authentic paella before.'

A lengthy debate ensued between Gavin and Lou as to whether such a thing existed, and if so, which region of Spain might rightfully lay claim to it. By the time the matter was settled, Neil had arrived with the champagne. Glasses were fetched, the cork noisily popped and a toast proposed to Lou and all who sailed in her. The paella rice was still opaque when the rain started — a fine wind-blown mist at first, which soon turned into un-ignorable drizzle. It took Neil and Gav's combined strength to bear the pan of charred chicken and saffron-infused rice back up the steps to the kitchen, where its sheer size, taking up all four rings of the stovetop, induced fits of incredulous laughter.

'I don't know what I was thinking,' Lou wailed. 'There's enough for an army. It's never going to cook.'

It did, however, and whether it was the sheer quantity of drink they had put away by then, the authenticity of the recipe, or the tang of wood smoke in the rice, Sara had never eaten better.

★ ★ ★

The filming had been intense, Lou told them, full-on. Everything that could go wrong had gone wrong. The sound man had gone on a bender and the lead actress had wanted to improvise; the hotel had had bedbugs, the catering had been diabolical and they shouldn't even *ask* about the budget. '*But* . . . ' she took a sip of wine and looked round the table, her coy smile turning triumphant, despite her best efforts ' . . . I think it might just be the best thing I've done.'

Sara clapped her hands childishly; Neil patted Lou on the shoulder; Gavin lifted his wife's hand, turned it over and bestowed a lingering kiss on the inside of her wrist.

'This is it,' he said, softly, 'this is your time.'

Sara smiled wanly.

134

'It's great to be back in London, though,' Lou said, 'Europe felt kind of *tired* to be honest. It was *so* the right thing for us to do — moving back here — creatively. In *every* way, really. You know when something just clicks? Anyway, tell me, what have you all been up to?'

'Not much,' Gavin shrugged and looked around the table for confirmation, 'just the usual round of domestic tedium.'

'Oh,' Sara protested, 'I hardly think so. *You* certainly did your best to relieve it, Gav.'

'Did I?' Gavin looked perplexed.

'The gallery trip?' She turned to Lou. 'He was a very naughty boy.'

'Was he now?' Lou gave her husband an indulgent smile.

'I couldn't believe it,' Sara laughed. 'One minute we're listening to this bright young thing telling us all about Picasso, the next Gav's got us doing a runner!'

'It was that or strangle the bloody woman,' said Gav. 'She's probably turned those kids off art for life.'

'How d'you mean?' Neil asked.

Gav adopted the woman's plummy vowels but, to Sara's relief, did not reprise the speech impediment. ''How many shapes can you see in the picture? Do you think Picasso was happy or sad when he painted it?' I mean, what the fuck?' He pronounced it 'fook'.

'She meant well,' said Sara.

'I know but, come *on*. A lot of those kids had never been to a gallery before. You've got one chance to engage them; get their juices flowing, let them see that art's not just pictures of posh people in gilt frames, it's something they might wanna participate in, live their *lives* by. And instead, they get some airhead Sloane handing out clipboards.'

'Bit harsh,' said Neil mildly.

'Not really,' said Gav. 'This is *Picasso* we're talking about. Greatest artist of the twentieth century. Bloke whose highest artistic ambition is to draw like a child. This guy *gets* kids. Kids *get* him.' He turned to Lou. 'Remember how Dash reacted when we took him to see *Guernica*?'

Lou nodded wistfully.

'So you voted with your feet?' Neil said, with a doubtful smile.

'Yup. Took them to Greenwich on the river bus,' Gav said smugly. 'Fan-*bloody*-tastic. Got to see Tower Bridge open up to let a liner through — made me feel like a kid myself. I've never seen that in all the years I've lived in London. Tell me that doesn't beat counting the number of lemons in a still life?'

'Yeah, that's pretty cool,' Neil conceded. 'Bascule bridge. That's physics.'

'Never mind physics,' Gavin said, 'it's *poetry*. The beauty of it. The *wit*. This kid, Darren . . . '

'Daniel,' corrected Sara.

' . . . Daniel — lairy little sod — wound up our Dash something chronic. But he sees this bridge go up and he's just gob-smacked. Chuffed to bits he was. Look on that kid's face I'll take to my grave.'

'His dad wasn't convinced,' Sara reminded him with a rueful grin.

'Oh, spare me the guilt trip,' Gav said, 'I know his type. Grew up around blokes like that. Doesn't give a shit about his kid, until there's a chance to take a pop at somebody else. Then it's all *'elf and safety.'*

'The school does have a duty of care, though,' Neil pointed out.

'Goody two-shoes!' Lou tapped him playfully across the knuckles and he grinned sheepishly, taking it rather better, Sara thought, than he would have done from her.

'Imagine if you could unlock the potential, in *every* child,' Lou said wistfully. 'If only education was about epiphanies instead of about testing and league tables.'

'Oh, I dare say there's the odd Eureka moment, even at Cranmer Road,' said Neil.

'I wouldn't bet on it, mate,' said Gavin. 'I was in the other week to do some art with the kids, around this Picasso trip. Went in with all these big ideas — collage, found objects, you name it. Turns out, 'Miss' wants me to focus on cubism because it ties in with their maths.'

He clutched his head in despair.

'Yeah,' said Sara, regretfully, 'they're playing it by the book at the moment, until the inspectors have done their spot check.'

'The inspectors?' asked Lou.

'Oh, er, yes,' said Sara, 'there was an OFSTED last term.' She made her voice heavy with irony. 'We didn't come up to scratch, apparently. Found wanting in the area of Gifted and Talented, among other things. Hence the sudden departure of all the little Hollys and Harriets.'

'Well I have to say,' said Gavin, 'I've got some sympathy with them now I've seen what goes on. Some of those kids can barely write their names. I can't believe we worried that Dash and Arlo might not make the grade. They're in a different *league*. I don't mean to sound big-headed, but it's true.'

'Oh dear,' said Lou, biting her lip, 'that must have been what Sonia Dudek was on about.'

'Who?' said Gavin.

'The Deputy Head. She took me on one side a while back. Said Cranmer Road didn't seem to be meeting Dash's needs. She wondered if it was really the right school for him.'

There was a pause, while they all contemplated the bleak educational future they had inflicted on their children.

'There's meant to be a good Steiner school in Clapham,' said Lou, hopefully.

'Don't like the sound of Steiner,' Gavin said, 'I knew a guy once went to one of those schools. Very, very fucked up. Can't make relationships *at all*.'

Lou shrugged and drained the remainder of the wine into their glasses. They sipped simultaneously, and a silence descended. Sara picked a congealed fragment of rice from the edge of her plate and chewed on it. Gavin reached into his pocket for his rolling tobacco. Neil took a surreptitious glance at his mobile.

'Am I the only one . . . ' Lou said, at last, folding her arms and looking around the table, ' . . . thinking the answer is staring us in the face?'

12

The next day, Sara noticed the crack. She stopped to pick up a balled sock off the landing and there it was. A jagged hairline fissure, running from the skirting board up the wall to the cornice, where it disappeared briefly from view, only to re-emerge on the ceiling, a fine but still discernible fault line. She frowned and touched it with one finger. So many things needing attention. In the old days, pre Gavin and Lou, she'd have nagged Neil until he agreed to get the decorators in. Shabbiness had depressed her. Now though, things were more complicated. Gavin and Lou's house was in much worse nick than theirs, and yet she preferred it. Lou had an eye for the aesthetics of decay. She would half sand a door, and then leave it, patched and mottled, like a piece of living archaeology. She would leave flowers in a vase until they drooped brown-veined petals onto the mantelpiece, not because she was too lazy to throw them away, but because she found the subtle hues of death strangely beautiful. She cultivated verdigris and patina, loved age-spotted linen and abraded chenille. And now that Sara had got her eye in, she too was coming to despise perky garage tulips and plumped up cushions. There was so much more texture and variation in old stuff, so much more *soul*. So, no, she wouldn't run straight for the Farrow & Ball paint chart, she would restrain her bourgeois tendencies; let the true character of the house reveal itself; make way, if necessary, for a bit of shabby-chic.

* * *

'Patrick? Caleb?' Sara called, sniffing the sock in her hand, before tossing it, with a grimace of distaste, into the laundry basket. 'Can you brush your teeth please? We should have left five minutes ago.' They moved at the speed of tectonic plates, only with more audible moaning. Even now, the gargling and hawking coming from the bathroom had an undertone of fraternal needle. Caleb's behaviour towards his younger brother, peevish at the best of times, had seemed to Sara to verge on bullying lately. His enthusiasm for school had waned since the start of term. Then again, he had had four different supply teachers in as many weeks and had been relegated to the bottom maths set, so it wasn't surprising. Now that Lou had raised the tantalising prospect of home-schooling, Sara couldn't think of a single reason to prolong her children's mediocre school career a day longer than necessary.

* * *

The doorbell rang.
   Well, perhaps there was *one*.
   'Hi, Gav.'
   'Hi,' he looked tired and distracted. 'Massive, *massive* favour?'

140

'Try me.'

'Could you take them to school? I've got to do a radio thing at nine-thirty.'

'Sure, no problem,' she said, disguising disappointment with a breezy smile. 'Lou busy, is she?'

'She's been up all night watching the rushes. Only crashed out an hour ago.'

'Oh,' said Sara. 'Fantastic. So we'll be able to see the film soon?'

Gav laughed sardonically and Sara smiled, unsure what she was meant to take from this.

* * *

She arrived at school late and out of breath. Chivvying the boys through the gate, she scanned the playground for Zuley's childminder, whom she spotted at last, slumped on a bench staring at her phone, while her small charges swarmed over the climbing frame. Seeing Mandy, Zuley leaned forward in the buggy and wiggled her fingers needily.

'Hello Princess,' Mandy said in the kind of fake baby voice Sara knew Lou despised.

'Sorry to keep you,' Sara said. 'Gav had to do a work thing at short notice.'

'I know,' Mandy said, 'he texted me.'

She glanced at her phone again and, smirked before putting it back in her pocket.

'It's a radio interview,' Sara told her, determined to pull rank. 'He tried to reschedule, but it's going out live so . . . '

Mandy stood up with an air of indifference

and slung her bag over the handle of the buggy. Zuley bucked eagerly, and Sara felt usurped, peripheral.

'Bye darling, have a lovely time,' she said, leaning down for a kiss, but the child screwed up her face with displeasure.

'I wouldn't worry,' Mandy said, 'she does that.'

Smarting from the rejection, Sara nevertheless forced herself to stroll alongside the buggy as far as the school gate. As they turned to go their separate ways, the childminder paused, and met her eye.

'Do you not get a bit sick of it?'

'What?'

Mandy smiled pityingly.

'At least I'm getting paid!' she said.

★　★　★

Sara was still inventing killer put-downs as she primed the coffee percolator half an hour later.

'Sick of living in a mutually supportive community where people don't keep score?' she wished she'd said. 'Sick of supporting important artists?'

Sara was so cross that she forgot to drink the coffee when it was brewed and so distracted that she had only made half a page of notes on Lewisham's Home Education policy when a ring at the doorbell brought welcome relief.

'Oh, good, you're in!' Lou said. 'Is that coffee I can smell?' She headed for the kitchen.

'I thought you were catching up on your

142

beauty sleep,' Sara said, following happily behind.

'I couldn't get off,' said Lou, 'my head's too full of the film.'

'I bet it is. Are you pleased with the way it's looking?'

'It's more of a cataloguing process at this stage, but, yeah I think it's going to be okay.'

She pushed a striped paper bag into Sara's hands.

'Forgot to give you this the other night.'

'What is it?'

'Just a little present from Belgium. A thank-you.'

Here, then, was the definitive proof. On a tight schedule, with egos to massage, crew to supervise, a film to bring in on time and on budget, Lou had still gone out of her way to buy Sara a gift.

She pulled off the tissue paper to reveal a bronze-coloured plastic cherub.

'Oh . . . ' she said. 'Cute!'

'It's a Pissing Boy drink dispenser,' said Lou, 'like the fountain in Brussels. Not that I was *in* Brussels, but anyway. You fill him up and he pisses out your drink.'

'Hysterical!' said Sara, 'I'll put him here, in pride of place.'

She stood the figurine on the middle shelf of the dresser and they both took a moment to enjoy the subversive kitsch of the gift.

★　★　★

'So what are *you* up to?' said Lou, at length. 'Oh God, don't say I've interrupted your writing?'

'Nope,' said Sara proudly, 'all finished.'

Lou turned to her with saucer eyes.

'Sara! That's amazing! God, you put me to shame.'

'I got loads done while you were away. Gav's got a great work ethic, hasn't he? I did my best to distract him, but he kept sending me back to my desk!'

Lou didn't seem to be listening. She pursed her lips as if making some calculation.

'Okay, that might work,' she murmured. 'If I take a look at your manuscript this weekend and give you my comments, then you could send it off next week.'

'Send it off?' said Sara.

'To literary agents,' said Lou. 'You'll need an agent, Sara. I'll talk to my friend Ezra. We might try his guy first. Won't hurt to use the connection.'

'Ezra?' Sara pricked up her ears.

'Ezra Bell.'

'You know Ezra Bell?'

'We do, yeah. He was one of Gav's early collectors, back when no one had heard of him.'

'Of Gav?'

'Of Ezra. Well, of either of them, actually. Their careers have risen in tandem, which is kind of nice.'

Sara digested this. Ezra Bell was a name to conjure with. Carol, she knew for a fact, would swap her Donmar Warehouse membership for a chance to touch the hem of Ezra Bell's corduroy

144

jacket. Gavin, on the other hand — celebrated, certainly; respected by the cognoscenti, but surely not quite as high-profile as the Pulitzer-prize-winning chronicler of post 9/11 America? Then again, Sara didn't necessarily trust her own instincts any more. Lou was always bandying about the names of people Sara had never heard of, with an air of reverence that suggested they were demi-gods. The fact was, until she met Lou and Gav, she had been ploughing a pretty narrow furrow.

'He'll be kipping on our couch next month when he comes over for his author tour,' Lou said. 'You can pick his brains then.'

'Oh, I can just see that,' scoffed Sara. 'Ezra, do you think I should hold back on the electronic rights until the marketing campaign's gathered momentum, or should I just go balls-out?'

Lou cocked her head on one side.

'You're doing it again,' she said.

'I know, but come on, I'm me and he's . . .'

'Ezra Bell; who, when we first got to know him was an ordinary self-deprecating guy who happened to have an unpublished novel in his bottom drawer. Sound familiar?'

Sara couldn't help smiling, whether at her friend's unfeasibly flattering comparison, or at the veiled suggestion that meeting Lou and Gav had itself somehow been the catalyst to greatness, she wasn't sure. And yet to dismiss Lou's hubris would have been to denigrate her own work and just lately, for the first time, Sara had started to believe in it. She had taken Lou's advice to heart, banished from her mind's eye

145

her mother's lemon-sucking face and written through her shame; plundering the furthest sordid reaches of her imagination and creating scenes of a rawness and pathos that had made her blink back tears even as she composed them. She had filleted her original manuscript in ruthless fashion, sacrificing paragraphs that had once seemed indispensable, but which now struck her as overwrought and pretentious. The resultant slender novel felt like something that had been waiting all along in the ether to be captured by her and her alone. When she looked at the wad of printed papers, nestling within their grey mottled box file, she wanted to pinch herself. It felt like a small miracle. The thought of exposing this final draft to Lou's critical gaze was daunting enough, but the idea that it might soon find its way, perhaps with a word of recommendation from the great man himself, into the inbox of Ezra Bell's literary agent, was enough to bring her out in a cold sweat.

'Just leave it with me,' Lou insisted, 'and get on with the next thing. What *is* the next thing by the way?'

Sara waved her notebook cheerfully.

'I'm all about home education now.'

'Ah!'

'It's actually much more straightforward than we thought. There's a process to go through, of course, but they can't stop you from doing it. And it's actually surprisingly common. Over four hundred families in the borough, and rising.'

'Oh,' said Lou doubtfully. 'Good.'

'You're not having second thoughts?'

'Christ, no. Just, I'd quite like to be involved in planning it but at the moment I'm too busy with the post — '

'The *post* . . . ?' an image sprang to mind of Lou sorting jiffy bags.

'Post-*production*. Always takes longer than you think. Realistically, I reckon New Year, don't you? Fresh start, new leaf?'

13

The end of term concert at Cranmer Road was a true test of Sara's resolve. As every year, the children forgot their lines, sang out of tune, corpsed, fidgeted and then killed it with a rousing rendition of 'Winter Wonderland', which would have melted the heart of Gradgrind himself. Even a failing school had to be failing pretty dismally to stuff up Christmas.

★　★　★

The dusk was already gathering as they walked home and the council Christmas lights had just come on. The route, past betting shops, newsagents and dry cleaners, whilst drearily suburban, had been the backdrop to a phase in Sara's life, which would never come again. Excited as she was to be on the brink of something new, something that she hoped would bring her children's lives rushing from two dimensions into three, as they discovered the transformative power of their own creativity, she was mindful now, suddenly and poignantly, of the value of ordinariness; of the consolation of being an ant on an anthill working, unthinkingly, to a common purpose. There was dignity in that too — and perhaps a kind of liberation.

'So, he didn't put up a fight, the Head?' said Neil over supper, as Sara reported back on the events of a momentous week.

'Not really,' said Sara, 'if I didn't know better, I'd say he seemed glad to get rid.'

'Probably had it up to here with pushy middle class parents,' said Neil, loading his fork with fish pie.

'Carol said he almost cried when she and Celia told him *they* were jumping ship.'

'Carol exaggerates,' said Neil, plucking a prawn tail from between his teeth and laying it carefully on the side of his plate. 'What did he actually say?'

'Oh, you know, he hoped we knew what we were taking on. He could assure us the school was back on track and that they wouldn't have any trouble filling the places. He firmly believed they were doing right by all ability groups. That was when Lou put him on the spot.'

'Oh?'

'She showed him Dash's reading record. She's got him on the classics: *Treasure Island; Tom Sawyer*; Salinger, even, which I don't think is really appropriate for a . . . '

Neil revolved his fork to indicate she should get to the point.

'Anyway, Dash has filled every page, and the teacher's put big ticks next to his reports and given him smiley faces, but when you actually read what he's written, he's just copied out the same review over and over again. And because she knows he's brainy, she hasn't bothered to read them.'

'Crafty little sod,' said Neil. 'What did the Head say?'

149

'He said Dash was a unique student whose specific learning requirements had tested the robustness of oh, some policy or other. He used a lot of jargon but I think he just meant they couldn't keep up with him.'

Neil snorted derisively and Sara was unsure whether this was a comment on the Head Teacher or Dash.

'Did he say anything about Patrick and Caleb?' he asked, as an afterthought.

'He said they would be greatly missed by the recorder group and the football team respectively.'

* * *

'Do we have to go next door?' Caleb was slumped on the sofa in his pyjamas, watching toddlers' TV. 'Their house smells funny.'

'No it doesn't,' said Sara, 'you'll have fun. You'll be with your friends.'

'Why can't they come here?'

'It's easier for me if we go there. It's where Zuley's toys are.'

'I hate Zuley.'

'Caleb!'

'She makes things up and she cries all the time.'

'Yes, because she's three. Come on. It's hard for her. She just wants to join in with you guys. Cut her some slack.'

'Why should I? She's not *my* sister.'

'You like girls.'

'No, I don't.'

150

'You like Holly.'

Caleb stared vacantly at the screen, before a thought flickered across his face,

'Why don't we see her anymore? Is it because you've gone off Carol?'

Sara adopted a deliberately light tone of voice.

'I'm very fond of Carol,' she said, 'and you can see Holly any time you like.'

★ ★ ★

There was no response when Sara rang the bell. She rolled her eyes and smiled to herself, imagining Gavin hard at work in the studio, deaf to the world on account of his headphones. He had once made her guess his favourite thing to listen to when working. She had squirmed and fretted, like the Princess trying to guess Rumpelstiltskin's name in the fairy story.

'Pearl Jam?'

'No.'

'Kraftwerk?'

'No.'

'Steve Reich? Muddy Waters? Patti Smith?'

'No, no and no.'

Turned out to be Magic FM. All that nostalgic slush, hour after hour, she could hardly believe it. But Gav said it took him to his happy place. It was the fish finger sandwich of broadcasting and it hit the spot. It amused her to think of him producing his tortured, existential sculptures to the strains of Air Supply and Lionel Richie. It would be nice not to have to wait on the doorstep in the cold, however, with the boys cursing and scuffing their shoes. Where were Dash and Arlo? At this rate they'd be waiting all morning. Eventually, repeated rings brought Zuley skittering down the hall in her pyjamas. Agonising minutes passed while she teetered on tiptoe, trying to reach the latch. At last, with a heroic leap, she succeeded.

'Go and ask Dash and Arlo what they want for breakfast,' Sara told the boys, then she marched through to the kitchen and started flipping open cupboards in search of basic provisions. The sink was filled with greasy dishes, half submerged in cold water and there was a smell of drains. She needed a coffee, but opening the stovetop pot, she found it full of mouldy grounds from days ago. She banged them out on the draining board, tossed the filter in the sink, squirted a river of washing up liquid in after it and turned the hot tap on full.

'Mary Poppins, as I live and breathe,' said a familiar voice.

'Oh, hi Gav,' Sara said, doing her best to ignore the plummeting sensation in her belly, 'looks like the washing-up fairy gave your place a miss last night.'

'God, yeah, what a tip. Listen, don't you be doing that.'

Sara was about to shrug it off, when Caleb hurtled into the room, skidded to a halt and announced breathlessly:

'Arlo wants rice pops and Dash wants prawn wonton!'

'Breakfast,' Sara explained, seeing Gav's look of bafflement.

'Prawn wonton,' Gav shook his head admiringly, 'cheeky fucker!'

'Bit of a stretch,' said Sara. 'You seem to be down to army rations.' She unscrewed the lid of a vintage canister and demonstrated, to add insult to injury, an absence of coffee.

'Jesus!' Gav sighed as though none of this were any of his doing, and Sara felt torn between sisterly indignation on Lou's behalf and a hint of schadenfreude that her friend's all-out pursuit of her career goals, had left her exposed in the house-keeping department.

'Oh well,' shrugged Gav, 'if there's no *coffee*, we've got no choice, have we?'

★ ★ ★

Sara didn't know when she'd enjoyed a fry-up so much. They had lived around the corner from Dimitri's for over a decade, but she had never before set foot in the place. Neil always said he could feel his arteries furring up just walking past the extractor fan. But this morning, the eggs were fresh, the bacon dense and salty, and the fried bread had a crunch and ooze that felt as sinful and delicious as, well, as flirting with one's best friend's husband over a weekday breakfast in a greasy spoon. As Zuley chased a button mushroom round her plate and the boys squabbled over *Angry Birds*, Gavin drained his coffee mug and smiled at Sara over its rim.

'I like a girl who can eat.'

Sara looked at the sunset streaks of egg yolk and tomato sauce on her plate and grinned.

Notwithstanding the occasional roll-up and a love of hard liquor, Lou was a health-food freak. She and Neil would be united in priggish disapproval if they could see their spouses right now. Every other week Lou subjected her family to some new nutritional fad. If she wasn't addressing Arlo's eczema with low gluten, she was urging Dash to new heights of intellectual endeavour with an abundance of omega 3 or enhancing Gavin's creativity and (wink) his all-round performance with cruciferous vegetables. But Sara had seen enough to intuit that his wife's anxiety and inconsistency around food got on Gavin's nerves, in the same way as her fussy subservience toward people like Dieter and Korinna did. There were not many domains, Sara knew, in which she trumped Lou, perhaps only in this — she was not neurotic. Here, then, was an opportunity to press home her advantage.

'Are you calling me a pig?' she said, a mischievous glint in her eye.

Gavin shrugged.

'Just saying you've got a healthy appetite.'

'Hmmm,' she said, poking her belly disingenuously, 'a bit too healthy.'

'It's nice,' he said, looking straight at her, 'nothing wrong with a bit of what you fancy.'

She forced herself to return his gaze and allow the silence to be meaningful.

'*Lou's* got a lovely figure,' she said with the merest hint of reproach.

Gavin looked at her levelly as if he could see right into her dirty conniving soul.

'Never said she didn't,' he said.

14

Arriving to babysit at the designated hour on Friday night, Sara's mother managed, as always, to take the wind out of her sails.

'Well, I suppose it's nice that you're still making an effort after fourteen years of marriage,' she said, giving Sara's outfit the once-over.

'Fifteen,' said Sara, 'what's the matter, don't you like it?' She fiddled self-consciously with the peplum of her cocktail dress. It wasn't as though, in her Country Casuals two-piece, her mother was an arbiter of style. And yet already Sara could feel her confidence ebbing away.

'Is everything . . . ' Sara's mother eyed her daughter's fishnet tights, doubtfully, ' . . . all right between you and Neil?'

'What do you mean?'

'You seem a bit dressed up for the pictures.'

'It's not just the pictures. It's a friend's film premiere,' Sara replied, 'in Soho.'

'Oooh,' said her mother, momentarily enlivened. 'Well, if they take your photo, don't forget to keep your shoulders back. You can look very hunched.'

'I say premiere; it's more of a preview. It's a short film my friend made. Very low-key.'

Her mother looked her up and down again.

'There's an after party,' Sara said.

'Oh dear, does that mean you're going to be

late? Only I've got Barnardo's in the morning.'

Sara, who was standing with her back to her mother, dunking a teabag in a mug of hot water, closed her eyes and counted to five in her head.

'I don't really know what time we'll be back, but we've got to put in an appearance. It's a thank-you to the people who helped with the film.'

No sooner were the words out of her mouth than she regretted them.

'How did *you* help with a film?' asked her mother, accepting her mug of tea.

'Oh we . . . er . . . just chipped in a bit. It was a sort of investment.'

'*Money?*' her mother said.

'Not serious money, just a contribution. Besides, if it gets taken up by one of the big distributors, which it probably will, we might even make a bit back.'

'I wouldn't have thought you'd have money to throw around, with you off work.'

Sara smiled tightly, determined not to be drawn in.

'We're managing,' she said.

★　★　★

They were. They were managing. Neil was CEO now, and the salary increase more than made up for the absence of Sara's meagre stipend. And if they'd had to raid the high interest account to loan Lou the last few thou to get her film in the can, well, what were friends for? Besides, it hadn't been her idea, strictly speaking. Lou had sat cross-legged on the hearthrug, plucking manically at its tufted pile with one hand, her eyes alight with passion and more focused than might have been expected at one thirty a.m. after several glasses of wine and a large spliff.

'But I refuse to be despondent,' she had said, 'because I *know* we'll find the money from somewhere. It's just not an option to leave it unfinished.' She had looked glassily from Neil to Sara and back again. 'It's just *not*.'

Sara had waggled her eyebrows at Neil, trying to telegraph the question '*Should* we . . . ?' when he had blurted out:

'Of course you must finish it. We can see you right for the shortfall, can't we, Sara?'

And Sara had felt at once moved by Lou's gushing reaction and slightly miffed that it was directed mainly at Neil, who had only voiced what she herself had been thinking.

'Oh, God, I never meant for you to do *that*,' Lou said, shuffling over on her knees and clutching Neil's hand like a medieval serf, 'but, thank you!' If he'd had a ring on his finger, Sara thought, she'd have kissed it. She had turned, belatedly and given Sara a hug and Sara had tried to savour the moment of being a dear, dear friend and a generous patron of the arts and not to make calculations in her head, but it was no good.

'How much *is* the shortfall?' she had found herself saying.

★　★　★

157

But that was water under the bridge now. They were in, and Sara had put her misgivings to one side, reassuring herself that the money they had been saving for the boys' university fees would soon be returned to their account. Meanwhile, she had started to compose a short feature of her own, which she ran from time to time in her head. It was a soft-focus montage in which she was ushered to the front of film festival queues, hung out with European intellectuals behind velvet ropes, cast her eyes tactfully downwards when name-checked in teary acceptance speeches for prestigious film awards. With any luck, tonight would be just the beginning.

First, though, she had further disapprobation to contend with.

'Is that right, what Caleb's just told me?' said her mother, returning from the sitting room and picking up a dish towel.

'You don't need to do that, Mum,' said Sara, 'we just leave them to drain. What's Caleb told you?'

'That you've taken them out of school.'

'Ye-e-e-s.'

'And that you're teaching them *yourself.*'

'Not on my own. With Lou.'

'And Lou's a teacher, is she?'

'No, she's the friend whose film we're seeing tonight. Her boys are best friends with Caleb and Patrick and she's as fed up with the school as we are. She's got great ideas — really imaginative. So as soon as she's finished this project, we're going to start in earnest . . .'

'You haven't *started*? But the schools must

have been back six weeks.'

'Five. I'm just waiting for Lou to finish her film.'

'I thought tonight was the premiere.'

'It's the rough cut, Mum,' said Sara with exaggerated patience. 'It's practically the finished article, except for a few tweaks, which she'll do before it gets released.'

Sara's mother set her jaw.

'So what exactly are my grandsons doing all day?' she asked. 'Watching the idiot box in their pyjamas, I suppose?'

'No actually, TV's banned. They've been reading books, and going to museums and making up plays with their friends next door.'

'Plays' was perhaps a generous term for the noisy war games that had laid waste to the house, but they had certainly exercised their imaginations.

'Do you not think it might be as well to pop them back to school for a bit, until you're properly organised?'

'We *are* organised, Mum, and the school's a shambles. I don't think you realise how impoverished education's become. If you'd seen how unstimulated they were, how frustrated.'

Her mother paused and marshalled her resources, before going in for the kill.

'What does *Carol* think about this?'

Sara took a deep breath.

'Carol took Holly out last term,' she said calmly, and her mother's relief was palpable. Here was rational endorsement of their decision. Here was sanity.

'Ah . . . '

'They've gone private.'

Her mother raised her eyebrows suggestively.

'No, Mum. It's not who we are. And anyway, we can't afford it.'

'I could hel — '

'*No*, Mum.'

'What about your career?'

And so to the argument of last resort.

'What about it?'

'You were so relieved when Patrick started school. I'm not being funny, love, but do you think you're cut out to be a stay-at-home mum?'

'I'm not *going* to be a stay-at-home mum. I'm going to combine home-educating my children, which I expect to be a rewarding and creative experience, with editing my novel that my friend Lou happens to think stands a very good chance of getting published.'

Her mother made the face. It was the face Sara had come to dread, growing up. The face that said, 'You are being ridiculous, irresponsible and selfish, but I am keeping my counsel because that is what mothers do.' She had made it when Sara had announced her intention to go travelling after university with two male friends, neither of whom was her boyfriend; she had made it when Sara had refused to be a bridesmaid for her cousin Liane because marriage was a patriarchal conspiracy (a line her step-father had worked into his speech, to great hilarity, three years later when she had married Neil). She had made it when, whilst suffering from undiagnosed post-natal depression, Sara

160

had fled to a friend's, leaving Neil to fend for himself with a colicky Caleb for a long weekend. There was no arguing with the face; no possible rejoinder that could mitigate its weary, self-abnegating prescience, so Sara pointed out that she had a train to catch and asked whether they could continue the discussion at a later date.

★ ★ ★

Spotting Neil waiting outside Burger King on the concourse at Charing Cross station, Sara wished she had insisted he come home and get changed, rather than go straight from his board meeting to the film.

'What?' he said, defensively as she approached.

'I just wonder how comfortable you'll be in your suit,' Sara replied.

'I'll be fine,' said Neil, 'besides, it's an occasion, isn't it? *You're* dressed up.'

'There's dressed up and there's dressed up,' she said.

He gave her a bemused look.

'We're going to Gav's club afterwards,' she reminded him, hooking an arm through his and leading him towards the exit, 'it'll be full of people in . . . ' she trailed off, realising that she hadn't the faintest idea how people would be dressed. She just knew that they wouldn't be dressed like that. But Neil was still grappling with part one of her statement.

'Gav's got a club?' he said. 'Who is he, Jeeves?'

'Jeeves didn't have a club. Jeeves was the butler.'

161

'Even so, a *club*!'

'God, Neil, it's not all quilted jackets and cigars, you know. It's an arts thing. A media thing.'

'I do know people have clubs, I've just never known anyone *personally* who had one.'

'Well, now you do.'

★ ★ ★

Nevertheless, by the time she had tottered the half-mile to Soho, she was feeling less than confident in the appropriateness of her own outfit. Lou had warned her that it was to be a low-key event, yet, remembering their house-warming, Sara had taken this with a pinch of salt. So she was a little disappointed to find herself outside an unremarkable looking office on a dingy backstreet wearing an outfit that would, at a stretch, have passed muster at Cannes. A discreet sign confirmed that this was the headquarters of Niche Productions, but not so much as a sandwich board confirmed there was a film previewing there this evening and when Neil tried the door it was locked. They buzzed the intercom, without success and were beginning to think they must have made a mistake, when a taxi drew up and disgorged another couple, he wearing ankle-skimming trousers and brogues; she, a cape.

'This has to be the place,' murmured Sara to Neil, as the pair swept past, pressed the buzzer and were immediately admitted. Luckily, Neil had the foresight to jam his foot in the door

162

before it swung shut again, and keeping a discreet distance, they made their way up the stairs.

★ ★ ★

The interior of the office was plusher than Sara expected: the corridor thickly carpeted and up-lit, the walls lined with framed posters, many of them advertising art house films that she had heard of, but never got round to seeing. A young woman was checking off guests' names on a clipboard before ushering them through to the projection suite with an obsequious smile. Sara tugged Neil's sleeve and quickened her pace.

'Hi,' she said breathlessly to the woman, 'Sara Wells and Neil Chancellor. We're here for *Cuckoo*.'

The woman's eyes roved up and down the list and Sara felt her hands growing clammy. 'I'm so sorry,' she said at last, 'I don't seem to have you here.'

Sara didn't trust herself to speak.

'May I?' Neil stepped up, all charm, and the flunky tilted her clipboard reluctantly towards him.

He shook his head and laughed.

'Typical Lou,' he said, affectionately, 'bloody awful handwriting.' He pointed. 'That's us, Sara and Neil. See, there?' The woman frowned, doubtfully, but ushered them through.

'*Was* it us?' whispered Lou. Neil shrugged, but there was no time to debate the point as the delay had cost them precious minutes, the house lights had dimmed and a reverent hush had already descended. Picking their way across an obstacle course of crossed legs, and booby-trap handbags to the two remaining seats, Sara felt her tights catch on a rogue winkle-picker and rip soundlessly from knee to thigh but she dared not stop to inspect the damage as they were already provoking a barrage of irritated sighs and tuts. As the curtains covering the small screen swished back, and the production company logo shimmered into life, she did a quick scan of the audience. Apart from one couple who looked vaguely familiar, the room was full of strangers — and even in silhouette, they were a daunting crowd. Between dreadlocks and trilbies, bandannas and beehives, it was a struggle for Sara to catch a glimpse of the screen and when she inclined her head on Neil's shoulder to get a better view, he squeezed her thigh warmly, in response.

'Love you,' he whispered, his eyes fixed eagerly on the screen.

'Shhh,' murmured Sara.

★   ★   ★

Sara had difficulty afterwards recalling what her expectations had been, so it was hard to figure out in which ways Lou's film had confounded them. The lack of plot was no surprise, but beyond that, she was at a loss to know whether the bewilderment she felt was the effect that Lou had intended, or was due to her own lack of critical acumen. It seemed to be a film that

164

worked on many levels. The eponymous 'Cuckoo' was played by a waif-like actress, whose accent hovered somewhere between Leeds and Leipzig. If the dreamlike episodes depicting Cuckoo's self-harm, binge-eating and exhibitionist masturbation were anything to go by, her character was aptly named. While in some sequences she was a person, delivering lines of more or less credible dialogue, in others she was a deranged, but benevolent sprite, who communicated her angst through interpretive dance. This was not the only ambiguity. Another aspect of the — narrative seemed the wrong word — mise-en-scène — was the idea of usurpation. Not only was Cuckoo cuckoo, she was a cuckoo in the nest. If Sara had understood it correctly (and it was a big if), Cuckoo was the product of an incestuous relationship between her father and one of his two other daughters. Cuckoo's unexplained return to the nest was a cause of jealousy and angst within the family and seemed particularly distressing for Cuckoo's mother/ sister, who, for no reason that Sara could identify, was played by a man in a dress. After a great deal of weeping, some sister-on-sister incest and a surreal episode involving maggots crawling out of a sink, Cuckoo was dispatched from the first floor balcony by all three members of her dysfunctional family. As the camera zoomed in, from a dizzying bird's eye view to a forensic close-up of the blood trickling from the dead woman's mouth, the credits rolled.

There was a moment of hush and then the auditorium erupted in applause. Sara clapped

165

until her palms stung. She stole a sideways glance at Neil, expecting to see bafflement written all over his face, but he too was clapping, smiling, nodding.

★ ★ ★

The house lights came up and Sara looked around her. All human life was there from skinny model types, frumping it up in paisley to hoary old intellectuals in donkey jackets. Sara was relieved to see that her own style of retro chic was not completely out of place, perhaps the ladder in her tights even added a certain something. Neil's suit didn't feel too dreadful a faux pas, now he had taken his tie off, although it was a world away from the nattily cut windowpane checks and old-school tweeds worn by some of the other men.

'What did you reckon?' Neil whispered.

'Yeah, pretty good,' she replied. 'You?'

'I thought it was fantastic,' he said and again she had to scrutinise his face for signs of irony. She couldn't believe this was the same man who had cried during *Saving Private Ryan*.

'Do you think it'll do well?' said Sara.

'I don't know if I even care any more,' Neil replied, 'I just feel really proud to be associated with it.'

Sara pursed her lips. It was like something from *Invasion of the Body Snatchers*. Someone had spirited away her down-to-earth, middle-brow husband, and replaced him with this cerebral, art house cineaste. But there was no

166

opportunity to probe further because a woman was arranging two mics and a carafe of water on a table in front of the screen and Lou was making her way out front, delayed by much air-kissing, and hand clutching.

★ ★ ★

'So,' said the woman, settling herself into one of two leather swivel chairs. 'It's my pleasure to welcome you all to this preview screening of *Cuckoo*. I'm sure my guest for this Q&A will need no introduction, as most of you here have been involved in some way with the film or are at the very least, supporters, admirers or friends.' Neil gave Sara's hand a squeeze.

'Please give a very warm welcome to Lou Cunningham.'

Whistles; whoops; extended applause. Lou, dressed like a bluestocking in a loose linen smock and Japanese sandals, leaned into the mic and murmured a husky, 'Thanks guys.'

'Lou,' the woman smiled, 'congratulations on a stunning film. Can I kick this session off by asking you just where Cuckoo came from? What, if you like, was the seed, the spur; the afflatus behind this character?'

'Oh God,' Lou squirmed and her breath boomed intimately on the mic. 'I hate this.'

'Well, of course, if you'd rather not say.'

'No, no, it's fine,' Lou said, 'I'm just . . . ' she clutched her hands to her breast and seemed for a moment too moved to speak ' . . . there's so much of *me* in Cuckoo.' There was a pause,

167

which threatened to become awkward. Then Lou rallied, looked up, with forced brightness, and winced into the spotlight. 'And yet when I was writing the script; putting her in that scenario, tormenting her in all those ways — I was almost laughing to myself, because it was just so ... *right*, if you will. Because a cuckoo essentially doesn't belong, you know? It's an interloper, a threat to the natural order of things and it's only fair that it be expelled, banished, whatever. I mean, Cuckoo, she's a very vulnerable, *very* damaged little thing, but you know, by the end, she's also well, come on, she's a pain in the arse,' she appealed to the audience and elicited a burst of warm laughter. 'Right?'

'I was going to ask you about that actually,' said the interviewer, 'there's a lot of humour in the film.'

'Yeah,' Lou nodded, smiled and took a sip of water. 'I'm glad you got that.'

Sara glanced at Neil. Had he got it? She certainly hadn't. Nor had she noticed anyone else rolling in the aisles; then again it obviously wasn't that sort of humour.

'I just think, you know,' Lou shrugged, 'you can't beat people about the head with this kind of thing: with anger, with pain, with humiliation, without acknowledging that actually, we may be doing the dance of death, but sometimes that can be pretty hilarious. I mean — it's preposterous isn't it, really? That we're born and we live these short, often sordid, apparently meaningless lives, and then we die.'

'Ah,' the interviewer pounced on this, 'would I

be right in thinking then, that that is the symbolism of the maggots — the sordidness? The life span?'

'I don't really want to talk about the maggots,' Lou said abruptly.

'Oh, right.'

'I'm sorry but, you know, I just don't think it's for me, the film maker, to confer meaning on the film; to *explain* it all. That's for you guys to do. You bring to it what . . . you bring.'

'No, quite,' said the interviewer, 'I see that, of course. It would be like asking Buñuel to explain the eyeball scene in *Un Chien Andalou*.'

'Well, I'd hesitate to compare myself to Buñuel,' Lou said, then added with a radiant smile, 'but if you *insist* . . . '

★   ★   ★

She was a class act, Sara thought, moving apparently effortlessly between self-deprecating humour and a self-belief that bordered on arrogance. Listening to her, Sara was converted. *Cuckoo* had not been incoherent, it had been uncompromising; the acting had not been amateurish, it had been raw; the seasick camerawork had been no accident, but a deliberate ploy to reflect the queasy moral world of the characters. But the further Lou's artistic stock rose in Sara's imagination, the further her own seemed to plummet by comparison, until she could hardly bear to think that she had actually entrusted Lou with the final draft of her manuscript to show to Ezra Bell. A manuscript, to make matters worse, that had incest as one of its central themes. People were sure to think she'd copied that from Lou. She shuddered at the thought. Compared to the assured, allusive, mood piece she had just seen, her own storytelling seemed schematic, and over-ripe. Lou's film was a work of art; Sara's novel merely a potboiler.

★   ★   ★

The discussion went on for some time and then it was thrown open to the floor. Sara no longer had the heart to ask the question she'd intended to put. These people were cleverer than her, they knew Lou better than her. They knew *film*. Everything on which her intimate friendship with Lou was predicated seemed flimsy and insubstantial now, for a whole aspect of Lou's character had been concealed from her. She might know that Lou's favourite book was *One Hundred Years of Solitude*; that the track that was guaranteed to get her on the dance floor was 'Deserts Miss the Rain', she might even know that Lou liked it rough in bed, but did she have a clue where she stood on the unconscious of cinematic discourse? No. These people knew Lou's body of work. The affection in which they held her was palpable and, judging by the way she bandied around first names and teased them with in-jokes, it was reciprocated. They questioned her about her decision to use analogue sound; the limitations of the hand-held camera, the redundancy of auteur theory, post-Dogme, and left Sara staring into the abyss of her own ignorance, vertiginous with self-disgust. Really, in film terms, compared to most of the people in this room, she and Neil were Neanderthals. It was with some alarm then, that she realised Neil now had his hand in the air. She gave him a friendly 'What the fuck?' kind of look, but he just smiled smugly back and left his hand where it was. The interviewer had said, two questions ago, that they were nearly out of time and people were getting restive, so why was the wretched woman still scanning the audience? Neil sat up a little taller, stretched his hand a little higher, just as he must have done in primary school.

'Yes, there,' she said, 'the man in the open-necked shirt.'

15

There was nothing so wrong with the after party, and yet Sara realised an hour in, that she was miserable. Lou had given her a fragrant kiss on arrival, and seemed gratified to be told that Sara had found *Cuckoo* really incredibly moving. Then a man with a goatee had come along, whose good opinion seemed to matter to Lou a little more than Sara's, so she had drifted away feeling like a spare part.

While Neil fought his way to the bar, Sara stood by the toilets observing the scene. The décor was a tongue-in-cheek pastiche of the traditional gentlemen's club, its rickety floorboards, button-backed armchairs and reading lamps undercut by artworks of lacerating modernity and a soundtrack of ambient music that would have caused apoplexy at the Drones club. There were a lot of people there. They couldn't all have been at the film, but since everyone was dressed in the same stridently non-conformist way, it was impossible to tell whether they were guests of Lou and Gavin or just regular club members. This made the prospect of mingling even more daunting and Sara determined only to approach people she had definitely seen before. She spotted a guest from Lou and Gavin's housewarming making a beeline for her, and readied herself with a smile, only for it to die on her lips when the woman barged straight past her into the Ladies. Neil bought her a drink and then left her in order to take Lou a congratulatory glass of Champagne. Her shoes were chafing and she was tired of standing in the gusts of jet-propelled air wafting out of the toilet, so she threaded her way through the crowd to a back room, where she subsided gracefully onto a leather Chesterfield next to an old woman wearing owlish glasses and magenta lipstick. The room was hot. Sara could feel sweat collecting on her top lip. She slipped off one shoe and rubbed her heel surreptitiously.

'Did you enjoy the prem-ee-er?' the woman said, in a gravelly American accent.

'You mean *Cuckoo?*' she said in surprise. 'Oh, I did. I absolutely *loved* it.'

The woman pursed her magenta lips, nodded sagely and closed her eyes. Sara waited for her to open them again and vouchsafe some finely honed critical response, but realised after a moment that her companion had nodded off. She sat, marooned, torn between her need for another drink and the dread prospect of making her way to the bar. She had all but resigned herself to sobriety, when she glimpsed, through the forest of legs, a familiar pair of battered suede brogues.

★　★　★

'Hello, stranger,' she said, tapping Gav on the shoulder. He turned, a little reluctantly, from a pretty redhead he'd been talking to.

'Oh, hi Sara,' he said. 'Rohmy, this is Sara.'

The redhead slowly relinquished her grip on

173

Gavin's lapels, which she had been clutching in a humorous attempt to convince him of her point of view, and acknowledged Sara with a grudging smile.

'Hey, maybe Sara knows . . . '

If Gavin felt any frustration at Sara's interruption, he didn't show it. 'Settle a little argument for us, will you?'

'I'll try,' she said.

'Johnny Thunders, right?'

Here was Sara's opportunity to admit that she had not, in fact, heard of Johnny Thunders and was therefore in no position to arbitrate.

'Sure, what about him?'

'How did he die?' Gav asked. 'Rohmy reckons — '

'No, don't *tell* her!' Rohmy interrupted. She turned to Sara, expectantly. Sara opened her mouth, and then closed it again.

'God, I *know* this,' she said. 'Doesn't it drive you mad when you know you know something, but you can't . . . ?' She screwed up her face in an attitude of all-encompassing concentration. 'Car crash, wasn't it? No, plane crash. One of the two. Actually, sorry . . . Johnny . . . ?'

'Thunders,' supplied Rohmy, smirking.

'Ah, no, in that case . . . '

'Who did you think we were talking about?'

She was really milking this.

'Yeah, no, I know who you mean. I just . . . ' She shook her head. 'Nope, it's gone.'

'Oka-a-ay,' Rohmy said, widening her eyes significantly at Gavin.

'Isn't she sweet?' Gavin pulled Sara into his

embrace. 'She *thought* she knew, but she doesn't know.'

Sara grinned sheepishly and submitted to the hug. She never found out whether Rohmy thought she was sweet or not, because another couple, Steve and Alexis, joined the group and settled the argument — guitarist from the New York Dolls; heroin overdose, *of course* — before moving the debate on to iconic deaths in general and then to a discussion of whether the net contribution of drugs to the rock and roll songbook had been positive or negative — a topic on which Sara judged it prudent to remain silent. It wasn't long before she found herself on the periphery of the group, listening to a bloke with a lot of facial hair telling her how he had once shared a bong with Tim Buckley. She had never been so grateful to see Neil, who scolded her for disappearing and thrust a glass of fizz into her hand.

'Great place, isn't it?' he said. 'I could get used to this.'

'Well don't. We've got to leave in five. I promised Mum we wouldn't be late.'

'I was just saying, Gav,' Neil called across, apparently oblivious to Sara's advice, 'I'm loving the whole Jeeves vibe.' He waved his glass to indicate the room at large.

'Yeah, cool isn't it,' Gavin agreed.

'May one ask,' said Neil, in what he must have imagined to be a Wooster-ish tone, 'how much membership would set one back?'

Sara winced.

'It's pretty reasonable, actually,' Gav replied. 'A couple of grand if I remember rightly. You might have to be patient though — I think the waiting list's pretty long.'

'Not a problem, old boy.'

'God Neil,' Sara hissed, pulling him to one side, 'you're embarrassing yourself.'

'What do you mean?'

'Can't you tell when you're being fobbed off? *You* can't join a place like this. It's for people in the arts.'

'I'm sure they're not that strict.' Neil looked hurt.

'I think they probably are. I mean, look at these people.'

'I'm looking.'

'Well, if you can't see it.'

'See what?'

'The difference.'

'What difference?'

'Between them and us.'

'I don't see a difference. I've met some nice people tonight. You'd be surprised how many of them congratulated me on the question I asked at the Q and A.'

'Well, that's great, but a question's not a body of work, is it?'

'Well, what about you? You're a writer.'

Somehow, Neil's faith in her as a novelist only made Sara feel more fraudulent.

'I'm not a writer, Neil, I'm just another unpublished wannabe.'

'Ah, but Lou's working on that.'

'Yeah, right.'

'No, she *is*,' Neil said, 'she's over there bigging you up right now.'

176

'Really? Who to?'

'Oh, er some nerdy American, name escapes me.' He snapped his fingers, pretending to fish for it. 'Eric? Esau?'

'Not Ezra Bell?' Sara gripped his arm. 'Is he here?'

'Might be.' Neil grinned.

'Oh my God!' she glanced over at Lou, her heart melting. What a woman. Her doubts all but evaporated and she felt herself grow in stature. She wanted to saunter over to Rohmy and ask if she'd ever heard of Ezra Bell. *The* Ezra Bell, the one who was shortly to endorse her — Sara's — first novel. That'd wipe the smug smile off her face. She turned back to Neil.

'What did he say? Did you tell him about my book?'

'We talked sport.'

'Jesus, Neil!'

'Chill out. You'll have plenty of time to schmooze him. He's staying next door.'

'God, I feel sick. Ezra Bell.'

Neil glanced at his watch.

'Anyway, I should just point out, we've got seventeen minutes to get to Charing Cross, if you want to get the last train.'

Sara grabbed Neil's wrist and stared at his watch as if willpower alone could make its hands move backwards.

'We've only just *got* here,' she wailed.

'Your mother; your call,' Neil said.

She thought of her mother. She thought of the face.

'Oh God,' she said, 'we can't just *leave*. We'll

have to explain.' She rushed over to Gavin, interrupting him mid-punchline.

'Sorry, Gav, we've got to go. Just wanted to say thanks for a great night.'

'Wha-a-at? You can't! I forbid it.'

'I know,' Sara gabbled, 'it's a real pain. Only, my mum's babysitting and she volunteers at Barnardo's on a Saturday morning, so . . . '

★ ★ ★

There was a pale glow behind the council flats as the taxi juddered to a stop. One by one, the stars were going out.

'Bye, amazing night, thanks.'

'Bye.'

'Bye Ezra, great to . . . '

Their final farewells were drowned out by the vehicle's thrum as it U-turned and set off back up the street.

'The driver was a bit narky,' said Sara to Neil, when the clunk of Gav and Lou's front door had finally severed the stream of merry banter. 'Didn't you tip him?'

'I barely had enough for the fare,' Neil said. 'I got a hundred quid out after work. Don't know where it all went.'

'They'll pay you back.'

'Yeah, yeah, I'm not worried.'

★ ★ ★

'Great night,' she shook her head fondly, then her eye fell on her mother's Golf sitting in front

178

of the house, neat and censorious with its Christmas-tree air freshener. 'Don't know how it got so late, though.'

Neil turned the key in the latch and they stumbled into the hall.

'Hello?' he said in a stage whisper.

'She'll have gone up,' said Sara.

'The light's still on,' Neil pointed out, nodding towards the sitting room door which stood ajar.

'Mum?' Sara poked her head into the room. Her mother was sitting on the edge of the sofa, coat on, handbag at the ready, as if waiting for a bus.

'What are you doing still up? It's after three.'

Sara's effort to disguise her tipsiness made her voice sound clipped and false. Her mother checked her watch.

'Quarter to four, actually,' she said. 'Patrick had a nightmare, but I sat with him for an hour and he's been fine since. I haven't heard a peep out of Caleb.' She stood up. 'I'd better get off now. At least the roads will be quiet.'

'Oh Mum, I'm so sorry. There was a bed made up in the spare room. It never occurred to me you'd — '

'Yes, well, I did say I've got — '

'Barnardo's. I know. I know. I wanted to leave ages ago, but we ended up getting a cab with our friends and it all got a bit later than I'd — '

'Would these be the same friends you're setting up a school with?' Her mother arched an eloquent eyebrow. Sara was aware of Neil listing drunkenly beside her.

'We're not setting up a *school*. We're just

179

teaching our own kids. Lou's a film director and Gavin's an artist, so it should be a fantashtically rewarding experience.'

Sara's mother weighed this claim in silence.

'Right. Well. I'd best get off,' she said at last. She brushed her lips past Sara's cheek and bid Neil a terse goodbye.

'Fuck!' murmured Sara as the latch clicked quietly behind her.

★   ★   ★

Sara and Neil lay in bed like two corpses, as grey light seeped round the edges of the curtains, and the burble and clatter of a waking neighbourhood drew them further and further from sleep.

'He's nice, Ezra, don't you think?' said Sara to the ceiling.

There was a pause, and she wondered whether Neil had dropped off.

'He's all right,' he said finally, 'but I thought he was a bit out of line in the cab.'

'Oh well, we'd all been drinking. I don't think Lou minded.'

'Just because he's a hotshot writer doesn't give him licence to . . .'

'I wonder what he'll think of my book.'

'Oh, I should think as you're young, female and attractive, he'll probably be predisposed to like it.'

'Thanks very much,' Sara propped herself up on one elbow. 'Now I'm going to feel bad about it even if he does.'

Another silence fell. A car door slammed in

the street. Its engine stuttered and then turned over.

'Why's *he* the arbiter anyway?' Neil said, his tone a little more peevish, Sara felt, than was warranted by Ezra's misdemeanour.

'Well, he is a pretty amazing writer,' said Sara, 'you said yourself that *Appalachia* was one of the best books you read last year.'

'It was all right,' Neil said grudgingly. 'Not a patch on Franzen.' He turned away from her and yanked the duvet up to his ear.

Sara lay motionless, her eyes gritty with exhaustion. Her mind was too busy now for sleep.

16

'You know that crack on the landing?' Neil said, putting down a tray of tea beside the bed.

'What about it?' said Sara, bleary-eyed.

'How long d'you reckon it's been there?'

'I dunno,' she replied, 'isn't it just old houses? Carol's got one in her sitting room. Something to do with the joists.'

Neil started muttering about movement and underpinning, but Sara tuned out.

⋆ ⋆ ⋆

Now that he had woken her, she wanted to talk about *Cuckoo*. Did he really think, having slept on it, that it was a masterpiece, as he had told Lou in the taxi home? He seemed unwilling to be called to account for his hyperbole of the previous evening, just muttering something about its being an impressive debut. Sara frowned.

'Did you feel sad, when she died? Because I didn't,' she said, eyeing Neil over the rim of her teacup.

'Did I feel sad?' Neil pursed his lips and stared into space for what seemed to Sara to be several minutes.

'Well, if you have to think that hard about it, I don't think you can have done.'

'I don't know if that was really the point.

There was a sense of inevitability about it.'

This felt like a cop-out to Sara.

'What about the humour?'

'What humour?'

'Lou said it was meant to be funny. Bits of it, anyway, but I didn't see you laughing.'

'I was laughing.'

'No you weren't.'

'I was laughing inside.'

Sara sipped her tea in silence.

★　★　★

In retrospect, it would have been better to stick with plan A and meet in the coffee shop. From the moment Sara stepped over the threshold of Lou and Gavin's place the next morning, carrying a bulging folder of educational material under one arm, she knew it had been a mistake.

'Goodness! What's all that?' said Lou.

'Oh, just some stuff off the Internet,' said Sara. 'I probably got a bit carried away, but I thought, as long as I had the printer on.'

Sara dumped the file on the kitchen table and Lou took out a sheet at random.

'Make your own Montessori spindle boxes,' she read.

'Oh yeah, they're for maths. You can buy the boxes from WHSmith and for the rods you just use . . . ' she trailed off, seeing Lou's face. 'We don't have to do it. It's just, you know, back up, really, I went a bit,' she flapped imaginary wings, 'crazy magpie.'

Ezra walked into the kitchen, wearing jockey

shorts, his face scrunched around a cigarette. Sara stopped flapping and watched him pad over to the sink, fill the kettle and grind out his fag-end in the compost container. With his hairy, barrel-chest and strutting gait, he looked like a dog that had learned to walk on its hind legs.

'Hi Ezra,' she said.

'Yeah, hi.'

'Ezra's a bit the worse for wear, aren't you poppet?' said Lou. '*Somebody* thought it was a good idea to break out the single malt when we got back last night.'

'Oh well, don't worry,' said Sara, 'we'll be out of your hair in a minute. We're off to Rumbles for a coffee.'

'Not that place by the subway?' growled Ezra. 'Shit they serve in that place they shouldn't be allowed to call coffee — *barfee* maybe. I can make you a coffee'll taste way better than that right here,' Ezra insisted.

'That's sweet of you, Ez,' said Lou, 'there you go, Sar. We can do the show right here.'

Sara was doubtful. She had left the boys at home, despite Neil having a paper to write for a child poverty conference, on the basis that she would be attending to the even more urgent business of their children's education. Did Lou really expect to have a meaningful discussion, with her kids bouncing off the walls upstairs?

'I suppose we could try,' she said, wincing as a particularly powerful thud dislodged a flurry of plaster dust from the ceiling.

Moments later they were all three installed around the kitchen table and Sara was trying not to grimace at every sip of Ezra's viscous brew. He and Lou were gossiping about an American artist she had never heard of.

'So, anyway,' she said, a little desperately, when there was a brief lull in their conversation, 'I've had a really good rummage online, and I think I've got a sort of skeleton curriculum together.' She turned to Ezra.

'I don't know if Lou mentioned? She and I are going to teach our kids at home for the next little while.'

She was rather proud of that 'next little while'.

'Why the fuck would you want to do that?'

'Because,' said Sara, drawing herself up in her chair, 'the education they're getting at school leaves rather a lot to be desired. The teachers spend their whole time cramming, and real education — proper, child-centred learning just goes out the window.'

Ezra stared at her and she wondered whether he had read her manuscript yet, or if he even knew who she was. She glanced at Lou, for moral support, but her friend had started leafing through Sara's resources file and didn't seem to be listening.

'So this,' Ezra jerked his head upward to indicate the racket coming from the first floor, 'is going to be your reality, five days a week?'

'I suppose it is,' Sara laughed a tinkly laugh, 'but the reason I'm here, now; and why I've downloaded all this . . . ' she nodded towards the bulging file ' . . . is so that we have some structure in place, so it *won't* be like this. Or not all the time at any rate.'

'Uhuh?' said Ezra, lighting another cigarette.

'This is incredibly impressive, Sara.' Lou looked up from the file. 'You must have been researching it for days.'

'Oh not really. There are some excellent home education blogs out there. Once you've weeded out the crackpots and religious maniacs, there are still loads of normal people like us, who just want to provide a nurturing, creative experience for their kids. And there's a very collaborative ethos, so nobody minds if you copy their lesson plans or worksheets or whatever.'

'Mmmm,' said Lou.

'But that's all practical stuff. What's fascinating to me is the educational theory, which I have to admit, I knew very little about.'

Lou looked bored.

'Anyway, it's all in there. Peruse at your leisure.'

'Thanks,' said Lou. 'What do you reckon, Ezra, want to join the faculty?'

Ezra gave her his dead-eyed stare.

'You could do a writing workshop with them,' Lou cajoled. 'A lot of people find working with kids very stimulating. It feeds back into their own creativity.'

'It does?'

'Definitely,' nodded Lou. 'I've got a couple of really good people signed up already.'

'Who?' said Sara, in surprise. She didn't know whether to be miffed that she hadn't been consulted, or gratified that Lou had shown some initiative.

'Well,' said Lou, 'remember Ismael, who

played guitar at our party? He's happy to trade some guitar lessons for a bit of help with his English.'

'Fantastic!'

'And then I have this friend Beth who's a puppeteer.'

'Not Beth Hennessy, from Little Creatures?' breathed Sara. Carol had crowed for weeks about the front row seats she had scored for their production of *Stig of the Dump*. In fact, it was a shame that they were no longer on name-dropping terms. She glanced at the fat grey file on the table, its ring binder straining to contain the wodge of worthy educational material she had so diligently collected. Ezra plucked a shred of tobacco off the end of his tongue, grinned and slowly shook his head.

'You got to be out of your minds,' he said.

'What do you mean?' said Sara.

'You ask me, you got someone whose job it is to keep your kids out of your hair eight hours a day, you got to be crazy to turn your back on that.'

'Ezra!' said Lou. 'You're such a tease.'

'I mean it.'

'Well, you would think that,' said Sara, 'you haven't got kids. But surely you'd agree that a child-centred model is best, rather than just teaching by rote, to the lowest common denominator?'

Ezra shrugged.

'You can't legislate that stuff,' he said, 'kid wants to write, he'll write; kid wants to paint, he'll paint. You think Herman Melville did *workshops?* You think Picasso did?'

'So you reckon writers are born, not made?' said Sara, thoughtfully.

The great man shrugged.

'Don't ask me,' he replied, 'all I know is, you try and make your kid into a writer or an artist, he's gonna be a plumber or a janitor to spite you.'

'Ha!' said Sara, cheerfully. 'Like Gavin in reverse.'

'How so?' Ezra looked suddenly interested.

'Oh, er . . . ' Sara darted an uneasy glance at Lou. 'Didn't he say that his mum wanted him to learn a trade? And his family don't really get his art because they're . . . '

A look of displeasure crossed Lou's face, but her phone was flashing up an incoming call.

'Sorry, I need to take this.' She snatched it up and, throwing Sara an exasperated glance, she hurried from the room.

Ezra smiled inscrutably and flipped his lighter back and forth on the table.

There was a long silence.

'I don't suppose you've had a chance to read my novel?' Sara at last plucked up the courage to ask.

'When did it come out?'

'Oh, it's not actually published yet. Manuscript, I should have said. Lou was going to ask you to have a look at it.'

'I guess she must be saving it up.'

'Mmm.'

'What's it about?'

'About?' Sara was nonplussed. 'Oh, gosh. It's a

kind of rites-of-passage thing about this girl coming of age — she's got a pretty unhealthy relationship with her father and she meets a boy from the wrong side of the tracks and they have a thing and the father gets pissed off and it all gets pretty intense and then . . . '

Ezra's gaze had drifted over to the newspaper that lay on the corner of the table.

'Anyway, it's quite short, so if you did have time to give me some pointers . . . '

'Sure.'

'Thank you. I loved *your* book, by the way.'

He smiled tolerantly.

'Mine's nothing like so ambitious in scope. I love how you made the family stand for the nation.' She had read this in a review.

'I did?'

'Oh well, that's what . . . Far be it from me, obviously. I just found it incredibly moving and surprising and tender.'

'Thank you,' said Ezra gravely. Sara was spared any further awkwardness by Lou's return. The excitement of the call had clearly supplanted any irritation she had been feeling at Sara's earlier indiscretion.

'Sorry about that, guys,' she said, glowing with pleasure and excitement. 'That was Cory Hamer from Niche. She's only got me on the judging panel for the Ann Arbor film festival.'

'Oh, that's wonderful!' Sara stood up and embraced her friend clumsily. 'Will you do that from home?'

'God, no! You have to *go*.' Lou gave Ezra a disbelieving glance. 'You can't judge the Ann

Arbor film festival *long distance*.'

'Well . . . when is it?' asked Sara stiffly.

'March the eighth to the twenty — oh crap!' Lou's face fell.

'Lou, we've already postponed it twice.'

'I know, I know. But listen . . . ' Lou was dancing an eager girlish jig. 'I will completely take them off your hands until I *go*, so you can get on with your . . . ' she waved her hand vaguely, '*stuff* . . . and then, if you can just hold the fort until I'm *back* . . . ' she flicked her finger excitedly up and down the screen of her phone, ' . . . yes, those dates work brilliantly — I have the *best* idea for a field trip.'

17

Spring had come to the West Country and the leaves on the birch trees shimmered like the streamers on a cheerleader's pompom. As the Volvo squeezed down winding lanes, between hedgerows feet thick, Sara sensed the proximity of buds unfurling, roots thrusting, catkins flinging pollen onto the breeze. She felt her pulse quicken and her heart lift.

'Weather doesn't look too clever,' Neil said, peering under the sun visor at the pregnant clouds.

'We're not climbing the north face of the Eiger,' Sara pointed out.

'Still won't be much fun if it pisses down.'

'We've got Carol's tent, Neil,' she said. 'It's probably more watertight than our house.'

★ ★ ★

Borrowing the tent had been awkward. Sara would have preferred to buy one, but the festival tickets had been pricey and the savings account was running low. It hadn't made it any easier that Carol was so nice about it.

'Don't worry,' she'd said, when Sara had made some pathetic excuse for not seeing much of her lately, 'We're all busy people. I'm having a Nespresso, do you want one?' She'd indulged Sara with fifteen minutes of friendly chitchat, then barely batted an eyelid when Sara brought the conversation round, none too subtly, to the subject of camping.

'A *festival*?' she'd said, with only the faintest whiff of condescension. 'Oh well, whatever floats your boat,' but she had volunteered the tent, as well as all its state of the art accoutrements, without having to be asked. Sara had forgotten that, beneath the preciousness and point scoring, Carol was actually a decent human being.

★ ★ ★

Neil's Eeyore-ish gloom about the weather wasn't fooling anyone. If anything, he was more excited than Sara about their weekend away. Amazing what the right line-up would do to a man's spirits — in this case, a predictable blend of acoustic hipster whimsy, grizzled old bluesmen and the odd superannuated punk. For her, the event held other attractions; forty-eight hours of unmediated access to Gavin and Lou, not least among them. Their company was usually parceled out so frugally — an evening here, an afternoon there, and always the sense of other people, other priorities, waiting to claim them. This weekend would be all theirs.

★ ★ ★

'Can we catch our own dinner, Mum? Like on *Man versus Wild*?' Patrick piped up, from the back seat. Sara felt a pang of guilt. She had perhaps overstated the self-sufficiency angle.

'I don't know about catch,' she replied, 'but

cook, definitely. I've brought some sausages.'

'Sausages are boring. Can't we catch a rabbit and skin it?'

'Like *you* could kill a rabbit,' said Caleb, 'you cried when the guinea pig died.'

A scuffle broke out in the back of the car.

'Nobody's going to be killing anything,' said Neil.

'Although there is archery,' said Sara, sunnily, 'look,' she passed a leaflet over her shoulder.

'Lush, two thous-and and four-teen,' Patrick read haltingly, 'Medlar's Farm, Devon, feat-ur-ing Crawdaddy, The Jeremiahs, They Might be Giants. This is boring.'

'Carry on,' Sara urged, 'you're doing very well. See where it says *Kids Lush?*''

' . . . Story-telling,' he went on, 'tug-o-war — what the . . . ? Circus skills, song-writing workshops.'

'There you go, Caleb,' Sara turned round and gave him her encouraging face. 'Didn't you and Dash want to start a band?'

Caleb stared moodily out of the window.

★ ★ ★

A splotch of rain landed on the windscreen and Neil turned on the wipers. For a few moments, everybody watched them stutter pointlessly back and forth, before he switched them off again.

'He-e-ey,' he said, after a while, glancing in the rear view mirror, 'what were the chances?'

Sara swivelled round in her seat.

'No way!' She said. The Humber was directly

behind them. Lou's bare feet were up on the dashboard, Gav was wearing a preposterous Stetson. They looked more relaxed than anyone who had left London, via the M4, during the rush hour had a right to.

'How did they manage that?' she said.

By now, Patrick had shucked off his seat belt and was rearward-facing, gurning and flicking Vs through the back window. Lou was laughing and flicking them back.

'Must have made good time,' said Neil. 'Mind you, it's got some poke, that car,' and as if to prove him right, Gavin swung out, as the road widened, and roared alongside, so that the two vehicles were briefly and hair-raisingly level. Lou wound down the passenger window and shouted something that Sara couldn't quite catch, then Gavin put his foot down, and with a volley of hoots and much waving, they accelerated away.

'Catch up with them, Dad,' begged Patrick, bouncing up and down eagerly.

'Yeah, overtake them,' said Caleb, indignation getting the better of him.

For a mad moment, Sara also found herself wishing that Neil would unleash some horse-power and show Gavin what he was made of, but Neil maintained a steady thirty, pointing out that country lanes weren't designed for drag racing and he, at least, would like to arrive in one piece.

★　★　★

For a small-scale event, Lush had created chaos on the roads. They turned off the A35, leaving

194

behind the Mercs and Audis towing their speedboats to the Cornish Riviera, and joined a slow-moving queue of festival-goers in VW camper vans, clapped out Morris Minors, Citroens, and Saabs, the vehicles' dilapidation as proudly worn as their rainbow mandalas and consciousness-raising window stickers.

★ ★ ★

'I've got a good feeling about this,' said Neil, grinning, as a dreadlocked man in a hi-vis jacket and lobe-stretchers fastened neon bands around their wrists and waved Neil cheerfully towards a parking space. 'I don't know why we haven't done this before.'

They unloaded the car and joined a steady flow of new arrivals dressed in split-knee jeans, flip-flops and beanies or bush hats. As they humped their cooler boxes and IKEA hold-alls onto the main site, this new contingent mingled with the old-timers who, having arrived a full twenty-four hours earlier, had already cast off the shackles of conformity and were traipsing from stage to portaloo to falafel stand to healing tent, in tutus and Doc Marten boots, onesies and Smurf outfits. Now and then, a sound-check from the main stage would send an ear-splitting whine of feedback echoing across the valley.

★ ★ ★

With the help of a friendly Dutch family, they found their pitch, conveniently situated between

195

the portaloos and the Kids' Big Top. Nor was there any shortage of advice when it came to erecting Carol's conspicuously up-market tent. Seeing them struggling, a young woman who introduced herself as Twink, left her partner breast-feeding their burly toddler on the step of their camper van, and came bounding over to lend a hand. With impressive dexterity she assembled the extendable poles, explained what went where, and returned, twenty minutes later, with reinforcements, to help them haul it aloft — the end result standing out like a butler at a barbecue. Again, however, nobody seemed to mind much, for the normal rules of society were here reversed — kudos accruing to the homespun and ramshackle, rather than the sleek and luxurious.

★ ★ ★

All that remained was to open a celebratory beer and wait for Lou and Gavin to show.

'I hope they're okay,' Neil said, 'the way Gav was driving . . . '

'They'll be fine,' Sara said, 'they always are.'

Neil nodded and took a swig from his bottle. He looked younger and more carefree already, Sara noticed. His stubble was coming in nicely. His hair had got past its newly-shorn 'executive' look and had a bit of boyish curl to it. She didn't even mind that he was wearing his hideous Hawaiian shirt — there were tragic dad-rockers as far as the eye could see — so for once, he had pitched it exactly right. She leaned across and kissed him on the lips, prompting an outbreak of faux-puking from Patrick and Caleb.

'Why don't you go and explore, guys?' said Neil. 'Here,' he fished in his pocket and handed Caleb a ten-pound note, 'Go get yourselves a lentil burger or something.' They set off across the field, Patrick at a skip, Caleb scuffing reluctantly behind.

★ ★ ★

'Fancy giving Carol's lilo a road test?' Neil jerked his head towards the open tent flap.

'What . . . now?' Sara didn't know whether to be pleased or appalled, but decided that a bit of spontaneity couldn't hurt, and followed him inside.

The lilo was off-puttingly bouncy and smelled strongly of rubber. She wished she had had a second beer. Although it was gloomy in their makeshift boudoir, it was still light outside and she could hear all the comings and goings of the families around them — Daisy being congratulated on the contents of her potty, Elijah refusing to eat wholewheat pasta. She raised her arms above her head, and allowed Neil to peel off her tee shirt, attempting a sultry look as he unhooked her bra and lowered it reverently on to the bed.

'Nice tits,' he said, cupping one of them and looking her in the eye. This was weird. She leaned forward to kiss him, but before she could, he had lowered his head to her left breast and licked it with a long, wet sweep of his tongue.

She gasped, more in surprise than pleasure. He paused, without looking up, and then licked the other side, as if evening up an ice cream. Soon he was licking it all over, with great thoroughness and apparent enjoyment. She closed her eyes and tried to surrender herself to the sensation. It felt quite sexy to be topless, in her jeans and hiking boots, but she was conscious that Neil was still fully dressed and that she ought perhaps to move things along. She made to unfasten his shirt, but he gently removed her hand and continued, not forcefully, but insistently, with his licking project. He switched to the other breast and she started to relax into it. Round and round he went, licking, licking, giving a wide berth, she started to notice, to the whole nipple area. It was nice now, very nice, but his refusal to take her nipple in his mouth was beginning to torment her and she realised that he was withholding this pleasure on purpose. She groaned and he broke off and looked into her face, smirking in acknowledgement of her need. Her nipple was stiff now, a gorgeous pagoda of nerve endings; larger than she had ever seen it. She thrust it towards his mouth, but he veered off towards its very edge, deliberately denying her. Now it was a game. He slowed down when she wanted him to speed up, pulled back when she wanted him to go all-out and every so often checked her expression to make sure his sadism was having the desired effect. Gone was his equal-opportunities policy on his 'n' hers orgasm, in its place, this pervy open-ended, teenage lick-fest which seemed to be doing the job for both of them. By the time he moved on top of her, she was in a frenzy and he had to put his hand over her mouth to quieten the pleading whimpers which she was barely even aware she was making. She had heard of women coming just from having their breasts stimulated, but had not believed it possible. And in fact, if the tip of his cock hadn't nudged her clitoris so decisively on the way in, she still might not have got there, but it did and she did.

★　★　★

'Well,' she said afterwards.

'Well.'

He dredged a screwed-up tissue from the pocket of his jeans and handed it to her.

'Thanks,' she said, manoeuvring it between her legs. It wouldn't do to return Carol's airbed with an unsavoury stain.

'Go, you,' she said, stretching out complacently, arms folded above her head.

'Go, me,' he agreed, leaning out of the compartment to pull a toilet roll from the nearby rucksack.

'Should've got you to a festival sooner.'

'Yep.' He seemed a little sheepish, now, about the scale of his achievement.

He clambered out of the sleeping area and let the flap fall back across the opening.

'Going for a slash,' he said. She heard him fasten his belt and put on his shoes. She knew those shoes — the lace on the left one had snapped and would only do up halfway. She

listened now, as he shush-slap, shush-slapped
away.

★ ★ ★

Sara lay in her cubicle, in a state of post-coital
languor, her head turned sideways on the
too-bouncy pillow. She plucked at a loose
rubberised thread on the lilo's edge and
eavesdropped on the conversations going on
outside, adults and children teasing one
another, remonstrating, negotiating. All happy
families were alike, someone had said, and by
implication, boring. Not hers though, not this
weekend. How good it was it to be out of their
comfort zone, out of their rut. Getting it on
under canvas — in broad daylight, if you please.
For this, and much else, they had Gavin and
Lou to thank. She remembered how small she
had felt at their housewarming party, how
peripheral. It was different now. It was OK that
the Humber had left them for dead on a
country lane. It was OK that Lou and Gav had
still not arrived, nor sent any word. It was even
OK (just about) that Lou had dumped the kids
on her and breezed off to France last month. It
was OK, because Lou admired Sara's writing
and Gavin just 'got' her. It was OK because
they had both taken Neil to their hearts. It was
OK because the four of them could riff off each
other until two a.m. on a weeknight, and still
have a spring in their step the next day. For the
first time, on this May afternoon, with her
husband's semen coagulating on her inner thigh

and the scent of cannabis drifting in the air, she felt that their friendship was where she wanted it to be.

18

It was a child's voice in Sara's dream.

'There it is, Mummy, the blue one.'

She was in a school cloakroom. A mother and child were looking for a coat on the other side of the rails. She could only see their legs — she wanted to tell the mother that they were making a mistake. The coat didn't belong to the little girl, it belonged to her but when she opened her mouth to speak, no sound came out. The impotent croak of her own voice woke her and she realised that the girl in her dream was Zuley. It was Zuley's voice she could hear now; their *tent* that was blue. She scrambled out of her sleeping compartment.

'Bloody hell, that's not a tent, it's a palace!' Gav bellowed. She had one leg in and one out of her jeans, when the outer zip whizzed open. She clamped an arm across her bosoms and froze, but it was Lou's face that loomed through the gap.

'Oops, sorry!' Sara felt Lou's gaze travel quickly over her naked torso before making eye contact again.

''S okay,' said Sara, 'I was having a nap. Must be the country air.'

'Not what I heard,' smirked Lou. She was wearing vermilion lipstick and a kerchief around her hair — a look, Sara thought wistfully, that only Lou could really pull off.

'Take your time,' said Lou, 'Neil's just giving us a hand with the tent. We're way up at the back, near that telegraph pole. Come join us for a beer when you're ready.'

*   *   *

Sara scooped up her bra from where Neil had thrown it, and put it back on. At first, she thought it must have attracted some shreds of leaf matter from the floor of the tent because as soon as she fastened it, it began to chafe her already over-stimulated breasts. But then she realised that her jeans felt tight and starchy too, as if fresh from the wash, which they weren't. She wriggled and flexed, but couldn't quite rid herself of the sensation, which, in any case, had a certain masochistic pleasure to it. She'd have put it down to hormones, except that Neil's idiosyncratic foreplay had made her think he, too, must be subject to some atmospheric juju — a nearby ley line, perhaps or an alignment of the stars. Smiling to herself at the recollection, she perched a magnifying mirror on the extendable flap of Carol's camping stove and squatted down in front of it with her make-up bag. She traced a little lip-gloss over her mouth with her third finger and gazed pensively at her reflection. The half-light of the tent was flattering. Gone was the suburban frau who could only meet the world from behind a protective layer of Laura Mercier. In her place, a dryad, lit from within by the spirit of the woods. She had been about to apply some mascara, but

203

liking what she saw, she replaced the wand in its tube, tossed it back in the bag and zipped it up. There was such a thing as gilding the lily.

★ ★ ★

It was quite a trek to find Gavin and Lou. Sara had automatically assumed that the two families would have adjacent pitches and struggled now to quell a pang of annoyance that their friends' late arrival had resulted in this less than ideal outcome. She had been pleased, initially, that she and Neil were close to the hub of the festival — a short walk from the main stage, handy for the toilets. But she couldn't help thinking now that Gav and Lou's pitch, with its elevated position and panoramic views, far from the hurly-burly and the food smells, was in many ways more desirable. There was more shade — oak trees dotted the gently sloping hillside — and the grass up here was still verdant and thick with clover, not trodden and muddy as it was down below. She stopped for a moment, and shading her eyes with her hand, surveyed the valley. A faint evening mist had turned the sky milky and given a slightly sinister purple cast to the motley colony of tents below. Penants fluttered, smoke drifted on the breeze, lanterns were starting to be lit. Somewhere, a Celtic folk band was tuning up. It was as though some elvish tribe with a taste for posh burgers and inflatables had crept up from middle earth to stake its claim on this idyllic corner of Devon.

* * *

She'd have picked Gavin and Lou's tent from yards away, for its flamboyant style and dubious practicality, even if the three of them had not been lolling on the rug in front of it, surrounded by empty beer bottles.

'Whoa!' she said. 'Party Central.'

'Hi.' Lou managed a lazy smile, Neil moved over and made space for her on the rug. It was left to Gav to scramble to his feet and greet her properly with an enthusiastic bear hug. Breathing in his scent of beer and tobacco and sweat, she felt as if someone had gathered up her internal organs and pitched them off a cliff. She sat down cross-legged and Neil handed her a beer.

'Where are the kids?' she asked.

'The boys took Zuley to play on the trampolines,' Lou replied.

'Oh that's nice,' Sara said, worriedly scanning the horizon.

'Relax,' Lou said, patting her hand, 'this festival's one big kibbutz. They *literally* cannot come to any harm. Aren't you *hot?*' she added, eyeing Sara's outfit.

'It was supposed to rain,' said Sara, defensively. She cast a sideways glance at Lou — her vintage floral tea dress, her slender ankles, her turquoise toenails. Everyone, Sara now saw, had made a sartorial nod to the festival spirit — Gav in his satirical Stetson, even Neil, in his silly shirt. Only she, in jeans, T-shirt and stout footwear, her face scrubbed free of make-up, looked like a conscript to a feminist boot camp.

Sara took a swig of beer and looked around. To their right, an innocuous dome tent, to their left a teepee from which could now be heard a flurry of muffled thumps, accompanied by a series of squeals, ascending in pitch.

'I think Pocahontas is getting some,' said Gavin drolly, jerking his head towards it.

'Oh God,' Lou said, rolling her eyes, 'I hope they're not going to be at it all night.'

'Upstaging you two, you mean?' Neil smirked.

'Oh . . . aha . . . ' objected Lou in mock outrage, 'you can talk!'

Sara felt the beginnings of a blush prickle her neck. 'Some of us are capable of restraint, aren't we, Gav?' Lou went on, with mock sanctimony.

'Going to have to be, aren't we, with the kids in the next compartment?' Gav said. 'Mind you,' he added, walking two fingers up the hem of Lou's dress, 'I always fancied myself as a bit of a stealth bomber.' Lou stopped his progress with a school ma'am-ish slap and Sara looked away, her face stained a vivid red with envy and arousal.

'So,' she said, when she felt enough time had elapsed, 'anyone fancy catching the Jeremiahs later?'

'Oh God,' said Gavin, frowning, 'I suppose we should.'

'They're pretty good, aren't they?' said Neil.

'Caleb certainly thinks so,' said Sara. This was an understatement. They were the only act at Lush in whom he'd shown any interest at all. If she couldn't get Caleb to The Jeremiahs' set, she might as well abandon any pretence at all of this weekend being about the kids.

'Yeah, Dash likes them too,' Gavin reached for his dope, 'but people, we're *grown-ups*.'

'They're great musicians,' said Neil, defensively. He had just downloaded their second album.

'Oh sure,' agreed Gav, 'but a bit folk-lite, don't you think? I mean, if you like that vibe, why wouldn't you go for the real thing — Jeff Buckley, Tim Hardin; Flatt and Scruggs, for that matter?'

'Aren't they all dead?' said Neil.

'Yeah, good point,' Gav laughed. 'Only thing is, if we go, I'll feel like we have to go backstage . . . ' He pulled a world-weary face.

'Do you know them?' Sara pricked up her ears.

'Their manager,' said Lou, 'lovely guy, lived upstairs when we were in Soho. Bit of a waster, in those days.'

'Even more of a waster now, I bet,' said Gav, 'all that money sloshing around. You know their first album went platinum?'

Sara watched Gavin's nicotine-stained fingers crumble a generous portion of hash onto a wodge of tobacco and tamp it expertly along the length of a Rizla.

'I don't mind, either way,' she lied, feeling like Judas — Caleb would kill for a chance to meet the band. She scratched unhappily at the label on her bottle of beer.

'Let's keep our options open anyway,' said Neil, standing up. 'I'll make a start on the barbie. Did you guys remember the briquettes?'

Lou winced and rolled her eyes. 'Still in the boot,' she said.

'Here you go, big man,' said Gavin, chucking Neil his car keys. Neil caught them nonchalantly and started to shamble away.

'Gav!' protested Lou, laughing.

'What?' Gav seemed bewildered.

Lou gave him an exasperated frown and scrambled to her feet.

'Hang on, Neil,' she called, 'I'll come with you.'

Any sense of grievance Sara may have felt on her husband's behalf was more than made up for by the unexpected bonus of time alone with Gavin.

'Slacker!' she said when Neil and Lou had gone, her tone more admiring than reproachful.

He slid a roach expertly into the end of the joint, smoothed his fingers lovingly along its length and then handed it to her.

'I'll be wrecked,' she warned him, raising it to her lips.

'You only live once,' he countered, touching a match to its end. She gave it a tentative toke. It was too early in the evening, and things were getting too interesting to jeopardise it all by getting off her tits. Turning her head away, she pretended to take a second draw, then, nodding in tacit appreciation, handed it back. Gavin had no such qualms, whittling the joint down to half its length, with one practised inhalation. He closed his eyes and tipped his head back, then, when Sara thought it had gone forever, exhaled the smoke in an insolent plume. They sat quietly for a while, Gav smoking, Sara studying the festival programme. At his request, she listed the other bands she was looking forward to seeing, and he disparaged them gently until she handed him the leaflet and demanded to know if there was a single act that was cool enough for him. He studied the line-up, and shook his head. Laughing exasperatedly, she wrenched up a handful of grass and threw it at him, but he ducked and it showered the back of his neck.

'Oh, shit!' she said, trying to flick it away, but succeeding only in driving it further down the back of his shirt. She knelt up and fished around for a bit, withdrawing her hand with an awkward laugh when she realised that her incursion had become a little too intimate.

'Sorry,' she said.

'Don't be,' he replied. Her hand was damp with his sweat. She sat back on her haunches. A new silence fell.

Drawing his knees into the crooks of his arms, Gavin sat forward like an eager boy scout and regarded her with interest.

'You're a funny one, Sara,' he said. His eyes were glazed, but he seemed sincere.

'Am I?' Sara said warily. He didn't expand on this assertion, but continued to stare at her in a manner which was as flattering as it was disconcerting. For something to do, she upended her beer bottle onto her tongue, liberating the last trickle. She was aware that he was watching her do this and that it was having the desired effect.

'You've grown on me.' His voice was quiet,

even a little hoarse.

'Ha!' she said.

'Oh, no, don't get me wrong. I always *liked* you.' He jabbed her knee, reproachfully. 'I just didn't *see* you.'

'And I'm meant to be pleased, am I?' she said gruffly. 'That I've become visible?'

She *was* pleased. She was ecstatic. What greater compliment could there be from an artist?

'Here,' he leaned behind him, took a beer from the cooler box and made to hand it to her. As she reached across, he jerked it out of her reach, laughing. He held it out again, she stretched, he snatched it away. Pouting with indignation and effort and amusement, she lunged. He snatched it away again and she collapsed, giggling, onto the rug and lay there, flailing like an upended beetle, his face blocking out the sunlight.

'Can't leave you two alone for a minute, can we?' Lou's voice sounded more amused than angry. Sara snapped back upright so fast she saw stars. She smoothed her hair self-consciously and tried to swig from a bottle that had not yet had its top removed.

'What took you so long?' Gav asked, without so much as a hint of awkwardness or compunction. 'We're wasting away here.'

'Couldn't find the car, mate,' Neil said, staggering towards him with a bag full of barbecue fuel. Gav shook his head in amused despair.

★ ★ ★

210

The next twenty minutes were spent in feverish activity. The men, stripped to the waist (a prettier sight in Gav's case than Neil's, Sara couldn't help thinking), took turns squatting beside the barbecue, blowing on the coals, tossing match after match onto the pyre, swearing good-naturedly when the wind changed direction. The two women dodged around each other, marshalling sausages, slicing open finger rolls, prising the lids off tubs of coleslaw, amid more pleases, thank yous and could I possiblys, than had passed between them in all their previous months of friendship. Sara couldn't say for certain which of them was responsible for this awkward politesse, only that the harder she tried to recapture their accustomed insouciant tone, the hollower it rang.

* * *

It didn't get any easier when the kids came back. Sara saw them first, bounding up the slope towards her. They looked carefree and rambunctious, the way children ought to look; the way hers hadn't looked in quite a while, she realised. Patrick was in the lead. As he got nearer, Sara watched his expression change, from childish insouciance, to incomprehension and then to indignation. Remembering too late, that she had promised he could cook his own sausages, she watched Lou ferry the last charred banger from the griddle to the warming rack, as if in slow motion. The children swarmed around them now, breathless, excited, ravenous.

211

'Here you go Patrick, first come, first served.' Lou held out the hotdog, but Patrick ignored her, training his eyes accusingly on Sara instead.

'What the hell!' he said. 'What the *hell!*'

'I know, darling, but if we're going to go and see The Jerem . . .'

'I don't care about The Jeremiahs.' Patrick's bottom lip was wobbling dangerously now. Sara could see him struggling to master himself in front of the bigger boys.

'I suggest you take this now, Patrick,' said Lou, tapping her foot, 'if you *want* supper this evening.'

'I don't!' said Patrick and he barged past her and stomped away.

'Well!' said Lou, in a tone of mock outrage. '*Somebody* got out of bed the wrong side this morning.'

'He wanted to cook his own dinner,' Sara explained in an undertone. 'I promised him he could.'

'In our house, 'I want' doesn't necessarily get,' said Lou, handing the hotdog to Dash, instead.

Sara gawped in disbelief. The irony of it — the overindulged princeling, who got every blessed thing he asked for, chowing down on Patrick's supper, while his mother counselled restraint?

'Just save him one for later,' she muttered.

'Well, if you think that's appropriate,' said Lou. 'Personally, I'd have thought a little tweak to the *ego* wouldn't go amiss.'

Sara stared at her, incredulous. That *she* should invoke ego — the woman who had put them all on hold for weeks while she faffed about with her pretentious film; the woman who had swanned off to Ann Arbor to suck up to some other bunch of narcissists in the hope they'd return the compliment, until the whole lot of them disappeared up each others' fundaments in a government-sponsored, grant-aided vortex of self-indulgence. The injustice was more than Sara could stand. She turned on her heel and walked away before she could act on an overwhelming urge to force Lou's face onto the barbecue and hold it there until it sizzled.

19

Patrick was standing a few feet away, hands clasped on his head, scuffing the earth with his toe. He had his back to Sara, but she could tell he was fighting back tears.

'Pat?' she called tentatively. He flinched at the sound of her voice and ran off, each lolloping stride carrying him closer to the mêlée, where, in a moment, he would be lost. Sara followed him, keeping her distance but never letting him out of her sight. Eventually he slowed and, affecting a macho indifference almost as heartbreaking to witness as his earlier meltdown, he paused at one of the stalls and began examining a glow stick.

'Want one?' she said, sidling up to him.

He scowled at her and shook his head.

'Quid each,' said the youth behind the stall, 'or six for a fiver.'

'We could take some back for the others. They don't look much now, but you snap them and they — '

'I know what a glow stick is,' muttered Patrick, 'we had them at Multicultural Day.'

'So we did,' said Sara.

* * *

For a moment, she was transported back to a summer's afternoon, when the school playground had echoed to the sound of a steel band

and the scent of curry had wafted on the breeze; when pearly kings had dispensed falafel and kameez-clad Somalis, cream teas. Sara had been put in charge of the tombola, which, alone, had raised sixty-four pounds thirty for Cranmer Road's sister school in Malawi. It all seemed a lifetime ago now.

★ ★ ★

Sara took one of the glow sticks, snapped it, and marvelled as it began to radiate fluorescent light.

'Amazing,' she said, fashioning it into an impromptu headdress.

'I wonder how they work. Remind me to Google it when we get home. We might be able to make our own. It'd be a great science project.'

'I don't want to,' said Patrick.

'Then you don't have to,' said Sara peaceably. 'The great thing about learning at home is that you'll be able to do stuff you *do* want to do. Fun stuff.'

'It won't be fun with her.'

'Oh now Pat, look.' Sara squatted in front of him. 'Lou didn't mean to be unkind. She didn't know I'd said about the sausages.' She fought down the bile that was rising in her at the memory of Lou's sanctimony and took a deep breath.

'She's going to be a really good person to learn from. She's got tons of ideas. Did you know she's even got a friend who makes puppets for her job? Really cool ones. And she's going to ask her to come and do a workshop with us.'

'I'm not a baby,' said Patrick.

'I know you're not, darling,' Sara said, 'but there'll be other stuff too. Grown-up stuff. *Much* more grown-up, actually, than the things you've been doing at Cranmer Road, because there won't be other less . . . motivated people to worry about.'

Patrick gave her a puzzled stare.

'I mean, when you think about it,' Sara went on, 'you had, what? Thirty children in your class at Cranmer Road?'

'Thirty-one, because that boy that can't speak English came halfway through.'

'*Exactly*,' said Sara, 'that's what I'm saying. Miss Nicholls has thirty-one students to teach, at least one of whom has English as a second language.'

'He doesn't have it as any language.'

'Which is *fine*,' said Sara, 'absolutely fine, but what I'm saying is, Miss Nicholls has thirty-one students to teach all on her own.'

'Well, now she's only got thirty again, 'cause I've left.'

'Yes, thirty then. At least *one* of whom struggles with English.'

'He doesn't struggle with it. He can't speak it.'

'No. Okay, well, that's very challenging, obviously, for Ms Nicholls. But *you*,' she said, turning a beaming smile on him, which he met with some suspicion, 'did brilliantly. So imagine, if you managed to learn as much as you did, even though there were thirty other children, all with their various . . . challenges, how much *more* you'll be able to learn in a class of four.'

'That's not really a class.'

'Well, it is. It's a small class, and you'll have two teachers, between four. Which is . . . ?'

'Half a one each.'

'Yes, very good,' she ruffled his hair affectionately. 'Or two to one, expressed as a ratio.'

★ ★ ★

By the time they had done a loop of the festival site and were heading back up the slope towards Gavin and Lou's pitch, Patrick seemed to have forgotten his grievance and was happily demolishing a burrito. As they came within sight of the tent, he broke into a run, eager to hand out glowsticks to the other children.

Lou was squatting by a tap, rinsing dishes.

'Hi,' Sara said, tersely.

Lou rocked back on her heels, squinted up at her and smiled the disarming smile of someone who has no inkling that her behaviour has caused offence.

'You're back!'

'I'd have done those,' Sara said, nodding towards the washing-up bowl.

'Oh, it's no trouble. I just thought if we're going to get to The Jeremiahs . . . '

'We are going, then?'

'The boys seem keen.'

Sara did her best to smile. It was nice of Lou to wash the dishes, she told herself. It was nice of her to go to the gig for the sake of the kids. It was *nice*.

'Okay. I wouldn't mind getting changed first, though.'

217

'You don't need to get changed,' said Lou, hooking an arm through hers, 'you're lovely as you are.'

The others were already heading down the slope, strung out in a line, Zuley perched on Gavin's shoulders, the boys chattering happily and bedecked in glow sticks, like a psychedelic Von Trapp family heading for the Swiss border.

★　★　★

The crowd in front of the main stage was dense by the time they got there but the vibe was relaxed, which was just as well, as Lou and Gavin had no hesitation in pushing their way to the front. Gripping the boys' hands, Sara put her head down and followed in their wake, surprised at the docility with which people were prepared to cede ground to those with an air of entitlement. Once they had muscled in, the four adults passed around a bottle of tequila and chatted amongst themselves as the sun went down. It was a young crowd, but to Sara's way of thinking a hip crowd. Lithe-limbed teenagers in cut-off denim, shared joints with their Peter Pan parents who, for the most part, could match them piercing for piercing, tatt for tatt; if this was The Jeremiahs fan base, Sara couldn't see what Gavin had to be so snotty about.

★　★　★

At last, to a roar of approval, the band came bounding onstage, a raggle-taggle bunch of geeks in jerkins and neckerchiefs, great shocks of hair on their heads, wisps of bumfluff on their chins. They struck up the opening chords of their breakout hit and, pleased to find that she knew all the words, Sara sang along, smiling indulgently at Caleb and Dash who punched the air in time to the music. During the second song, she committed a little further, tapping both thighs in syncopated rhythm. Neil, she noticed, was in seventh heaven, head bobbing, eyelids a-flutter, like a newborn rooting for the breast and, despite the unworthy thought that he looked a bit of a tit himself, Sara couldn't help envying him his wholehearted enjoyment. Gavin now showed some sign of being mildly entertained too, but it was always possible that his sporadic bopping was just to oblige Zuley, who was still perched on his shoulders. Certainly Lou looked less than enthralled. Two or three times she stood on tiptoe, cupped her hand and bellowed something into Gav's ear, to which he responded with a wry smile and a nod.

* * *

A final stomping chorus, a shimmer of brass and the set was over. The audience whistled, whooped, cat-called and finally, with a collective sigh of satisfaction, started to disperse.

'So what do you want to do now, guys?' Gav lifted a protesting Zuley off his shoulders and rubbed his neck. 'If we're quick we could still catch Billy Bragg in the Spiegeltent . . . '

'I thought we were going backstage,' said Sara.

'Oh God, really?' Gav pulled a face.

'I think we'd better, actually, Gav. I'm pretty sure Will saw me,' Lou said.

'Who's Will?' asked Sara.

'The keyboard player,' said Lou, with a pitying smile.

★ ★ ★

By the time they'd got through the cordon, to the Artists' Village, Sara was having second thoughts. The hallowed space into which they were ushered was just an oversized Portakabin designated HOSPITALITY, but the very act of admission seemed to confer a prestige of which she felt unworthy. Lou and Gavin, as always, exuded an effortless downbeat glamour. Even Neil just about passed muster with his six-o'clock shadow and his Converses; but Sara was still wearing the jeans and T-shirt she'd had on all day. She had sweat rings under her armpits, her face was greasy and her hair was limp with the heat. The only thing right with her outfit was her ACCESS ALL AREAS wristband.

★ ★ ★

The room itself was simply furnished, to cater for the band's essential needs. A table was laid out with bottles and snack food. Two beaten-up armchairs accommodated a couple of bored-looking girlfriends. The band members were wandering about, stripped to the waist, drinking beer. They looked spent but exhilarated. Gavin

220

and Lou did the rounds, fist-bumping, shoulder clasping, air-kissing. They introduced Dash and Caleb as big fans, and the band obliged them with selfies. Neil struck up a conversation with the sound engineer and Sara hovered for a while, but then got bored and drifted off to get a drink. A party atmosphere was cranking up, the decibels rising as more guests were admitted. She watched the room fill up with people who seemed to have a legitimate reason to be there and felt, more than ever, the imposter. She could see Lou and Gavin across the room, chatting with a good-looking bloke of fifty or so, who, despite his hooded eyes and incipient paunch, still radiated a plausible rock and roll charisma. This must be Mick, the band's manager. Gav was telling him some convoluted story, one arm slung matily around his shoulder, but Mick's attention was all on Lou. Neither the sleeping toddler on her hip, nor the proximity of her husband, could distract him for one second from her cleavage, to which he addressed his every remark. Lou didn't seem to mind in the least; on the contrary, she appeared to be enjoying it. Sara might almost have felt sorry for Gav, if she hadn't known only too well that he was prone to temptation himself.

Raised voices nearby caught her attention. Dash and Caleb were squabbling over the table football. It was getting out of hand and a few of the guests were beginning to cast disapproving looks in their direction. Sara started to make her way over, but was intercepted by Lou.

'Yeah, time they went home, probably,' she

shouted, over the din. 'We'll be right behind you when we've said our goodbyes. And as long as you're taking the boys . . . ?' She bundled a sleeping Zuley into her arms. 'Would you mind having this one, too? I knew we'd be pushing it bringing the kids.'

'I mean, what am I, the nanny now?' Sara stumbled across the campsite, Zuley's head bouncing against her shoulder with every step.

'You're waking her up,' said Neil, hurrying along beside her, 'let me take her.'

'I never even said I was leaving,' Sara went on, 'she just assumed.'

'Sar,' Neil warned her, 'the boys'll hear you.'

Sara stopped and faced him.

'I don't give a shit,' she said. 'She's got a bloody nerve!'

Zuley lifted her head and whimpered and Sara looked down a little guiltily.

'Poor little thing,' she said, 'should have been in bed hours ago. Wasn't exactly child-friendly, was it? All that smoke? And who thought it was okay to give the boys Red Bull, for God's sake?'

'They helped themselves,' said Neil. 'Lucky they went for that and not the Jack Daniel's. But I don't know why you're blaming everyone else — you were the one twisting Gav's arm to meet the band.'

'Yeah, I thought it'd be a quick autograph and then goodnight,' hissed Sara, 'not a love-in. Did you see that guy perving on Lou? I didn't know where to put myself. And that's another thing: one minute they're the least cool band on the planet, and it's a total drag to have to go and see them, the next it's all 'Oh, Will you were fucking amazing', 'Mick, mate, long time no see,' I mean . . . which is it? D'you know what I mean?'

★ ★ ★

They were back at the tent by now. Neil unzipped it and Sara clambered through the flap and deposited Zuley on Carol's airbed. The child's nappy was almost soaked through, but there was nothing to be done. In the outer compartment, Neil was trying to quieten the boys. From the sound of it, the Red Bull was just kicking in.

20

'Hello? Knock knock. Anyone for coffee?'

Sara opened her eyes to searing brightness. Her head was thumping. She tried to move, but found herself pinioned beneath Patrick's sleeping form, his warm, hay-scented breath whiffling past her nostrils. Gingerly she slithered out from under him, taking care not to pitch him sideways into the tangle of comatose children that surrounded them.

'Coming,' she whispered irritably, picking her way through the bodies. She unzipped the tent flap and stepped outside.

'Mornin'!' Lou thrust a cardboard tray at her and she helped herself, grudgingly, to one of the three coffees it contained.

'Ouch!' Lou said. 'You look like I feel.'

Sara glanced down at her shapeless night attire, then stared at Lou, radiating vitality, in her frayed shorts and Blundstone boots, hair coaxed becomingly into two tiny plaits. She could not bring herself to reply.

'Great party last night,' Lou said.

Sara winced.

'What time did you leave in the end?'

'Oh, not that long after you,' said Lou, 'we came by to pick up the kids, but it was so quiet we thought we'd better not disturb. You must have got them to bed in record time.'

'Er, not exactly.'

Lou had the grace to look a little shamefaced. There was an awkward pause.

'Nice coffee,' Sara muttered.

'*Isn't* it? It's Guatemalan. I've got some breakfast treats too. Come up when you've shaken off your hangovers. We're going to cook for you.'

'Could you not do it down here?' said Sara. 'Save us dragging the kids up the hill.'

'It's just a bit . . . public down here, isn't it?' Lou demurred, 'And we've got a guest for breakfast who might appreciate a little extra privacy.' She smirked mysteriously.

Sara knew she was supposed to ask who the guest was.

'Great,' she said. 'Whatever.'

⋆ ⋆ ⋆

All the same, by the time she and Neil were strolling up to Lou and Gav's pitch, later on, Sara's mood had mellowed. She was excited to see Gav, and curious, if she were honest, to know the identity of the mystery guest. For whom, after all, might *privacy* be an issue, at a festival of ten thousand laid-back stoners?

They breasted the slope and discovered the answer, sitting in a camping chair, wearing an OCCUPY WALL STREET T-shirt and a pair of khaki shorts.

'Ezra!'

Ezra shot them a wary glance, and Lou bent down and whispered something in his ear.

'Sara! Neil!'

'What brings you to these parts?' Sara asked, darting forward to give him a tentative kiss on each cheek.

'I'm on the run,' he replied.

Lou jerked her thumb at him.

'Absconded from Budleigh Salterton Lit-fest,' she said, chuckling. 'Put out an APB.'

Sara and Neil sat down beside Lou and Gavin on the plaid rug and, over an undeniably delicious breakfast of fried eggs and chorizo, listened to Ezra hold forth.

'You gotta hand it to the English chicks,' he said, egg yolk oozing from the corners of his mouth, 'they *love* to read.'

'They love to read *you*,' simpered Lou.

'They love to read anyone,' said Ezra. 'Misery memoirist, celebrity chef, deposed dictator, Deepak fucking *Chopra*. If you write it, they will come.'

'Isn't that a bit condescending?' said Neil.

'I guess if you *like* Deepak Chopra . . . '

Neil folded his arms implacably.

'Yeah, yeah, I hear what you're saying,' Ezra conceded, posting a last gobbet of bread into his mouth and proceeding to talk through it. 'I exaggerate for effect. But if you'd been held hostage at a book signing by a line of chicks — and it is always ninety per cent chicks — stretching from here to fucking . . . ' he waved his hand interrogatively.

' . . . Hay-on-Wye,' supplied Gav.

'Yeah, I gotta tell you, you'd be jaded too.'

'I thought you liked women,' Lou said reproachfully.

226

'I like *some* women,' he replied with a brazen leer.

'So what are *you* reading at the moment, Ezra?' Sara ventured to ask.

'At the moment, *Sara*, I am discovering the oeuvre of your own Doris Lessing.'

'Oh! I wouldn't have thought she was up your street.'

'I have a *street?*'

'Well, no, I just meant, wasn't she a big feminist?'

'On the contrary, I'd say she was refreshingly free of political correctness. She gives offence across the board, as any serious artist must.' He looked at her and raised a significant eyebrow.

She blushed with pleasure and disbelief. Did this mean . . . ? He held her gaze — his smile was knowing; provocative. He had. He had read her novel. She flushed with pleasure and tried to retain her composure. She was surprised and flattered. More than that, she was *ready*. Political correctness was the charge to which she was most susceptible, but she had rebutted this criticism in many an imaginary conversation with him. It was her second-favourite fantasy.

'Oh certainly,' she said, a rush of adrenaline bringing colour to her cheeks. 'I'm all for giving offence. I just don't think you need to reinforce negative stereotypes to do it.'

'You don't?' Ezra looked at her quizzically.

'No, I don't. I mean, okay, my drug-dealer character is *black*, which obviously lays me open to the charge of stereotyping at best, racism at worst, but I'm unrepentant on that score,

227

because it's appropriate to the setting.'

Ezra frowned and lit a cigarette.

'But if you think that's the reason I decided to give him a hinterland — to make him a morally ambiguous character with a backstory that demonstrates his many redeeming qualities, that's just not the case. He actually *needs* that duality to explain his fascination for Nora, who isn't just your garden-variety masochist. You know, it would have been easy just to write him as a thug and have been done with it, but I would argue that my giving him depth isn't knee-jerk political correctness, it's actually good writing.'

She sat back, feeling rather pleased with herself.

Ezra took a drag on his cigarette, exhaled and shook his head.

'You got me,' he said.

'What, you mean you agree with me?' said Sara, a little mistrustfully. He might at least have put up a fight.

'I guess I might if I had the faintest idea what you're talking about.'

Sara stared at him, and felt her cheeks grow hot again, this time with humiliation. There he sat in his canvas camping chair — a literary demi-god, cigarette pinched between his gnarly fingers, feet crossed neatly at the ankles, a look of polite bafflement on his face. What on earth had made her imagine *he* would read her manuscript? It was obvious now that he had never laid eyes on it, had no recollection of being asked to; had probably only the vaguest recollection of having *met* her before.

'Oh, I had the impression you'd read something I wrote, that's all. My mistake.'

She threw Lou a wounded glance.

'Would somebody please tell me what the hell it is I'm meant to have read?'

'Sara's novel, Ezra. I sent it to you.' Lou widened her eyes at him. 'It's fantastic. Really promising. Maybe you should check your junk mail. *Homecoming*, it's called.'

'*Safekeeping*,' Sara muttered.

'*Safekeeping*, yes. Maybe the attachment was too big.'

★   ★   ★

In the afternoon, the men headed off to watch a Bluegrass band and Sara and Lou took the children to a circus-skills workshop.

'This takes me back,' said Lou as they stood in line, breathing in the Big Top scent of warm turf and canvas.

'Lucky you,' said Sara. 'We never went to the circus, my mum thought it was common.'

'Oh, we never went either,' said Lou. 'I was *in* one, though.'

Of course, thought Sara, of course you were.

'Did I never tell you about Full Fathom Five?' Lou seemed amazed at her oversight. 'I suppose it wasn't technically a circus, more physical theatre, back in the days before that was really a thing. We used to train in a marquee just like this. It was founded by Jerzy Novak — fantastically talented Polish guy. He's married to Beth, you know, Little Creatures Beth, who's coming to do the — '

'Puppet-making,' Sara finished, nodding. She had been thinking about the puppet-making, and the guitar tuition, and all the other activities that she and Lou would need to plan and supervise, day in, day out, once the home-school was up and running. It had been on her mind.

'He's an alcoholic now, very sad,' Lou went on, 'he was absolutely amazing back then — the things that man could do with his body. I was a little bit in love with him, actually. Freaked the hell out of my parents. Flunked my GCSEs. Never forgot how to walk on my hands though, look!'

Suddenly, Sara was staring at the soles of Lou's feet as she paraded up and down the line of bemused families, her dress flopping over her face, her modesty spared only by a pair of black leggings. She righted herself with an agile backflip, to a spontaneous burst of laughter and applause.

★ ★ ★

When the children had been signed in, everyone sat on benches and two imaginatively-pierced instructors, Hepzibah and Dave, explained which behaviours were cool and which un-cool in a challenging health and safety environment such as this. As they listed the activities on offer, the buzz of excitement grew. A separate mat was allocated as a mustering point for each discipline — tumbling, stilt-walking, unicycling and so on.

230

Dash and Caleb opted for juggling, but the younger boys darted this way and that, unable to commit, their options diminishing with every second wasted.

'Tumbling!' Patrick yelled, finally, grabbing Arlo's sleeve, but before they could secure the final two places, Lou headed them off, stooping in front of them, palms sandwiched between her thighs, to deliver some homily. Sara couldn't hear what she was saying above the clamour, but she watched Lou turn her head repeatedly and nod in the direction of a different mat, one distinguished, as far as Sara could see, by its unpopularity. Patrick threw Sara a pleading glance. She half rose to intervene but, seeing that the last available spaces for tumbling had already been claimed, that *all* of the other mats were now full, she sat down again with a shrug of resignation.

'Mime!' Lou said, returning to her seat, with an air of satisfaction. 'I've always thought it would be Arlo's thing. Help him with his issues.'

Sara was about to say that it was not necessarily Patrick's thing, when he stomped back to the bench, bottom lip jutting.

Sara tried to put her arm round him but he shrugged it off.

'Come on, Pat,' she cajoled, 'you used to love Mr Bean.'

'Yeah, when I was five!'

'This is going to be *so* great.' Lou scarcely seemed to have registered Patrick's disappointment. She gave a little wiggle of delight and nudged Sara.

'The guy leading this workshop is from *Théâtre de Complicité*! I mean, what a privilege. Patrick?' She stood up and held out her hand. 'Not too late to change your mind.'

He regarded her stonily and Lou shrugged and sat down again, with a pitying glance at Sara, as if she had raised a delinquent.

★ ★ ★

They sat in a row on the bench and watched the various groups being put through their paces, yelps and giggles echoing under the Big Top. Sara was glad of the hubbub. She was not in the mood to talk, and nor, clearly, was Patrick. She was almost as angry with herself as she was with Lou. There was nothing she could do now to halt the approaching juggernaut of the home-school. It was happening. The world was watching. *Carol* was watching. But she would have to be a better advocate for her children than this.

After a while, she noticed Lou fidgeting beside her — groping around beneath the bench and tilting her ear towards the floor, as if she could hear, above the din, some other intriguing sound. Sara did not respond. She would simply not indulge another pathetic bid for attention. The woman didn't even know she was doing it. She was like a child. But Lou kept on. She was kneeling on the grass, now, peering between Patrick's feet, her hand outstretched.

'What's the matter?' Sara asked, eventually.

'Shhh!' Lou put a finger to her lips and smiled. Intrigued, in spite of herself, Sara

232

watched Lou rub her thumb and forefinger together as if to entice some small creature. She clasped her hands protectively around her knees and inched her body away, in case it was a rat. Lou seemed apprehensive but unafraid. She was making a curious crooning noise. Patrick had noticed now, too, and although at first he feigned indifference, curiosity gradually got the better of him.

'What is it?' he mouthed at Sara. She shrugged and they both looked back at Lou. Suddenly, she recoiled. Whatever it was, it was on the move. Patrick squealed, and Lou gestured downwards with her hand for calm. She crawled a metre or so along the floor and held out her hand as if offering food. Holding her breath, leaning forward, straining every sinew, she seemed close, now, to winning its confidence. She made a sudden snatch and, with an awkward writhing movement and a look of triumph, stood up. For a moment, Sara was confused. Lou's ungainly stance, her rapt expression, the repetitive stroking movement of her right hand, all suggested the weight of a hefty creature in her arms — a rabbit most likely. Sara had to do a double-take, to make sure, but no, she was not mistaken — there was nothing there. She felt the prickle of embarrassment on the back of her neck, the heat of shame. She actually is mad, she thought. And then she glanced at Patrick, all pique forgotten, round-eyed, smiling, approaching at Lou's tacit invitation to stroke the phantom creature.

21

Lou had been right about the festival being a field trip of sorts. How much the children had learned from it was moot, but for Sara it had been highly instructive; perhaps the chief lesson being that love and hate were intertwined. For every occasion when Lou's behaviour had taken her breath away with its narcissism, there had been another when it had beguiled her with its charm. Each act of staggering insensitivity had been redeemed with one of generosity, every harsh word balanced with a tender deed. Watching Patrick learn the power of mime through Lou's extraordinary performance had moved Sara. It had reminded her why she had set out, with such determination, to win Lou's friendship. And yet it was the hate she took away with her.

* * *

The journey back had only compounded it. It had been agreed that Arlo should travel in Sara and Neil's car, in order to make room in the Humber for Ezra, a decision with which Sara had had no problem until, ninety minutes into the journey, Arlo projectile-vomited all over the back seat.

'Couldn't Ezra have gone on the train? It's not like he's short of money,' Sara had hissed bitterly to Neil, handing sheets of kitchen roll into the back seat.

'Well, I could hardly say that, could I?' said Neil. 'Not with him standing there. We had a spare seat; they were one short. Maybe if I'd known Arlo was going to chunder, but I'm not a bloody mind-reader.'

'Funny, isn't it?' said Sara, bitterly, opening the window so that fresh air whipped through the car. 'How we always get stuck with the kids? Oh, my God, he's at it again!'

'Fuck's sake!' said Caleb. 'You've got to stop, Dad. There's, like, puke everywhere.'

'Yes. Caleb. Language. Don't you think I'm *looking* for somewhere to stop? We're on the motorway.'

Sara looked anxiously over her shoulder. Patrick was sitting worryingly still and had gone very pale himself.

'The Staines turnoff's coming up,' said Neil, doubtfully.

'Oh God,' said Sara, 'are you serious?'

★ ★ ★

'Well of course I don't mind,' said Sara's mother, 'come in, all of you. Only . . . What's his name? Arlo? If you could just stay in the porch a minute, Arlo love, until I bring you a change of clothes. Oh dear, you really *are* in a bad way, aren't you?'

Sara's mother loved nothing more than a crisis. She bustled about now, running the shower, fetching clean clothes, issuing instructions to Sara's stepfather regarding the steam-cleaning of the

235

car. For Arlo though, her overweening kindness was too much. He was used to a Spartan regime of hard floors and tough love, in which his needs came way down the pecking order. After a weekend when such fragile boundaries as he was accustomed to had all but collapsed, when he had eaten and slept erratically, hung out with rock stars, ridden an imaginary escalator and thrown up in a strange car, to find himself ankle-deep in Wilton carpet, being fussed over by a perfumed matron, was more than his constitution could stand. He shrank into a corner of the sofa and sobbed discreetly.

'Poor little thing, he wants his mummy, don't you, love?' Sara's mother patted his shoulder and fished up her sleeve for a hanky.

'He'll be fine, Mum,' said Sara, 'we'll get off as soon as the car's dried out.'

But now that the idea had been put in his head, Arlo was not letting go of it.

'I wa-a-a-ant my mu-ah-ah a h-ummmy,' he hiccoughed, until anything other than an emergency phone call to Lou seemed callous.

'I'll get the kettle on,' said Sara's mother.

'No need,' said Sara quickly, 'they won't be coming in.'

Richard shot his wrist out of his cotton twill shirt cuff and checked his watch.

'They might as well, Sara, it'll be nose to tail through London at this time.'

And, with that, Sara's last hope of preventing the collision of two remote and inimical planets fell away and she braced herself for impending catastrophe.

Pulling up in the Chase, alongside all the BMWs and Audis, the Humber might as well have been from outer space. As the doors opened, Sara got a whiff of leather and the signature scent of the Sheedy-Cunningham clan — a mixture of the pleasantly dank smell of their house, Lou's distinctive perfume and an un-nameable extra something, pheromones perhaps.

★ ★ ★

'Quick cuppa and we can all be on our way,' Sara murmured apologetically to Lou, leading the way up the block-paved double driveway. 'They just want to be hospitable.'

But Lou seemed in no hurry.

'Mrs Wells, what a gorgeous house,' she said, turning her charm up to full beam. 'I can't thank you enough for helping out with Arlo.'

'It's Mrs *Wentworth*-Wells, actually, since I remarried, Louise. I was old-fashioned enough to want to take Richard's name. But of course I didn't want to be disrespectful to Sara's late father, so I've gone double-barrelled, which to be honest I do find rather pretentious, when other people do it, but there we are. You can call me Audrey.'

'Hello Audrey,' said Gavin, with a winning smile.

'And you're the neighbours, are you?' Sara's mother said, sizing them up with a practised eye. Sara had hoped she might not make the

237

connection, but Gavin and Lou could not have looked more like an artist and a film-maker if they'd tried. In the interests of damage limitation, Sara prepared to head off any mention of home-schooling, lest the philosophical abyss that separated her mother's views on the subject from those of her friends, might become all too yawningly apparent. There was only one saving grace so far in this unhappy turn of events, and that was that Ezra had decided to stay in the car.

Shuffling their shoes off in the porch, as courtesy required, they all trooped into the house.

'Hey Buster, feeling better?' Gavin scooped a freshly showered Arlo onto his lap, and the child buried his face in his father's neck.

'Sara was just the same,' said her mother fondly, handing out cups of tea. 'Do you remember, darling? You always used to get carsick when we went on holiday.'

'I remember being sick *once*,' said Sara.

'Oh, no, it used to happen a lot. That time we went up for Gail's wedding, we'd only been in the car twenty minutes before you — '

'Thanks, Mum.'

'The key is to be prepared. I always kept a few plastic bags in the glove compartment — '

'We *had* plastic bags.'

'And you should have put him on newspaper if you knew he got carsick.'

'Oh, he doesn't, normally,' Lou said and Sara swivelled her head in disbelief.

'But I suppose he's used to our old jalopy, not a new car like yours. I think that syntheticky

238

smell can be a bit . . . off-putting sometimes. And then, they're so sort of hermetically sealed, aren't they, *proper* cars? Not like our rust-bucket. We get a Force Ten gale blowing through it even with the windows shut.'

Everyone smiled at the delightful eccentricity of Lou and Gavin's car, with all its quirky disadvantages, which actually turned out (who knew?) to be hidden assets.

'So, yes, it *might* have been the car,' she went on, 'but, to be honest, I'm more inclined to suspect the late night.'

Sara clutched the cushion on her lap, but before she could decide whether to hurl it at Lou or sink her teeth into it, Ezra's face appeared round the door.

'Pardon me, folks,' he said, 'can somebody point me in the direction of the john?'

★ ★ ★

Once Sara's mother had learned that, despite all appearances to the contrary, Ezra was not, in fact, a vagrant from the Bronx who had fallen through a worm hole into this leafy Middlesex suburb, but an important writer — who, now she came to think of it, she had definitely heard interviewed on Radio 4 — Sara knew they would never get away.

'It is ab-so-lutely no trouble whatsoever,' she insisted. 'I've got a couple of home-made lasagnes in the freezer and to be honest, Sara, that car's not going to be fit to drive for another hour at least. The *sensible* thing would be for you all to stay the night.'

'Oh no, Mum, people need to get back,' Sara said quickly. 'We'll just eat and then get on our way.'

It was amazing, she reflected, how her mother instinctively applied the techniques of Cold War realpolitik to parlay a quick cup of tea into supper. What was even more amazing was that everyone, Ezra included, seemed perfectly amenable to the plan.

⋆   ⋆   ⋆

Sara tried to persuade her mother to serve the food in the kitchen, but she was having none of it. Instead, they ate in her mausoleum of a dining room, off a rosewood table cluttered with placemats and cruets and Waterford crystal.

'Ezra?' said Sara's mother, in a casual tone that could nevertheless not disguise a certain relish in the exoticism of the name. 'Can I tempt you to some lasagne?'

If Sara hadn't been so fraught with nerves, she might have seen the funny side of her mother looming over this titan of literature, her sheer indomitability more than a match for his reputation. 'I hope you're not going to tell me you're a vegetarian.'

'No, ma'am,' said Ezra, watching apprecia- tively as she served him a generous portion. He seemed to be enjoying himself and Sara realised that, for him, this was a window onto a world he would otherwise never have seen. Just as, on a purely anthropological level, she'd have found it fascinating to dine with a bunch of God-fearing Texans on grits and red-eye gravy, so Ezra must, she supposed, be taking mental notes right now.

For his part, Gavin seemed no less interested in making an opportunistic survey of middle-brow aesthetics. Watching him cast an appraising glance over the artworks displayed on the dining room walls, Sara flinched. It was hard to know which was more lamentable, the hotel-lobby blandness of her mother's Impressionist prints, or the vulgarity of Richard's original Jack Vettriano, hung in pride of place over the coal-effect gas fire. She met Gav's eye, with a look in hers which, she hoped, conveyed an urbane amusement — an awareness that this was all beyond the pale, but must be tolerated, because, well, family was family.

'I understand you're a film director, Louise,' Sara's mother said, unfurling a serviette with a flourish and sitting down at last.

'*Writer*-director,' said Lou.

'That must be interesting.'

'Yes.' Lou seemed strangely reticent for once.

'And when will we be able to see your latest offering?'

'It's not going to be coming to the Staines Odeon, Mum,' said Sara wearily.

'Well, you know me, Sara,' said her mother, 'I have been known to schlep into town if there's culture in the offing.'

Her mother's unlikely recourse to Yiddish slang was almost as surreal as the idea of her making a cultural pilgrimage to the West End to catch an art-house short. Sara smiled to herself.

'Oh, well, the UK release is a way off, anyhow,' Lou said vaguely and turned away to attend to Zuley. Sara felt a stirring of unease. Lou hadn't mentioned *Cuckoo* the whole time they had been at Lush and, while it was typical of her to play her cards close to her chest, she would, surely, if she had secured the anticipated distribution deal, have wanted to share the good news with her investors.

★ ★ ★

At the other end of the table, Caleb and Dash seemed to have struck up a rapport with Sara's stepfather.

'So tell me,' Sara heard Richard say, 'who you saw at the pop concert.'

'It's called a music festival,' Caleb said kindly, 'and we saw a few different bands.'

'But who's your favourite? I need to keep up with this stuff. I've got *my* grandsons visiting tomorrow.'

'The Jeremiahs,' said Caleb.

'Yeah, The Jeremiahs were sick,' agreed Dash.

'Oh dear,' Richard stopped packing food neatly onto the back of his fork and looked up, 'but they still performed, did they?'

Dash and Caleb looked at each other, in delighted disbelief.

'Yeah,' Dash said, seriously, 'they still performed. They're very professional The Jeremiahs. Wouldn't want to disappoint the fans.'

Caleb snorted with laughter and Sara frowned at him.

'Maybe that's where young fellow-me-lad picked it up,' Richard said, nodding towards Arlo, who was pushing lasagne miserably round his plate.

'Could be,' agreed Dash seriously, 'could be a bug going around.'

This was too much for Caleb, who started to slide down his chair, clutching his belly in helpless mirth — or, Sara suspected, a simulation of it, calculated to flatter Dash. It was this, perhaps, her son's *sycophancy*, even more than Dash's slyness, or the meanness of the joke, that touched a nerve.

'Dashiell!' Sara snapped, when he opened his mouth to compound the offence. He met her gaze, innocent as a choirboy. The buzz of conversation and the tinkling of cutlery stopped. Sara was aware of Lou's eyes on her. She held Dash's gaze for a moment longer and then buckled.

'Would you pass me the bread, please?'

He handed it across with exaggerated courtesy. There was a pause and then the clatter and chitchat resumed. Neil engaged Richard in a conversation about golf. Lou started gathering up the dirty plates and the boys helped themselves to bowls of trifle.

★   ★   ★

'I'm so glad I read the book before I saw the film,' Sara's mother was saying, an unlikely rapport with Ezra apparently having blossomed, whilst Sara's attention was elsewhere.

'What book's that, Mum?' Sara inquired, queasily.

'*The Help*. Ezra and I are discussing American literature. They didn't do a bad job, but one never imagines the characters quite as they're depicted onscreen. I suppose it must be even more frustrating if you created them. Have you had your books adapted for the big screen, Ezra?'

'No, ma'am,' replied Ezra, 'I guess I don't write that kind of book.'

'Seriously, Ezra,' said Gavin, 'has no one optioned *Appalachia*? I'm surprised. I'd liked to have seen what the Coen Brothers made of it.'

'Nope,' Ezra shook his grizzled head regretfully. 'My agent was in talks with Francis Ford Coppola's people but it all fell apart. If the guy who made the greatest movie of all time says your book's un-filmable, I guess you're pretty much fucked.' Sara darted an anxious glance at her mother, but it seemed she was inclined to grant Ezra any amount of licence.

'*Godfather Two*!' bellowed Richard from the other end of the table.

Everyone turned and looked at him.

'He's forgotten to take his medication,' said Sara's mother in an undertone.

'Bang on the money!' Ezra bellowed back, pointing his knife. '*Two* every time. More nuanced than *One*; more heartfelt than *Three*. This guy knows his movies.'

★ ★ ★

244

The trifle bowls were scraped clean and collected up. 'Coffee' was served — a beverage so flavourless, as to make the much-maligned Rumbles Cappuccino seem like ambrosia. Soon, Sara told herself, soon she would be released from this purgatory and they could all go home. Emboldened from picking clean the carcass of Ezra's celebrity, her mother had now moved on to Gavin. His name was ringing bells, she insisted, although she couldn't claim to be completely *au courant* with modern art. Was it, by any chance, his work she had seen recently, gracing the courtyard of a Provençal Manoir in *Country Living* magazine? Gavin didn't think so.

'Never mind.' Sara's mother leaned across the table and patted his wrist, as if her inability to bring to mind his oeuvre were indicative of his obscurity, rather than her ignorance, 'You can explain it to me.' Sara wilted in shame, but Gavin didn't seem to mind in the least.

'I suppose you'd have to call it sculpture,' he said, 'in that I produce three-dimensional figurative works, but I don't like that label much because it locates my work in a tradition I don't feel very comfortable in — monolithic, *literally*, set in stone — whereas, for me, art is mucking about; it's childlike. The less you commit yourself to the idea of producing 'great art', the more chance there is you're going to make something worthwhile. That's why, until lately at least, I've worked with cheap materials — in plaster and wire. My finished works would be the *start* of the process for another sculptor — what they call maquettes.'

'So, let me get this right, they're *white plaster statues?*' Sara's mother was pulling her level three Sudoku face.

'Yes, figures really, more than statues, and not, generally, full-size. I tend to experiment with surface textures, so I'll use found objects — broken glass or feathers, ring-pulls even, you know, off Coke cans? To dirty things up a bit.'

'You like them *dirty?*'

Sara's mother's synapses seemed about to short-circuit, and Sara could no longer contain herself.

'Not everything needs to be *nice,* Mum,' she snapped. 'What Gavin's saying is that the medium reflects the meaning of the artwork. So, if it's a human being writhing in torment, then it's appropriate to give it jagged edges, or cancerous lumps and bumps because that conveys a feeling — makes an emotional connection with the viewer. And just because it's, you know, difficult to *dust,* doesn't invalidate it as art. Quite the opposite, in fact.'

'I see,' said Sara's mother, her eyes glinting with hurt. Sara looked defiantly around the table at the embarrassed faces of the other adults.

'Well,' said Lou at last, with a conciliatory smile, 'what a lovely evening.' She turned to Sara's mother. 'Thank you so much, Audrey, for your hospitality. I can't believe you conjured that wonderful meal out of nowhere. We should probably get off now. Get these kids to bed.'

22

The house had a neglected air on their return, as though they had been away for longer than a weekend. Junk mail had rained onto the doormat, dust had gathered in the corners, the light bulb on the landing had blown. Sara scuttled about trying to breathe life back into the place, dumping dirty washing in the utility room, putting away the provisions they hadn't used — the battered cereal boxes, a solitary bruised apple. She ran a bath for the boys and put hot water bottles in their beds. It seemed late in the year to be doing this, but there was a chill about the place.

* * *

Later, in bed, Sara's whisper echoed off the high ceiling.

'I never thought I'd like camping.'

'Mmmm.'

'We should get our own tent.' She reached for Neil's hand under the duvet.

'Maybe.'

She rolled towards him and insinuated her head into the crook of his arm. They lay in silence for a while.

'That thing you did . . . ' she murmured.

'Mmmm?'

'I liked it.'

Neil cupped her breast, with the awkward condescension of someone donating small change to a good cause. She faked a little gasp, but his hand just lay there. Tracing her toe down his calf, she received a valedictory squeeze of the tit, before his hand slackened and his breathing started to deepen. When she was sure that he was either asleep, or so committed to faking it, as to have forfeited any right to object, she slipped her hand between her legs and brought herself, quietly and resentfully, to orgasm.

★ ★ ★

The scent of his aftershave woke her — citrusy and sharp — he only wore it for work.

'I'm going to get Steve Driscoll to look at that crack. I think it might be structural,' he said.

Why are you telling me? she thought. What do I care?

'Okay,' she mumbled and closed her eyes again.

'Sara.'

Shut up, she thought.

'Sara?'

'What?'

'You said to make sure you were awake before I left. First day of term, yeah?'

Sara felt her heart lift. She would get the boys off to school and spend the day emailing publishers.

Then she remembered.

'Yeah, I'm on it,' she said.

She was not on it, not in the least. She felt

daunted and dispirited by the task ahead, and then almost immediately, guilty for feeling that way, and then, more comfortably, more *familiarly*, resentful of Neil for prompting such feelings in the first place.

★ ★ ★

'What's in those?' said Patrick, running his eye along the row of colourful stacking boxes beneath the kitchen window, each one labelled for a different subject area.

'Stuff for lessons,' said Sara, 'books, equipment, quizzes . . . '

Patrick brightened.

'Can I do a quiz?' he said.

'Wouldn't you like to get dressed first?'

'No.'

It couldn't hurt to let him stay in his pyjamas, Sara reasoned. Surely the whole point of home-schooling was to break down the boundaries between learning and life; keep things relaxed.

'There you go,' she said putting a printed sheet in front of him. She flicked through her sheaf of papers and found an age-appropriate quiz for Caleb on the same topic. Caleb gave it a cursory glance, then, smiling at her beatifically, folded it into a paper aeroplane and launched it across the kitchen. It was the kind of thing Dash would have done, Sara thought — a deliberate provocation. She would not be provoked. She strolled over to where it had landed, picked it up and examined its construction.

'Not bad,' she said.

Caleb smirked unpleasantly, but before he could think of a comeback, the doorbell rang and he hurtled out of the kitchen to answer it.

★ ★ ★

'God!' Lou walked in and gave Sara an absent-minded hug.

'That woman!'

'Who?' said Sara.

'The childminder. I swear I'd have sacked her by now if I had anyone else to fall back on. She's so blatant.'

'How do you mean?'

'It's so obvious she fancies Gav,' said Lou. 'I mean, big deal, on one level. She's not the first.'

Sara turned away and started filling the kettle.

'But she doesn't even *try* to disguise it. And she makes it pretty obvious she can't stand me.'

Seeing that Lou was in garrulous mood, the boys took the opportunity to drift away.

'Maybe we should talk about this later?' Sara said.

'Do you know what she said?' Lou sat down and took out a packet of cigarettes. 'Sorry, just the one. You see, *this* is what she does to me.' She shook her head. 'I'll open the window. Mustn't pollute the schoolroom!' She hauled up the sash.

Sara glanced anxiously into the garden, where the boys had started kicking a ball about. Patrick was still in his pyjamas.

'What did she say?' she asked Lou, filling the cafetière.

250

'Well, she thinks she's psychic — which is hilarious, considering how un-self-aware she is — and she's got the cheek to tell me that Zuley's aura's out of whack.'

Sara whirled one finger around her temple and went cross-eyed.

'Oh no, auras *are* a thing,' Lou corrected her, 'it's just the idea that *Mandy* can see them. Anyone less likely to be endowed with the third eye, you cannot imagine.'

'Right,' said Sara. It seemed like the safest response.

'Apparently, when she first started looking after her, Zuley's aura was lilac.' Lou laughed defensively and blew out a cloud of smoke. 'Now it's dirty grey.'

'Oh, for heaven's sake!'

Sara glanced through the open window and saw Dash make a reckless tackle on Patrick.

'Guys!' she called.

'So Madam wonders if everything's alright at home. 'Is Zuley wetting the bed?' for example. Er, no, she bloody isn't. She's been dry at night from the age of nine months.'

'Wow!'

'*Arlo's* the bed-wetter, if anyone.'

'Right.'

'Anyway, I'm going to start looking around.'

'For a new childminder?'

'Yeah. She thinks she's got me over a barrel, but Zuley's very resilient. It's a shame, at the end of the day, because she *is* happy there and she loves Sky to bits.'

'Sky?'

'Mandy's little girl. Anyway, sorry, good to get that off my chest.' She leaned forward and flicked her barely smoked cigarette out of the window. 'Gorgeous day . . . '

Sara glanced outside. It *was* lovely. The cherry blossom was in bloom; the chill had gone from the air.

'Shall we start off with some mind-body stuff in the garden?'

'Mind-body?' said Sara.

'A bit of yoga. Great for focus. I could do a guided meditation. See where that takes us.'

'How do you mean . . . ?'

'Creatively,' said Lou. 'See what they feel like after that: painting, writing, music-making — whatever.'

'Oh, okay, sounds good.'

Sara had pencilled in a session on symmetry, using the handbag mirrors she had bought from The Pound Shop.

'I really enjoyed the weekend,' Lou said, apropos of nothing.

'Oh, me too,' Sara said, forcing a smile; digging deep for the residual affection. 'Great atmosphere. We should definitely go again next year.'

Lou nodded happily.

'Your mum!' she said. 'What a character.'

'Yeah.'

'No, I really liked her. She was great. And Richard,' added Lou. 'You're lucky, Sara, I envy you.'

Sara stared in surprise, but before she could respond, Lou was on her feet.

'Listen up, guys,' she called through the open

window, 'we're going to do something fun now. Get yourselves into a space where you can spin round, arms outstretched, without touching anyone else.'

The boys looked sceptical, but to Sara's surprise, they lobbed the football into the shed and did as they were told. 'Yep,' Lou called, authoritatively, 'that's it. Wider, wider . . . *without* touching anyone else, I said.'

⋆ ⋆ ⋆

Considering the state of the house when he arrived home, Neil seemed pretty chirpy. He opened a beer, took a swig, and then started loading the dishwasher. Sara sat, slumped at the kitchen table, glass of wine in hand. She didn't even have the energy to go through the motions.

'Tough day?'

She gave him a look.

'You just need to get into a routine.'

'Thanks.'

He slammed the dishwasher closed with his knee and pressed start.

'Shouldn't this spare clay go away before it dries up?' Neil asked.

'That's not spare clay, that's Ulrik the Slayer.'

'Oka-a-y . . . '

Neil manouevred the coarse clay figure gingerly to one side and started to wipe down the oilcloth. Sara just about mustered the energy to lift her wine glass out of his way.

'There you go,' said Neil, cheerily, tossing the cloth into the sink, and sitting down. He topped up Sara's wine, sat forward in his chair and loosened his tie.

'Go on, then,' he said, 'today. Talk me through it.'

He was managing her, she thought — ironing out a human-resources issue.

'Oh, I don't know,' she said, 'it was just, I didn't realise it'd be so . . . that *I'd* be so . . . '

Her voice caught in her throat.

★ ★ ★

'Right. What next?' Lou had asked, leading the way back into the kitchen, breathless and pink-cheeked from her Sun Salutations.

'How about some poetry?' Sara had delved into her English workbox and pulled out a children's anthology. The boys had sat around the kitchen table, becalmed and amenable-seeming and Sara had leafed through the book, trying to find just the right poem to capitalise on their receptiveness — something fun; something relevant.

'Ah,' she'd said, smoothing the page, making eye contact with each of them in turn, clearing her throat.

'*Dis Poetry* by Benjamin Zephaniah,' she read.

> '*Dis poetry is like a riddim dat drops,*
>   *De tongue fires a riddim dat shoots like*
>   *shots . . . '*

Out of the corner of her eye, she noticed Dash grin and nudge Caleb, who groaned and lowered his forehead to the table.

> '*Dis poetry is designed fe rantin,*
> *Dance hall style, big mouth chanting,*'

Dash snickered, then clamped both hands over his mouth and lowered his eyes in mock remorse. Caleb remained face down.

> '*Dis poetry nar put yu to sleep*
> *Preaching follow me, like yu is blind*
> *sheep . . .* '

Even to her own ears, she now sounded more Welsh than West Indian and the more her confidence faltered, the worse her accent became. Dash was turning pink with the effort of containing his mirth. Patrick looked at her dumbly, his eyes beseeching her to stop.

> '*Dis poetry is not Party Political,*
> *Nat designed fe dose who are . . .* Right, that's it!'

She slammed the book shut and tossed it onto the table. 'You can bloody well read it yourselves.'

* * *

'I think you're being very hard on yourself,' Neil said. 'Just because the first session didn't go according to plan, doesn't mean the whole thing's a write-off. It's bound to take a bit of time to settle into it. The main thing is that you bounced back. I mean, look, you got through the

255

day. Everyone's still alive. You did clay *modelling*, for God's sake . . . '

He waved in the direction of the rudimentary clay figure on the table.

'Please don't patronise me, Neil,' Sara said. 'I worked my butt off getting ready for today.'

'I know. I know you did.'

'And Lou did nothing . . . well, unless you count boasting about all the airy-fairy people she's going to get to host workshops one day, when the stars are correctly aligned.'

'No, well . . . '

'So it's just a bit galling that when I get back after my meltdown, she's got them improvising street poetry.'

'Galling? I should have thought you'd be pleased.'

'Oh, overjoyed, yeah,' said Sara bitterly. 'She's a natural. The kids love her. No eye-rolling, no sniggering — just riffing off each other to create this really cool poem, all very Kate Tempest, very fucking urban.'

'Isn't that . . . ' Neil hesitated, ' . . . just the sort of thing you *want* them to be doing?'

'Oh, *just* the sort of thing,' said Sara sarcastically. 'Tapping into their creativity. Getting their juices flowing. And tomorrow, guess what?' She waggled her head and imitated Lou's eager, breathy voice: 'We might turn it into a little performance piece.'

Neil pursed his lips.

'That's if the muse condescends to drop in,' she added, 'if our chakras are in balance.'

'Sar . . . ' he said carefully.

She met his eye, with a glint in hers.

'I know Lou's a hard act to follow. She's got a lot of ideas, a lot of *charisma* . . . '

Sara picked up Dash's clay model and weighed it in her hand.

' . . . but I think it'd be a shame if you let a competitive spirit creep in.'

Sara squeezed the clay until her hand trembled with the effort of it.

'This is our kids we're talking about. I know Lou's got her shortcomings. She's a bit flakey. Nowhere near as methodical as you.'

Sara opened her palm and let the mangled clay tumble back onto the table, then raised her clenched fist above it.

'But she *does* also happen to be a bit of a geni — *Whoa!*'

The glassware leaped at the blow.

'Okay,' she said, peeling the pancaked clay calmly off the underside of her fist, 'got that. Thanks.'

23

Lou continued to be a genius for about a fortnight. Then she started going AWOL. One minute she'd be supervising papier mâché, the next Sara would glance out of the window and see her pacing the garden, phone clamped to her ear. It was amazing, since the home-school had started, how much more complicated and demanding all the other aspects of Lou's life had, coincidentally, become. There was Gav's admin to deal with, there was her own work to organise with that secretive demeanour of hers. And then there was The House. You would have thought, the way Lou talked about The House, that no one else had one, let alone an identical one, in which they were even now sitting, while Lou's children knocked bits off the already shabby décor. Lou talked about her house as if it were an adversary — a many-headed hydra needing to be slain. There was always something up — problems with the basement conversion, bills to be disputed, arcane insurance arrangements relating to its status as a business premises — it went on and on. Lou's mobile phone winked constantly on the corner of the kitchen table and whenever it rang, it was, 'Just bear with me . . .'

Then there were the late starts and the early finishes; the long lunch breaks when the queue in the post office had been 'unreal'. There were the times of the month and the times when she was sure she was coming down with something, which necessitated bunking off early, but did not rule out riotous returns by taxi at two the next morning, all too audibly the worse for wear. And yet, despite all of these absences, Sara was still seeing far more of her than was conducive to a healthy friendship.

★   ★   ★

Of Gavin, she wasn't seeing anything like enough. She missed him. She missed their banter on the school run. She missed their casual chats over coffee. She missed their flirtatious drunken arguments, their surreal jokes; the sense that she answered a need in him. The night they'd first discussed home-schooling, Gav had been all for getting stuck in. He'd promised to help the boys build a go-kart and take them beachcombing in Sussex. Perhaps those things would still happen, but it was starting to seem less likely.

Gav had a lot on his mind, according to Lou. The resin was doing his head in. It was a whole new way of working, learning to grapple with negative space. It was like, well, the only analogy she could think of was learning to walk again after a car crash. Sara wondered what Gav would have made of such hyperbole. She imagined he'd have laughed. Glimpsing him, by chance, from her vantage point at the bedroom window, he hadn't struck Sara as particularly tormented. There had been no outward signs of existential struggle. On the contrary, she had seen him whistling as he hauled industrial-sized tubs of epoxy from the boot of the car; watched him set off down the road on one of his many mysterious errands, singing along to whatever dross was pouring through his headphones. And on the odd occasion when she found herself, by happy coincidence, putting out the rubbish at the same time as him, he was no less cheery or flirtatious than normal.

★　★　★

Lou and Sara were supervising one of Lou's weird and wonderful art sessions when the doorbell rang. It was with some relief that Sara got up to answer it. It was only nine forty-five, but she'd already had enough of batik. It might be okay for the Women's Collective of Yoruba, as seen on YouTube, but to her way of thinking an intricate hot-wax-based dyeing technique was not the ideal artistic outlet for four boisterous boys.

She was so overjoyed to find Gav on the doorstep she felt compelled to be rude to him.

'What happened to your face?'

'Don't you like it?' Gav rubbed his hand self-consciously around an incipient beard.

'No, it's great. I just thought for a minute Caleb's guinea pig had come back to life and turned homicidal.'

'That's very funny, Sara, thanks. Not making me self-conscious *at all*.'

'Aw, thorry,' laughed Sara. 'It's lovely really.' She was reaching out to give his chin a stroke, when Lou materialised from the kitchen, all wifely solicitude.

'Gav? Nothing's wrong, is it?' she said, slipping between them with the guile and agility of a crack netball player.

'Nothing major. Just wondered if you could work your magic on the printer. Bloody thing's jammed in the middle of the White Cube contract.'

Sara gawped. If Neil had disrupted her day for something so trivial, well — he would know not to. But Lou was already halfway down the garden path, clucking, not at the pathetic incompetence of her other half, but at the regularity with which technology contrived to fuck up the lives of creative people. Gav gave Sara an apologetic shrug and was about to follow Lou down the path, when Sara had a thought.

'You could use ours if it's urgent . . . '

'Great!' he said, following her back into the house.

'Shouldn't we . . . ?' Sara gestured after Lou's retreating form, but Gavin flapped his hand dismissively.

'Needs sorting anyway,' he said.

Sara led the way upstairs to the study.

She shuffled some papers out of the way, pulled the office chair out for him, then flicked a switch and the printer hummed into life.

'It's all set,' she said, 'just bring up your document and away you go.'

★ ★ ★

261

She had got as far as the lower landing when Gav called her back. She could hear raised voices in the kitchen, a petty squabble, like a million others. She hesitated for a moment, thinking of the indelible natural dyes, the hot wax, the seven-year-old boys . . . Then Gav called again.

★ ★ ★

'Sorry, but is this your work? I didn't want to close it, in case it wasn't saved.'

'Oh Christ. Embarrassing.' She leaned over him and stabbed at the keyboard, desperate to get rid of the incriminating paragraph. She could feel the heat from his head, smell his earthy scent.

'Sorry,' he said, turning his face towards her so that their cheeks almost touched, 'I didn't mean to read it, is it a new novel?'

'It's crap,' she said, 'I'm not happy with it at all. I'm going to delete it.' She thought of her overripe prose, the plethora of adjectives, the sex . . . 'There you go,' she said, brusquely, bringing up Safari, 'I'd better go and check on the kids.'

'Hey,' he spun round on the chair and caught her hand, 'don't be mad at me. You'll have to get used to people reading your stuff when you're published.'

'Yeah, right.' She tried to pull away. 'Like that's going to happen.'

'Have some faith in yourself,' he said. 'Lou loves your writing.'

He gazed at her earnestly and she noticed a tiny fleck of brown amid the grey of his iris. Her breathing grew shallow.

'She's just being nice. I can't write. You've seen for yourself.'

The eye contact was too much. It was ridiculous. Look away, she told herself, *look away*.

'What I saw was *process*,' he said gently, 'nobody brings their work into the world fully-formed. You have to *permit* yourself to be an artist, Sara. You have to *permit* yourself to succeed.'

It was so much what she wanted to hear that she didn't trust herself to reply. Her throat was tight; her hand clammy. Embarrassed, she made to withdraw it but he wouldn't let her. The air felt charged. He circled his thumb in her palm and everything in her that was solid and resolved turned instantly molten and yielding. It was happening, the thing she had been fantasising about for months. He met her eye and smiled slowly, tugging her down onto his knee. The chair swung a little under the extra weight and she felt his erection press into her thigh. She moaned and buried her face in his neck.

The shouting downstairs had intensified, but it barely impinged any more.

It was a car crash of a kiss — clumsy and brutal and utterly thrilling. She arched her body away from him and fumbled at her waistband, cursing herself for wearing jeans. He reached down to help her, and the sound of her zip unfastening prompted a gush of readiness in her pants. She had shuffled the denim down as far as her thighs, when she heard the sound of footsteps clattering up the attic steps, the bleating cries of:

'Mum! *Mum!*'

By the time the door flew open, she was on her feet, jumper pulled well down, a full metre away from Gav, and still travelling.

'You've gotta come!' An ashen-faced Patrick yanked her hand. '*Come!*'

★ ★ ★

Adrenaline powered Sara's descent. She could hear a strange, otherworldly keening coming from the kitchen. Guilt and fear possessed her. She ran into the room.

'Arlo, *love!*'

Arlo was kneeling on the kitchen floor, clutching his face. Caleb crouched beside him, a tentative arm on his shoulder, while Dash hovered nearby, looking shifty. Sara lifted Arlo's hand gently from his cheek and gasped. A livid red weal ran from cheek to temple. His eyelid was swollen and glossy, beneath a film of solidifying wax.

'What happened?' Sara said, her voice tight. Both older boys started talking at once, but then Gav appeared and they fell nervously silent. He handed Sara out of the way, kneeling down and taking his son's face between his palms.

'Jesus Christ!' he murmured. 'Arlo, mate. How the hell did this happen?' He glanced around the room, taking in the rumpled squares of cloth on the table, the upset bowl of wax, the metal tools, flung every which way, then he looked at Sara — just one, fierce, uncomprehending glance. She hurried over to the sink and started soaking a teatowel in cold water to make a compress.

Patrick followed her, tugging at her elbow.

'It was Dash,' he hissed, with a nervous glance over his shoulder, 'he flicked wax in Arlo's face on purpose, 'cos Arlo was taking too long with the tool thing.'

Amid all the chaos — the running water, the wailing boy, the atmosphere of panic — Sara barely took this in. Afterwards, it would chill her marrow.

★   ★   ★

The doorbell rang.

'That'll be Lou,' said Gavin and for a moment, everyone held their breath.

'I'll go,' said Dash.

'Tell her to get the car started,' Gavin shouted. 'Tell her we're going to the hospital.'

★   ★   ★

Afterwards, Sara would seethe, rehearsing in her mind all the reasons Lou was just as much to blame as she was. Hadn't batik been her idea? Hadn't she breezed off to fix Gav's printer, leaving four small boys unsupervised? But if her anger was tempered with the shaming knowledge of her own complicity, Lou's seemed untainted by self-doubt. She had entered the kitchen like an avenging angel, screaming at everyone — Sara for letting it happen, Gav for not phoning an ambulance, Patrick and Caleb for getting

265

underfoot. Even poor Arlo got a mouthful, for crying so loudly she couldn't hear herself think. Only Dash, it seemed, was blameless, which might have struck Sara as ironic, had she had time to think about it.

★ ★ ★

When they had left, Sara began to set the room to rights. Caleb and Patrick joined in, subdued and purposeful. Only Dash, apparently incapable of matching his mood to the sombre circumstances, prattled cheerfully. As he scraped away with a kitchen knife at the solidified wax on the kitchen table, he explained that Arlo had been waving the tool around, taunting everyone with it, that he had tried to remove it for his brother's own protection, but that Arlo had dropped it and the wax had splashed back into his own face, which kind of served him right when you thought about it. Sara smiled tersely. You are a psychopath, she thought.

★ ★ ★

Neil's key rattled in the door.
'Hi Sara!'
His sing-song voice told her he wasn't alone. Footsteps rang down the tiled hall and they appeared in the kitchen doorway, two interlopers from the real world.
'This is Steve, from work,' Neil said, 'Chartered Surveyor extraordinaire. He's come to have a look at the crack.'

266

'Hi Steve,' Sara said, attempting a smile. 'Neil, can I have a quick . . . ?'

'Got them clearing up then?' Neil interrupted her. 'I told you you'd get into the swing. I'll just take Steve up for a gander, he'll be wanting to get home.'

They were gone for some time. Sara couldn't tell what was being said, but she could hear Neil talking in his work voice — bluff and authoritative. She wondered if the day would ever end. She was itching to pour herself a glass of wine, but until Lou and Gav got back with news of Arlo, it didn't seem appropriate. To distract herself, she went into the living room and turned on the news. She felt restless and a little bit sick. She couldn't get the thought of Gavin out of her head, but it was all wrapped up, now, with the shame and anxiety of Arlo's injury. Maybe that was just how it was when you embarked on an affair. How hard she had made it for herself, though. To be living next door to him, to be best friends with his wife, to have remade her whole life — even the children's education — around an idea which this charmed and charming couple had seemed, uniquely, to embody; yet to be contemplating an act of treachery that would blow it all apart.

★   ★   ★

Neil poked his head round the living-room door.

'Do you want to mute that a minute?' he said.

He and Steve came in and sat down, bringing with them the blotting paper scent of work.

267

'So they're mates, are they, next door?' Steve said.

'Yes,' said Sara with less than total conviction.

'That's good, because I could do with having a look from their side. You don't happen to know, do you? If the crack goes right through?'

Sara had been up and down Lou and Gavin's stairs many times, but it had never occurred to her to check. She shook her head.

'Never mind. I'll be back again to monitor it. Best to look in daylight anyway.'

'We'll be insured, will we?' said Sara, more to show an interest than because she really cared.

'Probably,' said Steve, 'depends on the cause. Could be a number of things — soil shrinkage, tree roots, worst case scenario; subsidence. You said they'd had work done, next door?'

★ ★ ★

As Steve was walking down the path, the Humber pulled up next door. Sara watched Gav unstrap Zuley from her car seat and lift her onto one hip, before scooping Arlo, his face half-obscured by a large dressing, onto the other. He carried the two of them towards the house, as if they weighed nothing. She was so busy admiring the effortlessness of it, that she didn't notice Lou approaching.

'For you,' her friend said, handing her a bunch of garage flowers. 'Sorry.'

'What on earth for?' said Sara.

'I was out of order, blaming you. I just freaked.'

'Oh,' Sara smiled uncertainly, 'thanks. How's

Arlo? What did they say?'

'It's not as bad as it looked, thank God. Only first-degree. There might be a bit of scarring, but his eyesight won't be affected.'

'Phew,' said Sara, 'I'd never have forgiven myself.'

'Ah, ah . . . ' Lou held up an admonitory finger. 'Not your fault.'

Sara hugged her.

'Anyway — it's a wake-up call,' said Lou. 'I've been thinking for a while, that working together isn't really doing us any favours.'

'So, what? You don't want to home-school any more?'

Despite all the frustrations of the past few weeks, Sara felt suddenly bereft.

'Oh, no, I *do*,' said Lou. 'I just think, for very good reasons, because we've been so focused on the kids, we've lost sight of our own needs. And I think we should fix that, for their sakes as much as ours. I think we need to be a bit more selfish, Sara. I think we need to make some time for *us*. When did you and I last do anything together? We don't even *swim* any more.'

★ ★ ★

If Sara had not been feeling so kindly disposed toward Lou, she'd have pointed out that the reason they no longer swam, was because these days, Lou could never fit it in. The pressure of a fast-approaching British Film Institute grant deadline had edged it out of her itinerary. Only she seemed to have forgotten that, whether or not she wanted to hone her body with aerobic exercise, some mug still had to drive the boys to the leisure centre for their Taekwondo class. For the last five weeks, that mug had been Sara.

She hadn't even minded that much. She liked the place. She liked its melancholy strip-lit atmosphere and its comforting aroma of chlorine and chips. The cafeteria was a good place to write. She felt anonymous there. There was no one to judge her; no hipsters in cropped trousers or brainy-looking women in funky tights. Coffee only came one way — hot, weak and foamy.

It had been a surprise, therefore, on her last visit, to be interrupted mid-sentence by a familiar voice.

'Hello, stranger!'

Carol wore her body warmer like a suit of armour. Her hair lay sleek and damp against her head. Under the unflattering light of the cafeteria, the strain of the forty-two years she had spent doing only the done thing, was showing. Sara was surprised, nevertheless, at how pleased she was to see her.

'Hi,' she said, closing her laptop and sliding it surreptitiously into her bag. 'You're slumming it, aren't you?'

'I know.' Carol lowered her voice and jerked her head towards Holly, who was queueing at the serving hatch, 'Had to give up my gym membership. Bloody school fees!'

There was an awkward silence. Sara pushed a moulded plastic chair towards Carol, and she perched uneasily on the edge of it.

'How's she settling in?' Sara asked.

'Oh,' Carol wobbled her head equivocally, 'you know. A few teething troubles, but I'm sure she'll come through. How're *you* getting on with the . . . ?'

'Home-schooling?' said Sara. 'Oh, it's going well. Really, really well.'

Carol nodded.

'That's good,' she said. There was another silence.

'She hates it,' Carol burst out, 'every day I want to run in there and rescue her. It's competitive and cliquey and she's in the bottom set for everything. She cries every night and I can't bear it.'

'Oh no!' Sara felt a pang of real pity. She reached out and clasped Carol's manicured nails.

'Have you thought about moving her back?' she added hopefully.

'Oh, I couldn't do that,' Carol said. 'Not now you and Celia have gone. I was talking to Deborah Parry and she says it's a war zone. She said, 'Carol, I'm not exaggerating, it's like Sarajevo in there'. No, the more I look at it, the more I think maybe you had the right idea.'

'Huh!' Sara said. 'I wouldn't be so sure. Home-schooling's no picnic, I can tell you. It's exhausting trying to keep them engaged all day and with the best will in the world, Lou can be a bit of a . . . '

Carol's eyes lit up and Sara saw, belatedly, the trap that had been set for her. She could have sidestepped it, but she chose not to. She jumped in with both feet.

'To be honest, she can be a bit of a nightmare.

271

She's full of great ideas, but she forgets that Patrick and Arlo are only little and then they get left behind and start misbehaving and my *God*, she's got a temper on her.'

'Oh I've seen it, don't worry,' said Carol. 'I once made the mistake of telling her eldest off for kicking a football at our garage doors. Well . . .'

'And she's always disappearing and leaving me to hold the fort,' Sara interrupted her, 'and she's got this way of being really condescending when she thinks what I'm doing isn't arty enough. Well, her ideas are brilliant on paper, but half the time they don't come off. She was supposed to be getting Beth Hennessy — you know from Little Creatures Puppet Theatre? To come and do a workshop with the kids.'

'Oh, now that *would* be something.'

'Yeah, well, I'm not holding my breath. I just saw in the paper that they're touring Eastern Europe at the moment. She's full of bullshit, Carol. If it isn't all about her, she doesn't want to know. I don't know how Gavin puts up with her.'

'Ah, the lovely Gavin,' said Carol sarcastically.

'Gav's not so bad,' Sara said, realising that she had already been shamefully disloyal.

'Oh, but he's so fake,' said Carol, 'he puts on this big show of being matey when you bump into him in the street, but you can tell he's not really listening to a word you say.'

'I don't agree,' said Sara, hotly. 'I find him very genuine. And he's not poncy about his art, either. Not at all.'

'Nor should he be, quite frankly,' said Carol. 'Talk about the emperor's new clothes. Really, Sara, I'm no philistine, I like modern art as much as the next person, but Simon and I saw a couple of his pieces at a gallery in Copenhagen, and we just looked at each other and shrugged.'

'Really?' Sara was starting to feel annoyed. She had forgotten about Carol's small-mindedness, her determination that anything she didn't understand must be a con.

'I find it rather beautiful. I think he's got a lot to say about the human condition and I think because his work's figurative, it's easy to think it's more straightforward than it is.'

'Oh well, of course, you've seen more of it,' said Carol huffily, 'so I'll have to defer to your superior knowledge.' The barriers were up again. 'But, Sara, a word to the wise . . . '

Sara never did find out what Carol's word to the wise was, because at that moment the boys came barging into the cafeteria, flushed and adrenaline-fuelled from their martial arts session, and by the time Sara had calmed them down and doled out change for the vending machine, Carol had made her excuses and left.

* * *

Recalling this conversation, as she stood on the doorstep, holding Lou's flowers and listening to her friend suggest ways in which they might reconnect, Sara felt a pang of guilt.

'There's this yoga retreat in Kent,' Lou enthused. 'I know Shani, the woman who runs it,

273

so we'd get mates' rates.'

'Sounds perfect.'

'I'll give them a call,' said Lou, 'but we might have to wait a week or two. It's open studios next weekend and the one after's my birthday . . . '

'So it is,' said Sara, 'the big four-oh!'

'Which reminds me,' Lou said, 'save the date, won't you? We want to take you out for dinner.'

24

'Sign this,' Sara said, putting Lou's birthday card in front of Neil. He demolished his last mouthful of toast, licked his crumby fingers, and dashed off a signature.

'Is that it?' said Sara. 'No kiss?'

She had drafted her own birthday greeting on the paper bag that the card had come in, so as to appear fluent and spontaneous on the real thing:

~~Dear~~ Darling Lou,

Wishing you everything you wish for yourself, in this, your fortieth year. Your precious friendship means the world to us. Can't wait to celebrate with you.

Love and ~~kisses~~ hugs, Sara xxxxxxx.

Neil took the card back and put two kisses next to his name.

'It's her forty-*first* year,' he said.

'She's forty, Neil. I think I would know.'

'But her fortieth birthday is the beginning of her forty-first year.'

'Oh for God's sake!' She snatched the card back.

★ ★ ★

All his little tics and habits were driving her mad at the moment — the way he wore his jeans too

275

high on his waist, his fastidiousness about keeping food in airtight containers, his latest obsession with testing his breath, after brushing his teeth, by exhaling into his cupped hand. It was hard not to compare him unfavourably with Gav, whose clothes hung so well on him, who was endearingly un-house-trained, who, thanks to his cavalier attitude to personal hygiene, had a sort of earthy, fungal thing going on, that drove Sara insane.

* * *

She had hardly seen Gav lately, but it was only to be expected that he would avoid her. There was, after all, nowhere for them to go with their feelings for each other — nowhere, apart from the obvious place, anyway. It was all Sara could think about since it had happened. It was humiliating to have to admit to herself that a fumble with her best friend's husband, had been the most erotic experience of her life to date, but there it was. It wasn't that she hadn't had good sex before. She had. She had even had some of it with Neil. But she had never before been so pole-axed by desire that she had forgotten whom and where she was. It hadn't even been a proper kiss. It had been a glancing, painful skirmish, lasting perhaps three seconds, at most. Their teeth had clashed. She had come away with blood on her lip, and he with drool in his beard. She had worried afterwards that she might accidentally have leaned too hard on his penis, in a way that he may not have found erotic. Even as fumbles went, it had been clumsy and ignominious, yet she had been unable to think of it since, without melting at the recollection. She had even been moved to go to the bathroom in broad daylight and masturbate.

* * *

She had been happy in her marriage to Neil; never tormenting herself with what ifs, never self-sabotaging by succumbing to passing temptation. There had, in fact, only *been* one passing temptation — Tim Hughes, her line manager in her first job, who had seemed Byronic and alluring for about three weeks, until she went out for a glass of wine with him after work, and noticed for the first time how oddly long his neck was. That had put an end to it, all right. She loved Neil. She loved his smile, at once self-conscious and cocky, like a kid in a school photograph. She loved his unfussy manliness, his competence, the way he occupied space. She loved that he was playful, but essentially serious. She loved his hands — the way he held her life and the lives of their children in them — steady and sure.

* * *

Had he ever made her swoon though? Had he ever made her feel so ripe, so loaded with nerve endings, that she might explode, like a seed pod, at his touch?

* * *

It was doing her head in, this thing with Gavin. She understood why he was avoiding her — even respected him for it, but she did not have the self-discipline to do the same. She was her own worst enemy — she would loiter guiltily on the landing, for the pleasure of watching him take a fag break in the garden; she would take more trips than necessary to empty the shopping from the boot of the car, because each trip afforded her a glimpse of the back of his head, as he sat on the sofa watching television. She knew it was a kind of madness, but she couldn't help herself. And the more she was deprived of his company, the more reckless she became.

* * *

One morning, she was washing up, when she saw him set off on his bike, with Zuley in the toddler seat. She knew it was his habit to call in at the newsagent's on his way back from the child-minder's, to pick up a copy of the *Guardian*. She glanced at the clock. She had twenty minutes before Lou would be round with the boys. She went upstairs, changed her top for a more flattering one and swiped some Jo Malone behind her ears.

'Just popping to Samir's,' she called to Caleb, but her voice was drowned out by the clamour of cartoons. There was a chill in the air as she set off down the road. It was nearly time for other people's children to go back to school. Sara walked as slowly as she could whilst still appearing purposeful. When she came within

278

sight of the newsagents, she got out her phone and whiled away a few minutes scrolling through her inbox, whilst keeping one eye on the corner of the road. Her twenty minutes were almost up and still there was no sign of him.

She went into the shop and dawdled up and down the narrow aisles like a criminal, acutely aware of the CCTV camera winking in the corner. Glue seemed a plausible item to be buying, so she examined the three brands on sale, as if writing them up for a consumer magazine. At last she chose one and stopped on the way to the counter to pore over the newspaper headlines. She stood there for more than a minute, one ear cocked for the two-tone electronic beep that alerted Samir to new customers. Any moment now, Gav would speak her name or grasp her elbow. She felt sick and elated at the thought of it. But the queue of harassed commuters had diminished and she was now Samir's only customer. Gavin must have deviated from his normal routine. She paid up with a sigh and hurried home, her breathing ragged, her reflection, glimpsed briefly in the window of the dry cleaner's, that of a mad woman. As she turned up the path, and took out her key, she heard the whirr of wheels and the *ker-thunk* as his bike mounted the pavement.

'Hi, Sara!' he called cheerfully. Turning, she glimpsed the top of his head whizzing behind the privet and moments later, heard their side gate judder and slam shut.

★   ★   ★

Located in a back street of Camberwell, down basement steps, Lupercal was very Gavin and Lou. Its discreet signage ensured that by the time they found it, Sara and Neil were even more fashionably late than they'd intended, though not quite as fashionably late as their hosts, who had still not arrived. The maître'd showed them to a cosy wood panelled booth, lit by a retro wine-bottle candleholder and promised to return momentarily to take their drinks order.

'I told you we'd be early,' hissed Sara accusingly.

'We're not early, they're late.'

Neil squeezed onto the banquette next to her, inadvertently crushing her full-skirted dress as he did so. She sighed and yanked it out from under him.

The waiter came and Neil ordered dry martinis, with a decisiveness that surprised Sara.

'Great place.' Neil examined the menu. 'Bit pricey though.'

'Who cares?' shrugged Sara. 'It's on them.'

'You think we should let them pay? On her *birthday*?'

'Oh, no,' said Sara sarcastically, 'let's buy her dinner as well as an expensive present. Oh, and let's throw in a babysitter as well.'

This was disingenuous, she knew. When Lou had called round in a flap, to tell Sara that her babysitting arrangements had fallen through, Sara's mother had been quick to volunteer her services.

'Bring them round here, by all means, Louise,'

Audrey had insisted, only too pleased to make herself useful once again to the delightful family who had parachuted a Pulitzer prize-winner into her dining room, 'the more the merrier.' But it was one thing to accept Sara's mother's kind offer, in Sara's opinion, quite another to dump the kids an hour early in order to 'swing by' a private view, en route to the restaurant.

'Jesus. Who rattled your cage?' said Neil. 'Your mum was well up for it.'

'Yeah well, she doesn't know Dash.'

'You've got it in for that kid.'

Sara stared at him stony-faced. Already they were off on the wrong foot.

Neil took a deep breath.

'Nice dress,' he said, 'is it new?'

'I didn't buy it specially, if that's what you mean.'

'It's okay if you did.'

'Well, I didn't.'

★ ★ ★

A lie. She had gone into town to buy Lou's present and got sidetracked. It was a *Madmen*-type number that showed off her shoulders and made her look as if she had tits; not the kind of thing she normally wore, but once she'd put it on, all she could think about was Gav taking it off her again and so she'd bought it. The guilt of the purchase had ensured that she spent double what she'd meant to on Lou's present.

★ ★ ★

Sara took a sip of her drink. It was delicious — clean and cold, like the slice of a scalpel. Belatedly, she remembered to clink glasses with Neil.

'Shaken not stirred,' he said in his Sean Connery voice.

'That was awful,' she said.

★ ★ ★

Lou and Gav's arrival seemed to cause a bit of a frisson in the restaurant, whether because the other diners recognised them, or because they entered like people who expected to be recognised, Sara wasn't sure. Lou certainly wasn't courting anonymity, in her leather skirt and tight Nirvana tee shirt. Seeing her, Sara had the usual pang of doubt about her own outfit, until she noticed Gav's eyes flicker greedily over her cleavage and felt instantly better.

When the hugs and happy birthdays were done with, they sat down and Neil nodded to the waiter to bring two more martinis.

'Sorry we're late, by the way,' Gav said. 'Had to show our faces in Shoreditch. Private view of a mate of mine.'

'Any good?' asked Neil.

'Naaah.'

They all laughed. There was a pause while they settled into one another's company and rode out the inhibiting curiosity of their fellow diners.

'Mmmm, these are lethal!' said Lou, sipping her martini happily. Gav swivelled round in his seat, caught the waiter's eye and ordered another round just by spiralling his finger. The first drink had already made Sara a little woozy, but Gav's proximity prompted her to take a large gulp of the second one to calm her nerves. He always looked well-turned out, but tonight he had refined his left-field aesthetic to perfection. He was wearing a dark denim shirt under a jacket, which though knitted, somehow managed to look better-tailored than Neil's Jaeger twill. His eyes glittered like jet in the candlelight and his cheekbones looked sharp enough to shave parmesan. All the same, there was a vulnerability about him — something different that she couldn't quite put her finger on. Then it came to her. He had shaved off his beard. She remembered how mean she had been about it, and felt guilty and exhilarated at once. The dolt, the adorable fool. There had been no need, she wanted to tell him; she loved him either way.

⋆ ⋆ ⋆

Neil gave her a nudge and, remembering herself, she reached into her bag for Lou's present and card.

'For *me*?' Lou's eyes boggled with gratitude as if a present on her birthday surpassed her wildest expectations. She opened the card and made a little moue of gratitude, then ripped into the package. She had, Sara thought, never looked more beautiful or more damaged. Even with her hair scraped back in a scruffy topknot, barefaced, save for a slick of eyeliner, she still

283

managed to make Sara, with her well-buffed glow and her expensive dress, feel obvious and suburban.

'It's nothing much,' Sara lied. 'I wasn't sure if you'd like it, but they're happy to exchange. There were two or three nice ones but I just thought this one seemed the . . . '

Lou laid a hand on Sara's and she trailed off foolishly. 'I love it,' she said, 'it's beautiful.'

She put the bangle and its tissue wrapping to one side and turned her attention to the menu. 'Now, what do I want to eat? Do I want confit of duck? Or do I want black rice with monkfish? Oh God, I can't choose.' She snapped it shut. 'Neil, order for us will you?'

Neil looked up in alarm, as if the teacher had asked him to take the class, but soon rose to the occasion with a highhandedness that Sara feared exceeded his brief. Before long they were feasting as if it were the last days of the Roman Empire, dishes arriving thick and fast from the kitchen, each one containing an obscure animal part or salad leaf of which Sara had never heard. Not to be outdone, Gav ordered a bottle of wine costing eighty pounds, which they downed in half an hour, and followed with a second.

★ ★ ★

It was a pity, Sara thought vaguely, not to be paying more attention to the delicately rendered juices, the subtle dressings, the witty garnishes. Who knew when she would eat so well again? But the food might as well have been sawdust.

How could she taste, when there was so much *looking* to be done? She had endured weeks with barely a glimpse of Gav, and now here he was, just inches away from her, smiling his crooked smile, waggling his fork to make a point. Sara struggled to tune in to what he was saying — something about a guy he'd met at the private view, a short beefy bloke called Matt, with an impressive moustache and a slightly incongruous alto voice.

'I knew I knew him from somewhere,' Gav said, 'I just couldn't work out where. And then the penny dropped — it was *Matilda*. This girl I'd known at art school. She'd transgendered. It was a shock, you know, but also great. He was so *together* — so much more himself than *she*'d ever been.'

Sara dangled her wineglass halfway between lips and table, smiling, shaking her head.

'And I was like, 'mate, great to see you, welcome to the fold,'' Gav went on, 'only, for fook's sake, can you not stand next to me with that six pack 'cause you're making me look like a wuss!'

Everyone laughed, but then Neil embarked on a lecture about hetero-normative assumptions, which slightly killed the mood and Gavin, though nodding and smiling, started delving in his pocket for his rolling tobacco. Here, Sara thought, was her chance. Before Gav could declare his intentions, she got in first, announcing that she needed to pee. She skipped off the bench, leaving Gav for dead, and made straight for the Ladies, where she checked her appearance in the mirror, and pushed the button on the hand dryer, for authenticity's sake, before taking a sneaky detour via the courtyard, where she knew, by now, Gav would be ensconced.

★ ★ ★

'I'll have one of those,' she said.

He was sitting on the steps, partly obscured by a topiaried bay tree.

'*Please*,' he said sternly.

'Pretty please.'

He surrendered his freshly rolled cigarette and began making another one. When it was finished, he sparked his lighter and they both leaned in. Seeing his face in the glow, his hooded eyes, his thin, sardonic mouth, she felt a mule-kick of lust.

'Mmmm,' she said, inhaling, lest he be in any doubt that she was enjoying herself.

'Careful now,' he said. 'Don't make yourself poorly.'

'I can honestly say I have never felt better.'

She had had just enough alcohol to remove her inhibition, not so much that she didn't know, with forensic clarity, what she was doing. She cupped his newly shorn chin in her hand.

'You didn't *need* to shave it off, you know.'

'I know.'

'But I'm flattered you did.'

She dropped the barely-smoked cigarette and taking his hands, pulled him up to a standing position. She could smell the wool of his jacket, the astringent scent of his cologne and beneath them both, his own slightly musty aroma, a scent she had come to prefer to any on earth. She knew they couldn't fuck, not here; but a kiss would suffice. A kiss, on Lou's birthday, would be fine. She tugged his head towards her, turned her face upwards and closed her eyes.

'I'm sorry,' he murmured, his breath sweetish and acrid from the wine and tobacco.

'Don't be.' She jostled his mouth with hers, but he caught her jaw in his hand.

'No,' he said, gently, 'I'm sorry.'

25

As if in a trance, she walked to the water's edge and felt the sand suck her feet down a little further with each step, as she drew nearer to the rush and bubble of the approaching waves. She picked up a piece of bladderwrack from the shore and weighed its heft in her hands. It was slimy and its air-filled pods felt more substantial than her life. She hung it over her face, like a veil. It felt right, to be thus obscured, by watery, putrid stuff, by primitive plant life. She had come from water and she would return to it. Her feet sank inexorably into the sand and the tide swirled around them. By the time they came looking for her the next morning . . .

'Sara?'

'Jesus!' Sara swung round in her chair.

'What are you doing?'

Neil's eyes looked baggy with tiredness. He was only wearing pyjama bottoms and Sara's eyes were drawn to the whorls of springy hair around his nipples.

'I'm writing,' she replied.

'At two in the morning?'

'What's it to you?'

'I can't sleep.'

'Well, I'm not stopping you.'

'Just come to bed.'

'And when will I get to write?'

'At the weekend.'

'You'll take the boys out, will you?'

'Ah, I *could*, only . . . '

Sara shrugged and turned back to the screen, irritated, yet somehow also gratified by him continuing to hover guiltily behind her. She heard him sigh, and push the door to. He went over to the ugly wingbacked armchair they had inherited from her mother and perched watchfully on its inhospitable edge. Sara continued to stare pointedly at her computer screen.

'So this is what, a re-write?' he ventured at last, 'only, shouldn't you wait until you get some professional feedback?'

She looked at him witheringly.

'I've had all the 'professional feedback' I need, thanks. This is something new.'

'Well I don't think, just 'cause you've had a few rejections, you should write it off.'

'With respect,' she said, swivelling the chair towards him, 'you don't know what you're talking about.'

'Lou does,' he said.

'What?' Sara said, rudely.

'Lou read your book and loved it. Presumably, her opinion counts for something?'

'She *said* she loved it.'

'Why would she say it if she didn't mean it?'

'God, you can be naïve sometimes.'

'What's that supposed to mean?'

'How about, so we'd lend her eight grand to make her film? I don't think we'll be seeing that again anytime soon, do you?'

Neil gawped at her and she was reminded, fleetingly, of his essential goodness — the quality that had first drawn her to him. She had loved that he saw only the best in people, that he believed in progress and regarded sin from a sociological, rather than a moral standpoint; even as she despaired at his credulousness, his unfashionable stalwart sunniness, his conspicuous lack of existential gloom. Perhaps the times had changed, certainly the company had — at any rate Neil's naïve optimism about human nature now struck her as silly. Silly, and deeply unsexy.

'You think Lou's that calculating?' he said.

'Maybe not consciously, but I think that's the game she's playing. The game they're *both* playing. They've been cultivating us.'

'Christ! When did you get so cynical?'

'Maybe the eighth or ninth time Lou dumped the kids on me while she rang her agent, or filled out a grant application or, let me see, *storyboarded an entire short film while I stopped her kids from killing each other.*'

'I thought you said she was an inspirational teacher.'

'She was. For about two minutes. Until she got bored.'

Neil looked crestfallen and Sara softened a little.

'Honestly? If I'd known it was going to be like this, I never would have taken the kids out of school. I don't even care that I've fucked my life over, but I can't bear the thought that we've done it to them. At least they were happy at Cranmer Road. God, I'll never slag off teachers again. I never realised how much energy it takes, how much ingenuity. You have to stay one step ahead all the time. You have to make boring stuff interesting. You have to really get stuck in. I must have been mad to think I could do that and write as well.'

'You're being too hard on yourself. Something like this — it's bound to have ups and downs. You've done a really, really courageous thing — to try and lead a creative life. To role-model that to the kids and make space for *them* to be creative in their turn. That's a huge thing. If you can pull that off, that's going to be way more of an achievement than anything I've ever done. But it was never going to be easy. Something like that — it's not a straight line.'

'But that's just it,' she said, 'those two things — leading a creative life yourself and providing that environment for the kids,' she shook her head, 'mutually exclusive. You can't have your cake and eat it. Finally, I get where Ezra was coming from. Creativity is selfish. At least the kind that results in art. How can I carve out the time I need for myself, as well as help the kids realise their potential? I can't.'

'That is so pessimistic. You're buying into a stupid romanticised view of what creativity's about — starving in garrets, cutting your ear off — the whole tortured genius myth.'

'Oh, what do *you* know about it?' she said angrily. 'The most creative thing *you've* ever had to do is choose the font for the annual report.'

Neil looked hurt, but rather than recant, she went on, her strident whisper becoming hoarser and hoarser as she pressed home her point.

'It might be a mystery to you, Neil, but I can

291

tell you, from first hand experience, that art comes at a cost. Writing isn't something you can tinker with on the sidelines. It's a serious commitment, or it's nothing. Why do you think I'm up in the middle of the night? It's not because my creative juices flow better at two in the morning, I can tell you. It's because it's the only time I can bloody well carve out. Is it any wonder my writing's shit? Is it any wonder I've got an inbox full of rejections? I'm an amateur, Neil, and I write like one. To be a proper artist, you've got to make sacrifices. You've got to be prepared for your work to eat you alive — and for it to eat everyone *around* you alive.'

'Oh for God's sake, don't be so melodramatic. What about Lou and Gavin? *They're* both artists, but they don't make a meal of it . . . '

Sara flung herself backwards in her chair, in a spasm of disbelief.

'You have got to be kidding!' she squeaked.

'Well, it seems to me they get it about right,' said Neil, defensively, 'they have their work; they have their family . . . '

'Neil, *I* have their family! You do know I'm childminding Zuley at the moment?'

Neil looked taken aback. 'Really?'

'Yes, really. Lou's fallen out with Mandy. She thinks she's got her claws into Gavin. So now *I'm* running a fucking crèche. On the itinerary next week — a day trip to Tower Bridge to learn about levers. Can you imagine? With Zuley in tow?'

'But Lou'll go too, surely?' said Neil.

'Oh, she *says* she will,' said Sara, 'she probably

even *thinks* she will, but come Monday morning you can bet there'll be some catastrophe that only she can sort out. She'll have to go and camp out at the passport office, or she'll get asked to do some urgent script edits or something. Christ knows what, but I'm willing to bet the *house* that she won't be within a million fucking miles of Tower Bridge. *That's* how it works for Lou and Gavin.'

'Well, no, that's not on,' said Neil, his indignation a little underpowered to Sara's way of thinking, 'you'll just have to tell her.'

'*I'll* have to?'

'*We* will. We'll bring it up tomorrow night.'

Overwhelmed by Neil's generosity in footing the bill at Lupercal, and somewhat the worse for drink, Lou had insisted on inviting them round for dinner. 'Lou's birthday round two,' she had modestly called it.

★ ★ ★

At the time, Sara had smiled tersely, determined that wild horses would never again drag her over Lou and Gavin's threshold for the purposes of socialising, but it was starting to dawn on her that such an assignation might, after all, have its uses.

26

Sara slid down the bath into the scalding water and watched her body turn a startling sherbet pink. Only her knees, protruding above the Plimsoll line of pain, remained flesh-coloured. Beads of sweat bloomed in her hairline and trickled down her face, but she stayed put. It was a test of will.

★ ★ ★

Later, she sat naked, on the edge of the bed, massaging body lotion into her legs and rehearsing the evening ahead. On reflection, she decided, she'd be mad to leave things to Neil. A couple of glasses of wine, and they'd have him eating out of their hands. It made her cringe, the way he crept around them lately — laughing at Gav's lame jokes, indulging Lou's selective memory syndrome. He didn't seem to realise what a bad look it was — they could scarcely be blamed for booting his backside if he was determined to stick a target on it and bend over. But she was damned if *she* was going to take a kicking. She'd had enough.

★ ★ ★

Red weals were starting to appear on Sara's flesh by now, from the force with which she was pummelling her thighs. She stopped, a little shocked

294

at herself, and caught sight of her reflection in the dressing table mirror. Her hair, released from its towel, but not yet combed through, stood out from her head in a tangled heap. Her eyes were dark as coals. She looked like one of the furies of Greek mythology — snake-haired avenger; righter of wrongs. Might as well dress the part, she decided, unearthing a bodycon number that she had bought on a whim one day with Carol. Its bandage-y, chest-flattening look seemed to strike the right note of sexy androgyny. Just the thing to remind Gav what he was missing; *what he had turned down.*

★ ★ ★

' . . . And I don't want to stay late,' she muttered, as they stood on Lou and Gavin's doorstep waiting to be let in.

'Why don't we wait and see?' said Neil, his tone only superficially friendly. 'We might even enjoy ourselves.'

A shadow loomed behind the stained glass and Lou's voice could be heard, light, warm, pleased with itself, as she threw some remark over her shoulder. In the moment of the door's opening, as the familiar dank scent of their house met her nostrils, Sara's resolve weakened momentarily. She remembered all the times she had stood here feeling blessed — blessed to be spending an evening in their company, blessed to know them. A tightness came in her throat and she swallowed hard.

But here was their hostess, in a halo of light,

bra-less in a faded T-shirt and Thai silk fisherman's trousers. She had done something weird with her hair again and she was wearing an unusual amount of eye make-up.

'Hell-o!' she said, as if they had not seen one another for ages. 'Come on *in*.'

She gathered Sara to her, without making eye contact, and inclined her head on her guest's shoulder, in an odd gesture of supplication.

'Hi,' said Sara, stiffly. She disentangled herself and watched Lou greet Neil, in what seemed, by comparison, a cursory manner.

'Dinner smells good,' she said, relenting a little. In truth she was spooked to find a meal already under way — this had never happened before. She even wondered whether it might be a tactic on Lou and Gav's part — had they somehow guessed that they had overstepped the mark? Were they hoping to smooth things over with the help of Ottolenghi? If so, they had better think again.

★ ★ ★

Entering the kitchen, she almost tripped over Gavin, perched on the low windowsill, legs crossed at the ankle, bottle of beer in hand. She thought she had prepared herself for this moment, but seeing him felt like a physical blow.

'Here she is,' Gav said, all pantomime goodwill, 'here's my girl.'

He yanked her towards him with a comic flourish. For a moment she was back in the restaurant courtyard, her nose full of the ripe fug of his body, her thigh pressed hard against his. He puckered up for a chaste kiss, but she turned her face away, coldly. That was when she saw the other guests.

'So, yeah,' said Gavin, after he had given Neil a man-hug, 'Sara, Neil, meet Claudia and Chris.'

Sara stretched her mouth into a smile. She should have known. She should have known they would pull the rug from under her; conspire somehow to put her on the back foot. There had never been other guests before, only the four of them. It felt like a slap in the face. It might have been just about tolerable if their fellow invitees had been drawn from Gavin and Lou's usual coterie of movers and shakers, but these two were well below par. Claudia was a mousy little thing, dressed older than her years, in a long, ribbed cardigan and dangly earrings. A decent stylist could have done wonders with her dirty-blonde hair, but it hung either side of a middle parting in two limp hanks. She waved at them feebly from the other side of the table. Chris was, if anything, even less charismatic, his only distinguishing features two unruly beige eyebrows, which clung below his receding hairline like tumbleweed to the side of a precipice. He was wearing a sports shirt with the collar turned up. He leaped up and shook hands, making lots of eye contact. Even Neil looked depressed to be meeting him and Neil would give anyone a fair crack. It was as if, scenting controversy, Lou had dragged the nearest couple in off the street to deflect any unpleasantness. And yet, they were getting the full treatment, the candles, the flowers, a Sufjan Stevens album playing quietly in the background. While Lou cooked up a pot of frijoles refritos on the stove, Gavin chatted away to Chris as if he were interested in what he had to say.

★ ★ ★

Claudia chinked her glass against Sara's with a conspiratorial look as though drinking wine were a little bit naughty.

'So, how do *you* know Gavin and Lou?' she asked.

'We live next door,' Sara replied, her tone barely civil.

'Sara and Neil took us under their wing when we first came back,' Lou said, over her shoulder, to Claudia. 'God, what a state we were in, Sara — do you remember?'

Oh yes, she did. She remembered. She remembered the sense of dizzying good fortune at being selected, of all the women in the street, to be Lou's friend. She remembered sipping coffee, and listening, rapt, to Lou's fairy tale of Spain. She remembered barely breathing, as the confidences had poured out, in case Lou took fright and stopped talking. And now, as she watched Claudia, slack-jawed with admiration, gobbling up every word Lou said — she remembered her old self — the credulous, grateful acolyte she had been.

'It was so funny, being around people again,' Lou recalled fondly, 'we were practically feral. And the *language*. I kept breaking into Spanish.'

No, you didn't, thought Sara. Now the spell was broken, she could see how transparent, how *juvenile* were her hostess's attempts to impress.

Lou didn't seem herself tonight, Sara thought. Some subtle thing was different. She seemed tired and a little apprehensive. Perhaps she could sense the tide of Sara's affection running away from her.

'It must have been difficult, making the adjustment,' piped up Claudia. 'London's so anonymous, isn't it?'

'Well, I know what you mean,' said Lou, diplomatically, 'but this neighbourhood kind of bucks that trend.'

'Is it a trend?' asked Sara. 'Or is it a cliché? I must say I've never found Londoners particularly unfriendly.'

'Well, I didn't mean it was unfriendly, exactly,' stammered Claudia, the colour rushing to her cheeks. 'I suppose I've just always found it rather daunting.'

'Why, where are you from?' Sara demanded.

'Well my family's actually from Derbyshire, but I had quite an itinerant childhood because of my father's work. We were all over Europe, really.'

'Claudia is Jerzy's daughter,' Lou explained. Sara dredged her memory. Which one was Jerzy? Ah yes, the bendy ringmaster with the fatal charm and the drink problem. Now it made sense. These two kids may have had the charisma of pond slime, but they were part of a dynasty. They were creative by *association*.

'Oh okay,' said Sara, 'so you must be involved

with Little Creatures, then?'

'No, actually,' Claudia sounded apologetic, 'that's Beth's thing. She's my stepmother. No, it's wonderful, how it's all taken off for her, but I'm not really a theatre person.'

Sara had been about to ask what kind of person Claudia was (although, God knows, she could happily have lived without knowing), when Lou put a dish of food on the table alongside a basket of home-made tortillas.

'Dig in,' she said, pulling up a battered stool.

Sara slopped a spoonful of the rich, coriander-flecked goo onto a tortilla and rolled it up.

'Guacamole? Salsa?' Chris passed various dishes back and forth, as if he, not Gavin were the host. Claudia num-nummed appreciatively. For a while no one spoke.

★ ★ ★

'I thought you'd be bringing the boys over, Sara.' Lou's tone was a little wary.

'They weren't really up for it,' Sara replied, meeting Lou's eye with a callous stare. She felt giddy with daring. How liberating it was to have burned her bridges, to no longer care that she might be hurting Lou's feelings — to actually *want* to hurt them.

'Oh,' said Lou.

'They didn't want to miss *Top Gear*,' Neil said apologetically.

★ ★ ★

At close quarters, Lou really did look quite peaky, Sara noticed. There were broken capillaries on her cheeks and a spot on the side of her nose. No, it wasn't a spot — it was the hole where her nose ring should have been — it seemed to be turning septic. Not a good look. She still managed to look irritatingly attractive though — like some consumptive courtesan wasting away for love.

★   ★   ★

Lou turned to Claudia and said, with a brittle brightness, 'It was such a stroke of luck, moving next door to these guys. Sara and Neil's boys are almost *exactly* the same ages as Arlo and Dash and they get on brilliantly. We hardly see them when they're all together, do we? They just go off and . . .'

But Claudia and Chris never found out what it was they just went off and did, because a piercing shriek stopped Lou in mid-sentence. Footsteps clattered on the stairs and Dash burst into the room.

'I need you. To get Zuley. Out of my room!'

'Sweetheart . . . ' Lou had the grace to look a little embarrassed, 'calm down and tell me what the problem is . . .'

'The *problem*,' he shrieked, 'is that Zuley and Arlo have made a den in my room.'

'Darling, it's Arlo's room too.'

'And they've used my duvet cover and knocked over all my Warhammer stuff, so can you please come up now and fucking well get them out?'

'Dash!' barked Gavin, without much conviction.

He frowned at Lou, who seemed at a loss.

'Why don't *I* come up and see?' Claudia said, squeezing past Sara's chair. She grasped Dash gently by the shoulders and steered him, with a surprising authority, out of the room. For all Sara loathed Dash, she found herself egging him on now; anticipating the backlash with no little relish — the barrage of swearing, Claudia's red-faced return. It didn't happen.

'Amazing, isn't she?' said Lou, seeing Sara's expression. 'And they only met on Wednesday.'

'But I thought you went way back?'

'The family, yes; but me and Claud haven't really seen that much of each other. I suppose I just feel a closeness, because Jerzy was like a father to me, growing up.'

A father you wanted to fuck, Sara thought.

'So when we heard they needed a place to crash we thought, why not?'

'And how long will that be for?' Sara asked, turning to Chris.

'Just a few months,' he said, through a mouthful of guacamole, 'until we can get a place of our own.'

'Months?' said Sara. 'Gosh.'

'Chris and Claud are looking to buy in Deptford,' Gavin said, leaning forward to top up Sara's wine.

★   ★   ★

It was the first chance she'd had to look at him properly, since she'd arrived. She wasn't over him, she realised, not at all. The sight of him still

302

turned her inside out. The thought of his hands on her, the thought of his mouth, his tongue . . . But he was behind glass now. Nothing spoke more eloquently of his indifference, than the impersonal affability with which he had treated her since she arrived. She could see now that his seduction had been half-hearted. He probably wouldn't even have bothered on his own account. Flirtation was second nature to him — Korinna the art-house avatar; predatory Rohmy, from the after party; Mandy the childminder — they had all fancied their chances with Gav, not realising that they were just walk-on parts in a wider drama — a game of cat and mouse between Gavin and Lou. But Sara had thought herself different — above them all — pre-eminent in Gavin's affections. She had known he would never leave Lou — she wasn't stupid. But she'd believed she answered a need in him that Lou couldn't — she had been quite certain of it. Just as she had been certain they would make love; that the opportunity would arise, and that it would be transformative.

It had not happened, and now it never would, and she was forced to sit here watching him waste his charisma on these replicants; these *non*-people. They laughed and chatted, apparently welcome inside the charmed circle, from which she was now excluded. Her time was past.

* * *

' . . . Because prices have gone up by eight percent just in the last six months,' Chris was saying, 'so it's now or never, essentially.'

God, he was dull.

'Well, you'll be in a strong position,' Neil said, 'as first-time buyers.'

'Hopefully.' Chris darted a doubtful glance at Gavin. 'We're just hoping we won't have trouble getting a mortgage, because I'm self-employed and Claud hasn't got a permanent post yet.'

'What's your line of work, Chris?' asked Neil pleasantly.

'I'm an accountant,' said Chris.

Sara stifled a yawn.

'Should be a pretty safe bet then,' Neil said.

'I expect so,' agreed Chris, 'but they'll want to dot the i's and cross the t's.'

'Let them dot,' Gavin said, shrugging, swirling the wine in his glass roguishly, and knocking it back, 'let them cross. We're in no hurry. Be great to have you guys around. Get us out of our rut.'

★ ★ ★

Claudia came back into the room, then looking quietly pleased with herself.

'All quiet on the Western Front,' she said. 'Arlo's had a story and Zuley's nearly asleep.'

'Oh, you angel!' said Lou. 'I'd better pop up and see her. She'll never forgive me if I forget her magic cuddle.'

Magic cuddle? Sara almost choked on her wine. Did the woman have no shame? Had she forgotten that Sara knew what went on around here? Then again, perhaps Lou was more interested in recruiting new members to her fan club, than in presenting anything resembling an authentic personality to a friend whose good opinion of her seemed to matter less and less with each day that passed.

★ ★ ★

'She's bright as a button, isn't she?' Claudia said, applying herself, enthusiastically, to her cold tortilla.

'Who, Zuley?' Gavin grinned smugly, 'Yeah, not bad.'

'Not bad?' Claudia affected outrage. 'She's a Key Stage One reader, I'll have you know.'

Gav looked bemused. 'Is that good?'

'At four? It's amazing,' Claudia said. 'I've taught kids of seven who couldn't read as well as that.'

'So you're a *teacher*, Claudia?' Sara said.

'Newly qualified.' Claudia blushed and plucked at her earring. 'I'll probably be doing supply for a bit, while I find my feet.'

'How does that work?'

'They just call you up when someone goes off sick or whatever.'

'And the rest of the time?'

'Well,' said Claudia, happily, 'I shall be here, I suppose. Helping out where I can.'

★ ★ ★

So there it was. The home-school had been outsourced. No wonder Gavin and Lou were rolling out the red carpet for these people — they were

305

worth their weight in gold. While Claudia honed her teaching skills on the kids, Chris would no doubt be running an eye over Gavin's tax affairs. Sara almost wanted to laugh, it was so perfect. Didn't they say sharks had to keep moving or they'd drown?

★ ★ ★

'They asked *us*, by the way.' Claudia leaned towards her and spoke in a defensive half-whisper.

'*Sorry?*' said Sara. The poor woman was still tying herself in knots of humility and gratitude.

'They asked *us* to come and stay,' said Claudia. 'We didn't ask *them*. I was only ringing to find out about the area, I never dreamed they'd offer to put us up.'

'I dare say they could use the rent.'

'Oh, we're not paying rent,' said Claudia, 'they wouldn't hear of it, which, when you consider that it's an open-ended arrangement and a very generously-sized room, says a lot about them, don't you think?'

Gavin came back, whistling, a bottle of Burgundy in his hands.

'An oldie and a goodie,' he said, 'had this one laid down for a bit, but as long as we're celebrating. Have I missed something?'

'No,' said Neil, with false bonhomie, 'we were just commending your hospitality. What are we celebrating?'

'Didn't Lou tell you?' Gav rolled his eyes. 'Typical. We've just heard that the BFI is

306

releasing *Cuckoo* in a new series of DVDs celebrating contemporary women film-makers.'

'Fantastic!' said Neil.

Claudia and Chris swooned.

Sara was confused. Was this a coup or a comedown? In the real world, when a film went straight to DVD, it was considered a flop.

'Does that mean it won't get a cinema release?' she asked, a little too eagerly. And yet her schadenfreude was self-defeating. If the damn thing didn't make any money, it was she and Neil who stood to lose out.

'Oh probably, yes, at some point,' said Gavin vaguely, 'but either way, this is fantastically prestigious. It's a huge boost for her career.'

★   ★   ★

Lou came back into the room, to a smattering of sycophantic applause.

'What did I do?' she said, affecting bafflement. 'Oh, the *film*? Oh, for heaven's *sake*.'

Gavin poured the wine with great ceremony and stood to propose a toast. Reluctantly, Sara raised her glass along with the others.

'To my gorgeous, sexy, prodigiously talented wife. Thank you for never, *ever* being boring.'

'To Lou,' Neil said, rushing into the respectful silence a little too quickly.

'Lou,' cooed the others, in unison. Sara mouthed the shape of the word.

Lou flapped her hand dismissively in front of her face. Tears came to her eyes and she caressed her breastbone, as she had done post-screening, when the emotion had all been too much. She sat down, but then almost immediately stood up again.

'Actually . . . ' she said, with a catarrhal gulp, 'sorry, Gav, but you're not getting off scot-free here.' Her tears welled again. 'This man . . . ' she said. She half laughed and shook her head, '*this man*. If talent is a word that could ever be applied to me, which, incidentally, I dispute . . . '

Mutinous tuts and mutterings from the sycophants.

' . . . then some other term will need to be coined for him. For *you*.' She looked into her husband's eyes, excluding, in that moment, the rest of the company. 'I can honestly say that, without your example, I would be nothing and no one. Your art is the linchpin of our lives. It is beautiful and inspiring and important and I thank God for it and for you, every day.'

There was a respectful silence, and then another ripple of obsequious applause, which seemed to remind Lou where she was.

'Oh, and did I mention he's not bad in the sack either!' she added, with a bawdy wink.

A burst of nervous laughter told Sara that she was not the only one for whom this was a confidence too far. Lou started clearing the dishes away and Claudia sprang up to help her, scraping and stacking like a dinner monitor on the head girl's table.

'That was gorgeous, Lou,' she said, 'I must get the recipe from you.'

★　★　★

308

Gavin changed the music and topped up their glasses, and when Lou had finished clearing up, she bought a platter of cheese to the table and introduced each one, in turn.

' . . . And this one's Grazalema,' she said, loading a cracker with a generous portion and passing it to Claudia, 'from Andalucia, where we lived in Spain. I don't buy it very often, because it makes me homesick, but it's a special occasion, so . . . '

'That is *divine*,' said Claudia, holding her fingertips discreetly over her crumb-filled mouth. She swallowed, and sighed. 'England does seem rather narrow, doesn't it? When one's lived abroad.'

There was a wistful silence.

'Oh, now while I remember,' Sara said, keeping her tone deceptively friendly, 'remember that guy, Steve?'

Neil shot her a warning glance.

'Steve?' Gav narrowed his eyes, thoughtfully.

'You know, Neil's mate from work. The surveyor?'

'Do we want to do this now?' murmured Neil.

'*I* do,' she shot back, fiercely.

'Steve . . . ' Gavin narrowed his eyes. 'Steve, Steve, Steve . . . Oh, the hi-vis guy, Lou, remember? With all the kit?'

Lou wrinkled her nose in amusement.

'Oh, yeah — he was like a Lego man, wasn't he? With his hard hat and his little bag of tricks.'

'That's him,' said Sara, cheerfully, 'well, so, hi-vis. Steve reckons we've got a bit of a problem.'

'Which we maybe don't want to go into right

now,' repeated Neil, widening his eyes at her.

'Hey, man, let her get it off her chest,' Gav said, turning towards Sara and resting one arm, complacently, along the back of her chair. 'What's the problem, Sara?'

'*Thank* you,' Sara said, 'sorry about this, Claudia and . . .'

'Chris,' Chris reminded her.

'Yeah. Only, once you're homeowners, I'm sure you'll appreciate, that, you know, the place you live very quickly stops being just bricks and mortar and becomes something more than that. You invest in it emotionally. We have done anyway. We've lived here nine and half years now. Patrick, my youngest was born here. It feels like the place we were always meant to be.'

'Jesus, Sara!' said Neil.

'Well, if you'd brought it up, like you said you would.'

'It's subsidence!' snapped Neil. He said it like a swear word and threw Sara a furious glance afterwards.

'Well, I think we knew that much,' said Gav, looking only slightly less pleased with himself than before, 'but you expect a bit of movement, don't you? With old houses?'

'It's more than a bit of movement, mate,' mumbled Neil grimly.

'The work you had done,' Sara said, warming to her theme, 'has undermined the foundations of the building. I don't know who drew up your plans, but they've botched it. Your studio, where you make all your beautiful, inspiring, important artwork, has fucked up our ordinary, uninspiring

310

home in a major way. *That's* what Hi-vis Steve figured out, with his . . . ' She drew inverted commas in the air. ' . . . little bag of tricks.'

Backs grew a little straighter, smiles a little more fixed. Lou stood up abruptly and walked over to the fridge. She opened the door, but seemed to forget what it was she was looking for, and closing it again, returned to stand behind Gav, rubbing her hands briskly back and forth across his shoulders, as if he were a talisman.

'I don't think that can be right,' she said, with a twisted little smile, 'that can't be right, can it, Gav? Because it was supervised by a really good mate of ours, Jerome.' Correctly apprehending that name-dropping was no longer likely to cut any ice with Sara, she turned to Claudia instead. 'He did the Pebble Gallery in Bury St Edmunds. So I think we can assume he knows his stuff.'

'Didn't that one win an award?' offered Claudia, helpfully.

'Look,' said Neil, gesturing downwards with his hands, 'let's not have kittens here. We're mates, aren't we?'

They all tried to look as if this were the case.

'Steve's preliminary investigations suggest that your building works *might* have contributed — '

'Ninety-nine per cent likely — ' murmured Sara.

'That it's *probable* your building works contributed to the, er . . . '

'Yep! Okay, okay,' said Gavin, slapping his thighs, 'I think we get the message. Obviously, we're as keen as you are to investigate further, so we can rule out that possibility.'

'Good luck with that,' said Sara, earning herself a look of pure hatred from Gavin, which, despite her having courted it, still wounded her.

'So, please, just tell us what you need from us,' he finished.

'Great!' said Neil. 'Thanks. It's not complicated, really. Steve just needs to see the original drawings, plus a copy of the planning consent, and if you can tell him what system you used for the underpinning.'

'The underpinning?' said Gavin.

★ ★ ★

Sara lay in the dark beside Neil. His eyes were closed and his face was turned implacably to the ceiling, like a figure carved on a medieval tomb. She knew he wasn't asleep, because his body was tense with resentment, but he wasn't letting on. He hated unpleasantness, always had, but this unpleasantness was not of her making. She didn't see why she should get it in the neck for Gavin and Lou's colossal negligence. And that was how it felt. As though he was on *their* side, instead of hers.

She put out a hand in the darkness and touched his hand. He twitched away, as though in fear of leprosy.

'It had to be said, Neil,' she whispered, 'there was never going to be a right time.'

Silence. Well, then, she would find forgiveness how she may. She trailed her hand gently over his thigh. He went tense at her touch, but didn't stop her. Slowly, now, she tilted her body towards him. His erection bobbed up, and she made to touch it, but he pushed her hand out of the way.

★ ★ ★

With no preamble, and no tenderness, he clambered over her, supporting himself on one hand, while he wrenched up her nightie with the other. His eyes were dark hollows in his face. He handled her roughly. This was not like Neil. To Sara's dismay, she grew wet with the unexpectedness, the difference of it. He licked his thumb and rubbed it matter-of-factly over the end of his erection. There was to be no kissing then, nor any of the usual nuzzling or ear biting. Certainly breast licking was off. He positioned the end of his cock and, pausing briefly to gather momentum, thrust inside her without making a sound. She gasped in shock. Their usual call and response was dispensed with. The interrogative pushing and gyrating that were supposed to pleasure both of them, yet hadn't, for years, really pleasured either of them, were now replaced by greedy, priapic thrusts. And. It. Felt. Good. Her bottom chafed against the sheet, air rushed in her ears, her hair slithered against the pillow, up down, up down, faster and faster. And then a sharp pain made her yelp in surprise. Something — it felt like a fishhook — had embedded itself in the soft flesh at the base of her buttock, and with every thrust, was digging itself a little deeper.

'Ouch! Jesus. Jesus, *stop*!' she yelped. But Neil

313

was oblivious. One, two, three more thrusts and he was finished.

'Get off,' Sara whispered. 'Can you get *off*? I've got a . . . something's *stuck* in me.' He rolled off her and she fumbled for the offending article and wincing, unhooked it from her flesh. She grasped it between thumb and forefinger, and held it out in the dark. It was hard to believe that something so tiny had caused her such pain.

'Christ!' said Neil, angrily. He leaned across her and turned on the bedside light.

They blinked at each other in the unaccustomed brightness and she held the object under the lampshade, to get a good look at it. It was a hinged silver hoop, about the size of a split pea. She frowned in incomprehension and looked at Neil, just in time to see him recognise it, and then pretend not to.

★   ★   ★

Neil shook his head, slowly at first, and then urgently, emphatically.

'It's not what you think.'

'Not what I think? Lou's nose ring turns up in my bed and it's *not what I think*? How the *fuck* did it get here then? Was she reading you a bedtime story or what? No! No!' She pushed both hands over his mouth. 'Don't make it worse. Oh I can't bear it, I can't *bear* it.'

She keeled over on the bed. The pain was visceral, astonishing. She heard a guttural groan, scarcely aware that it was coming from her own mouth.

314

'Sara, listen. It was nothing. It meant *nothing*!'

He wittered on for a while, '*accident . . . meaningless . . . lonely . . . so very ashamed.*'

At last, when he had finished, she raised her head, slowly, as if from a swamp, and looked at him, this man who had betrayed her, this man whom she no longer knew.

'When?' she said. 'When were you even *alone* with her? Oh. God. *I* know. Taekwondo. I was at the leisure centre, looking after her kids. Oh, that's beautiful. That's perfect.'

Neil continued to shake his head, eyes shut, like a little boy denying that he had raided the biscuit tin.

Sara looked again at the tiny shred of silver still clamped between her thumb and fingernail. It was almost nothing. And yet it was everything. Absence and presence, both. A little O, a hole through which their marriage had all but leached away.

'Perfect, perfect, perfect,' she kept repeating, rocking back and forth, until the words elided into a continuous keening wail.

27

Eighteen months later

It was one of those winter mornings when the sea, shrouded in mist, heaved its surf onto the pebbles with a muffled splash. The land felt clean, anaesthetised by cold. Even the rubbish, blown into the corner of a shelter on the esplanade, looked like pop art. The dog skittered about, yanking Sara this way and that, cocking its leg on the rusty iron balusters and yapping after seagulls. She hadn't wanted a dog at all, let alone this needy little mongrel, but she could see that it was A Good Thing. It compensated the boys, in some small measure, for the upheaval of the move and provided some welcome noise and chaos in a household that had become uncharacteristically subdued. The requirement to take it for a shit, onerous as it was, got Sara out of bed in the mornings, which was preferable to lying there waiting for the dawn to reacquaint her, gradually, with the strange contours of her new bedroom.

★   ★   ★

She still dreamed of the old house. She would be standing on its doorstep, turning her key ineffectually in the lock, or walking downstairs only to find herself teetering on the edge of a

316

precipice. Once, she dreamed she opened the airing cupboard and discovered a hidden wing, with a ballroom and a Wurlitzer organ. She'd woken up happy, until she remembered that there was no ballroom and, in fact, no house. Not for her, not any more.

★ ★ ★

They were further along the promenade than usual — way past the bingo hall — before the dog condescended to open its bowels. Sara stooped to wriggle the still-steaming turd into the plastic bag she had brought for the purpose. Yet even this act of self-abasement could not quite take away the day's wide, blue optimistic sheen. She felt, not happy, no, but reconciled. This, she had discovered, was the only realistic aspiration. Yet even this, until very recently, had seemed wildly ambitious. You could not afford to look back. You could not afford to compare. It was as if a new regime had swept away the customs of the old country. You had to turn amnesiac; let it all slip away. If you got out the accoutrements of the old way of life — started to recall its rituals, you would go mad with grief and resentment.

★ ★ ★

Caleb claimed not to like his new school, but at least he wasn't being bullied. That had been Sara's fear. On the contrary, as far as she could tell by hacking his Facebook account, his

317

disaffected air and world-weary cockney swagger had turned him into a bit of a cult hero. At the weekends, though, he would mope in his room, only emerging to pour himself a huge bowl of cornflakes and disparage whoever was in the kitchen at the time. He tended to reserve particular scorn for Neil, who was only *there* at weekends and whose attempts to ingratiate himself, during these brief, tense sojourns, were heartbreaking. He had always been the better parent. His instinct had been sound, his love had been steady, his authority — stemming, as it did, from his integrity — had been respected. Now, that integrity was shattered, and his authority gone. His instinct was all over the place. He made bad call after bad call. Only his love remained but that, it seemed, was not enough for Caleb.

★   ★   ★

She hated to see Neil brought so low in the eyes of his eldest son, and yet she struggled not to feel slightly smug. He had, after all, brought it on himself. He had admitted as much during the counselling. He had looked Sara in the eye and apologised, and then he had begun to weep quietly. She had wanted to forgive him, had reached out her hand, but inside, her heart had been stony. The counsellor had heard the whole sorry tale, minus one salient fact on Sara's side, which would have cast her in an altogether less favourable light. Over the course of several weeks, Sara had striven to disentangle her anger

318

with Gavin and Lou, from her anger with her husband. Work had been done.

★　★　★

Eight months living next to her sworn enemies had been enough. Eight months of hiding behind the hedge, waiting for the Humber to pull away, before she braved the street. Eight months of telling the postman that no, actually, it wouldn't be convenient to take in an Amazon order for number nine. Eight months of remembering that the kids were just kids, and that Arlo must still be congratulated for performing an excellent manouevre on his skateboard, even if such congratulation met with a hostile stare.

★　★　★

The anger, the stigma, the paranoia, had turned Sara from gregarious neighbour into social pariah. She crossed the street, now, rather than face awkward questions from well-meaning acquaintances, but she could tell, by the way people looked at her, that they knew. Meanwhile, Gavin and Lou seemed to have no shame. Sara could not say for sure that they were recruiting allies, but over the course of a few months, they seemed to have transformed themselves from enigmatic outsiders into pillars of the community. *They* were now the takers-in of parcels, the cat feeders and plant waterers, the signers of petitions, the hosts of Boxing Day drinks parties.

★ ★ ★

That had been a tough one. Sitting in the front room, among the debris of Christmas, *The Snowman* turned up full blast on the telly to drown out the sounds of partying next door. Sara had been unable to resist glancing up every time Gavin and Lou's garden gate squeaked. All the usual suspects had come and gone that day — sharp-suited Hoxton types, grizzled intellectuals — and harder still to witness, neighbours like Bronte and Mac, Marlene, Sandra from across the road, with her new baby, all apparently, happy enough to transfer their allegiance, for the sake of a tot of whisky and a mince pie, from Neil and Sara to the arty newcomers, who had only just bothered to learn their names.

★ ★ ★

When the house had been on the market for six months, and a property developer with an instinct for desperation, had offered them six fifty for it, they'd snapped it up. It was worth it to get the hell out. It meant that they couldn't afford Brighton — or not a four bed anyway, and as the train service from Hastings didn't allow for daily commuting, Neil would only be able to visit at weekends. This had seemed an apt punishment to Sara at the time. For even though she had conceded that the subsidence was not his fault, his behaviour *had* contributed in no small part to the toxic atmosphere, which had made living next door to Gavin and Lou untenable, and thus precipitated the untimely and therefore unprofitable move. In view of this, allowing him to sleep on a futon in the box room three nights a week seemed downright generous.

★ ★ ★

The dog was pulling again, trying to get round to the business end of a Labrador whose owner had been too busy looking at his mobile to give them a wide berth. He raised his eyes from the screen now, and a vague flicker of interest crossed his face that told Sara, despite her early morning dishevelment, she was still recognisably female. She didn't acknowledge him, only called the dog and tugged gently on its lead until it scurried unwillingly after her, but the subliminal message of the encounter added, incrementally, to the auspiciousness of the day.

Not that she was interested in men, not at all. If there was one thing that the whole sorry episode had taught her, it was that; to keep your eyes on the pavement — not to look up. She and Neil had been just fine the way they were. More than fine, actually. Unpacking after the move, she had come across a wallet of holiday snaps. One had shown her and Caleb sitting on the steps of a caravan in the Dordogne, sharing a salami-filled baguette — she had been heavily pregnant with Patrick at the time and Neil had counselled against unpasteurised cheese.

Just looking at herself in that photo, recalling the feel of the nubbly, sun-baked aluminium beneath her feet, the complacent weight of her

321

belly, the slight discomfort of squinting into the light, as she waited for Neil to frame the shot, she yearned to be that person again. Even in the mild exasperation of the moment, she had been, she now saw, sublimely content. There had been love in the wry smile, which urged Neil to get a move on, love in the air of exaggerated patience with which she maintained the pose. Love was everywhere in the photograph — filtered through the weave of the canvas umbrella, bouncing off the moulded plastic furniture, leaking through the photographer's lens.

They wouldn't get back to that — not now; but nor would they founder. Even as she had lain sobbing in the bed, she had known, in some cool, rational chamber of her brain that they were not finished, her and Neil.

But she hadn't known it would be this hard. The easy, elegant dance of their marriage, to which Sara had not even had to learn the steps, had turned into a weary, ill-coordinated shuffle. Long after Sara had moved back home, after a fortnight spent spaced-out on Diazepam at her mother's; long after relationship counselling had supposedly put her and Neil back on track, they were still attempting to conceal their mutual resentment in a pastiche of cooperation.

'That thing's on at nine o'clock,' a typical exchange might go, 'but never mind if you're watching the football.'

'Turn over then, go on.'

'Not if you're watching. I mean, it's nil-nil, and they're not even teams you care about, but if you're watching . . . '

'I said, turn over. I'm not bothered.'

'No, forget it, I've missed the beginning now.'

At this point, Neil would get up and leave the room, and Sara would sit, stubborn and miserable, in front of the football. And that was on a good day.

* * *

To say it had been a relief to leave London was an understatement, even if it had been a decisive move down in the world. Everything about the Hastings house was a compromise: Hastings itself, by dint of not being Brighton; the location of the house; in the old town, but not on one of its favoured streets; the lack of a seaview, unless you stood on a chair and opened the velux in the attic. But the biggest comedown had been the house itself. The need for a fourth bedroom had militated in favour of Sea Crest, a former B&B in an undistinguished Victorian terrace. Its pebble-dashed frontage, high-gloss, sky-blue paintwork, and front wall of latticed concrete bricks hinted at the reason for its demise. Inside and out, it was a temple of kitsch, which would have appalled Carol as much as it would no doubt have delighted Gavin and Lou. And it was a measure of the lingering power of her old adversaries' unconventional aesthetic that Sara actually considered, for about five minutes, retaining the mirror-backed 1980s bar in the front room. And yet the *house* did not depress her. She supposed, at some point, they would get around to stripping it back to its constituent parts, knocking down a few interior walls, revealing whatever period treasures might be hidden behind its stud-partitions and built-in wardrobes, but she was in no hurry. There was something very restful about living with other people's choices. God knows Sara had made enough bad ones of her own, though not, perhaps, chiefly in the area of interior décor.

At any rate, as she tossed the plastic-swathed dog turd into a rubbish bin, and crossed the road towards her own front gate, it felt, for the first time, a bit like coming home. The postman had been, and after she had closed the porch door and unclipped the dog's lead, Sara tugged a bulky A4 envelope from the over-sprung letterbox, prompting a cascade of smaller items onto the doormat. The main event turned out to be Neil's copy of *Inside Housing*, which, Sara noted, he'd had redirected to Sea Crest, despite being on probation as a permanent resident. This, she found, didn't annoy her as much as she might have expected. She flicked through the rest of the post — car insurance reminders, junk mail, several unimportant looking missives for the former residents — and was about to toss them into the recycling, when she came across an ivory-coloured envelope, hand-addressed to her and Neil.

28

'I just think they might have considered us, that's all,' Sara said, accelerating into the overtaking lane, with the recklessness of one who has been stuck behind a Honda for twelve miles of single carriageway. 'They could have hired somewhere. It's not as if they're short of money.'

'I think they're entitled to have a party at their own house,' said Neil mildly. And Sara had to acknowledge that they were. All the same, it wasn't going to be easy, standing in Carol and Simon's front room, looking across at Lou and Gavin's place. She hoped that she'd been right to accept the invitation. It had felt right. It had felt about time. Either they wiped their past life from the record, stopped sending Christmas cards, ceased the sporadic phone calls, discouraged the boys' occasional trips down memory lane; or they brazened it out. By making this strategic visit, Sara hoped to cauterise the wound. She had, of course, first established that Lou and Gavin were not going to be at the party. There was cauterising the wound and there was self-immolation.

* * *

Even so, as the car began to navigate its own way along the last few familiar streets, she found herself feeling both teary and slightly nauseous.

'The Glovers' extension's finally finished,' said Neil, peering with great curiosity through the passenger window, 'looks all right, actually. And those people next door to Marlene have cleaned up their act,' he went on, 'she must have got on to the council.' He continued to provide a running commentary on the superficial differences he was able to discern between the street now, and the street as they had left it, apparently impervious to Sara's brooding silence, right up until the moment she stopped the car.

'Okay,' Neil slapped his thighs, a little too heartily, 'let's do this thang.' He made to open the passenger door.

'Are you coming?' he said, but Sara kept hold of the steering wheel as if it were a life raft. Objectively, the suburban Victorian street resembled a hundred others, yet, attuned as she was to the *these* paving stones, *these* hedges, *these* bricks, the atmosphere of belonging, of identification, seemed to rush through the air vents like ozone. Here was the National Trust green of Carol's front door, here the dent in the lamppost made when Neil had reversed too hastily en route to the labour ward. The failing light, the glowering privet, the sheen of drizzle on the wheelie bins, all brought a sense of nostalgia almost too intense to bear.

★ ★ ★

Neil bounded up Carol and Simon's steps and rapped smartly on the door.

Under cover of reaching behind her seat for

326

Simon's present, Sara snatched a glance across the road. Their house was hidden behind scaffolding, halfway, no doubt, to being turned into three 'generously-sized apartments.' Lou and Gavin's on the other hand looked more or less the same except for a rusty hunk of metal in the front garden, which she took to be a sculpture. It didn't look like one of Gav's.

'Sara! About time too.'

Carol's middle class drawl made her wince with equal parts pleasure and embarrassment. She backed out of the car and found herself engulfed in *Must de Cartier* and cashmere.

'Hello,' she said, her voice cracking a little.

'Don't you dare!' Carol gripped her by the shoulders, so that it hurt. 'Don't you dare stay away so long again.'

⋆　⋆　⋆

They had tea at Carol's scrubbed-oak kitchen table and Simon got in trouble for not using the strainer. Sara had forgotten the pleasures of small talk; the layers of familiarity, going back ten years — the broad consensus on where was worth holidaying, what was worth reading, what one might aspire to for one's children. It was a game, really, a bonding ritual — they might as well have been dingos or orangutans. She wondered, in retrospect, how she had managed to get so worked up about it all — how she had become, overnight, so desperate to define herself as 'other'. Of course Carol still indulged in one-upmanship and Simon could bore for

England on the subject of ethical investment, but they were funnier, more self-deprecating, *wiser* than she remembered. Simon's brother turned up with his wife and they had another pot of tea and chatted about how the south coast was on the up, and the smart money was now on Margate and although some snarky things were said about Tracey Emin, that would once have raised Sara's hackles, she found the whole experience far more congenial than she'd expected.

* * *

Other guests began to arrive in dribs and drabs, the tea things were cleared away and someone handed Sara a glass of champagne. They moved through to the living room, where *Reggatta de Blanc* was playing through the iPod speakers and Carol had set up a slideshow of Simon's life in photographs, which turned out to be an excellent ice-breaker. She stood next to one of Simon's colleagues, and they nudged each other and smiled as the story unfolded: Simon wearing a nappy and a bashful smile; Simon at Cub Scouts, minus his two front teeth; Simon wearing a dodgy beret and brandishing a ticket for the Blow Monkeys; Simon leading Carol through a shower of confetti, looking like the cat that got the cream; Simon in red braces and a truly misjudged pair of 1990s spectacles. The carousel went on, each image a staging post in a fortunate, but otherwise unremarkable life; a life not dissimilar to Sara's own, except that where

Simon had accepted his privilege with good grace, Sara had chafed against hers; where Simon had cheerfully borne the responsibilities of marriage and parenthood as if they themselves were creative challenges, Sara had felt constrained by them; where Simon had never doubted his individuality enough to bother asserting it, she had come within a whisker of throwing over her whole life, in order to prove hers.

*   *   *

Since the move, Sara's writing had got better. It was the only thing that had kept her sane to begin with, apart from the dog-walking. She had abandoned her novel, which, in retrospect, she was very glad Ezra hadn't got round to reading and had been honing her skills on short stories instead. She had even had one short-listed for inclusion in a small anthology. It hadn't made the final cut, but it had given her hope.

*   *   *

The slide show was on its second circuit now and she had run out of small talk, so with an apologetic waggle of her empty glass, she drifted away.

*   *   *

Seen from Carol's well-appointed living room, Lou and Gavin's house, while still projecting an air of otherness, looked dilapidated. Nearly three years on and they still hadn't painted the window frames. The lavender border that she had planted herself, years ago, to mark the boundary between the two properties, was leggy and sparse. It had the look of razor wire. If only it had been, she thought. If only she had known to defend herself against their incursions, instead of inviting them in, to run amok.

She had been so naïve, so easily impressed and all too ready to take their failings for strengths. She had mistaken the physical neglect of their house for some kind of aesthetic statement and worried that, by comparison, her own place looked shiny and shallow. Even when Lou had praised her home-making skills, she had scented condescension. Only now could she see that the compliment had been genuine, that for Lou, 'home' was as theoretical a word as 'studio' was to Sara. It wasn't, she could now see, that Lou and Gavin *meant* to be neglectful and exploitative, they had just bitten off more than they could chew. Their art came first — before their house, before their children, before their friends, maybe even before their marriage. Perhaps there was something noble in that, after all.

★   ★   ★

Turning her attention back to the party, she noticed Neil watching her pensively from the other side of the room. He met her gaze with a slightly rueful smile and, reaching for his drink,

330

seemed intent on joining her but before he could, Carol ushered in a bevy of new guests.

'Hi Sara, how are you?' Toby Warricker was an acquaintance from Cranmer Road days. Carol and Simon had been very thick with him and his wife Alyson, who was even now bearing down on a beleaguered-looking Neil.

'Hi Toby,' she said, 'how are things?'

'Yeah, fucking good actually. I suppose you've heard I've set up my own production company? Only way to go, these days, unless you want to spend your life filming tedious middle Englanders 'escaping to the country'.' He held up his hand. 'No offence, by the way.'

'None taken,' Sara replied, doubtfully.

'How's that going by the way?'

'Hastings?' she said. 'Yeah, very well. We like it. Neil's always wanted to live by the sea.'

'Made Al a bit restless, you going,' Toby said.

'Really?' Sara was surprised. The nearest she and Alyson had come to friendship, had been running the lucky dip together at Cranmer Road's Christmas Fayre.

'Yeah, you know how it is,' Toby shook his head, 'someone's kid gets mugged at the bus stop and the next thing you know everyone's upping sticks. First it was Matt and Jude, then you guys. Doesn't worry *me*, but Al's very susceptible.'

★ ★ ★

Toby droned on. Sara's gaze drifted toward the window. It was dark outside now, and she could see her own reflection superimposed like a hologram on the house across the road. Their curtains were half closed but the cold blue flicker of the TV could just be seen. She imagined Gavin lounging in the Eames chair with a glass of red, Lou lolling barefoot on the sofa. They might be watching an art-house movie together — or perhaps just slumming it with Saturday night telly. It was all too easy to conjure — the flea-bitten hearth-rug, the aroma of Pinot Noir mingled with woodsmoke. Even after everything that had happened, the scene still had its allure.

★ ★ ★

From their vantage point, Carol's place would be a goldfish bowl — blinds open, lights blazing, a room full of people and more arriving. Sara hoped they had noticed. She hoped their exclusion would hurt, but she doubted it. Her focus shifted, once again, to her own face, a ghostly smudge in the sheen of the windowpane.

★ ★ ★

' . . . But it's just a one-off and that's what people need to realise.' Toby was smiling at her, with barely disguised impatience and she realised, with a flush of embarrassment that she had not taken in a word he had said.

'Hello!' He leaned forward and made as if to rap her on the forehead with his knuckles.

'Anybody home?'

Acknowledgements

Thanks to the members of Clifton Hill Writers' Group, Melbourne, for their constructive criticism of early drafts, especially to Trish Bolton; to Polly Jameson for her editorial input and encouragement; to Sallyanne Sweeney at MMB Creative for her continuing support and to Kate Mills at HarperCollins for getting it. Above all, thanks to Adam Goulcher for being first reader, unsparing critic, and empowering friend.

We do hope that you have enjoyed reading this large print book.

Did you know that all of our titles are available for purchase?

We publish a wide range of high quality large print books including:
Romances, Mysteries, Classics
General Fiction
Non Fiction and Westerns

Special interest titles available in large print are:
The Little Oxford Dictionary
Music Book
Song Book
Hymn Book
Service Book

Also available from us courtesy of Oxford University Press:
Young Readers' Dictionary
(large print edition)
Young Readers' Thesaurus
(large print edition)

For further information or a free brochure, please contact us at:
Ulverscroft Large Print Books Ltd.,
The Green, Bradgate Road, Anstey,
Leicester, LE7 7FU, England.
Tel: (00 44) 0116 236 4325
Fax: (00 44) 0116 234 0205

16TH SEDUCTION

James Patterson and Maxine Paetro

Fifteen months ago, Detective Lindsay Boxer's life was perfect. With her beautiful baby daughter and doting husband, Joe, she felt nothing could go wrong. But Joe isn't everything that Lindsay thought he was, and she's still reeling from his betrayal as a wave of mysterious heart attacks strikes seemingly unrelated victims across San Francisco. And at the trial of a bomber Lindsay and Joe worked together to capture, the defense raises damning questions about the couple's investigation. A deadly conspiracy is working against Lindsay, and soon she could be the one on trial . . .

THE LYING GAME

Ruth Ware

The text message arrives in the small hours of the night: *I need you.* Isa drops everything, takes her baby daughter and heads straight to Salten. She spent the most significant days of her life at boarding school on the marshes there — days that still cast their shadow over her. At school, Isa and her three best friends used to play the Lying Game. They competed to convince people of the most outrageous stories. Now, after seventeen years of secrets, something terrible has been found on the beach. Something that will force Isa to confront her past, together with the three women she hasn't seen for years. Theirs is no cosy reunion; Salten isn't a safe place for them, not after what they did. It's time for them to get their story straight . . .